MURDER ON THE
17TH HOLE

MURDER ON THE 17ᵀᴴ HOLE

A Golf Mystery

Thomas P. Evans

Murder on the 17th Hole
A Golf Mystery

iUniverse books may be ordered through booksellers or by contacting:

*iUniverse
1663 Liberty Drive
Bloomington, IN 47403
www.iuniverse.com
1-800-Authors (1-800-288-4677)*

*ISBN: 978-1-4502-0906-9 (sc)
ISBN: 978-1-4502-0907-6 (e)*

Print information available on the last page.

iUniverse rev. date: 03/18/2015

CHAPTER 1 – PRO-AM

———— ▼ ————

The dream woke John Rollings almost every night. He couldn't read a putt...

He squatted and plumb-bobbed, closed one eye, then the other. He tried lining up the putt from off the green, then from just behind the ball. He adjusted for green's speed, told himself to aim two inches outside left of the cup and stroke it firm.

In the dream, some mysterious caddy crouched behind him. "Everything breaks toward Indio," the caddy said confidently. "Dead center, slam-dunk it."

When John turned to see who the caddy was, the caddy's face disappeared. What does he mean Indio? John thought. We're on the East Coast. It wasn't John's regular caddy, Chump. He took his putting stance, but he couldn't pull the trigger. John stood over his ball so long a PGA official showed up in his white shirt and bow tie.

"Too much time," he said. "Two stroke penalty on Rollings."

Then John sat upright in bed. He was sweating in his air-conditioned motel room. It was 3:18 A.M. His starting time in the Hartford Pro-Am was 10:32 A.M. Seven hours until tee time.

A half hour before their starting time the 10:32 group was on the driving range warming up. Each of the three amateurs in the group had paid $6000 to play a round of golf with a PGA professional. Each of the three also had a caddy, as there were no golf carts allowed.

"I'm Chump," a middle-aged, stocky caddy said by way of introduction. He wore a yellow shirt panel with "ROLLINGS" embroidered across the back of it. He walked down the line and shook hands with the amateurs.

"I'm John Rollings's caddy and you may as well know where I got my name. My real name is Philip Williams, but when I started out caddying twenty years ago I always complained about the 'chump change' caddies made on the tour back then. They shortened it to Chump and that's been my name ever since. You'll find John easy to play with. He enjoys giving the amateurs some pointers. It doesn't bother his game at all. But don't you be giving him pointers. He's been on the Tour for twenty years. You'll see. It'll be a very enjoyable round."

Just then John Rollings showed up on the driving range. After playing hundreds of Pro-Ams over the years he'd found it was better if his caddy set the amateurs straight about what behavior of theirs could derail his round. John found it paid to keep on the good side of the amateurs. He was what they called a journeyman in the PGA golfing world. He had made a decent living hitting a golf ball, but he wasn't anywhere near the top golfers in earnings, many of whom flew from tournament to tournament in their private jets. But John found that many of the amateurs he played with were corporate executives, and often their companies owned corporate jets. More than once in years past one of his East Coast playing partners had his corporation's jet fly John and Chump to Florida or the West Coast. In fact one corporate president played as John's Pro-Am partner for ten years straight on a West Coast tour stop, and had his driver shuttle John and Chump anywhere they wanted to go when they were in town. John knew it paid to stay on the good side of the amateurs.

Rollings shook hands with each of his amateur playing partners. There was Carl Buffsky, a short, balding man of about fifty who owned a machine shop in New Britain, who was an enthusiastic golfer, although with an 18 handicap, not a very good one. Unusual in Pro-Am events because he was so young was Jason Sombery, a recent graduate of Western Connecticut State, who carried a respectable two handicap. The only amateur approaching celebrity status was Web Miter, the recently retired CEO of United Eastern, whose chauffeur/caddy Sanjay drove him up from his ten million dollar estate in Greenwich.

As each of the amateurs pounded out practice balls from their driving range bucket John Rollings methodically warmed up by hitting a couple balls with each club.

Nearby Wayne Sedlock watched the pros putt on the putting green. Sedlock, an insurance investigator for Alco Insurance Company, had taken advantage of one of his company's free passes to spend the afternoon at the Pro-Am. He had been quite a golfer himself in his youth and the annual outing at the Lordship course stirred up that urge to play again.

Sedlock, now 35-years-old, grew up near a nine-hole golf course, the type of course working men played after getting out of work. He discovered that if he cleaned up the golf balls he found in the rough he could sell them to golfers for a quarter a piece. Sometimes he even got caddying jobs, where he made a dollar fifty a round. Old Man Headle, who owned the golf course, got so tired of chasing young Sedlock off the property that he decided to give him chores to do. Before long Sedlock was cutting grass on the course and Old Man Headle let him hit practice balls after his day's work was done. Sedlock used a baseball grip and played on summer days with his friends. There was something magical about crushing a ball with a wood and sending it far down the fairway. After watching him flail away for a full summer, Old Man Headle, who had been a crackerjack golfer in his day, taught Sedlock the proper way to grip the club and gave him pointers on his swing. By the time Sedlock was seventeen he was the de facto club champion, meaning he was shooting the lowest scores of anybody on the nine-hole course. He played on the high school golf team and beat all the country club kids from the other side of town. He played in the state tournament his senior year, and he missed being the state small school high school golf champion by a single shot.

But his showing in the state tournament was good enough to get a golf scholarship to Trinity College. There he fell in love with writing, along with golf, and he majored in journalism. By his senior year he was the number one seed on the college golf team, and even had aspirations of perhaps turning pro.

So each year he watched the pros when they came to Lordship, and each year he thought of what might have been. He hadn't picked up a club in thirteen years.

Carl Buffsky teed off first. Chump yelled "Fore!" as Buffsky's drive sliced far right of the spectators about 220 yards from the tee. Jason Sombery poked a drive right down the middle about 270 yards. John Rollings was impressed by the youngster's tempo. Web Miter had an awkward, herky-jerky swing, but he managed to put his ball about 260 on the left side of the fairway.

Finally, John Rollings hit his drive. All of his amateur partners were impressed with how effortless his swing seemed and he put his ball straight down the middle 280 yards away. As the group walked down the first fairway John said to Carl, "With that outside in swing of yours you might want to aim a little left of your target, Carl."

"I'm just out here enjoying the beautiful weather," Carl said.

"Did you play golf in college, Jason?" John asked.

"Sure did," Jason said. "Western Connecticut."

"You've got a great tempo in your swing. And how about you, Web? When did you take up this game?"

"I've been playing on and off for years, John. But it's only been in the past couple years since I retired from United Eastern that I've been able to get out on the course and finally get some kind of feel to my shots. I know my swing is one only my mother could love, but I feel I'm finally starting to strike the ball decently."

"Believe it or not you've just described what every pro on the PGA tour is constantly striving for – that feel you need to hit a golf ball right."

Carl Buffsky hit first. He sliced his ball out of the right rough right and short of the green into a greenside bunker. Web Miter hit a solid six-iron just short of the green. Jason hit a nine onto the green twenty feet below the hole. John Rollings hit a pitching wedge just six feet from the cup. After Rollings and Sombery marked their golf balls, Miter hit a pitch and run just three feet from the cup. Carl took two to get out of the bunker, where he lay a good thirty feet from the hole. He was still away.

Carl lined up the putt then stroked it eight feet by the hole. Jason two-putted for his par, Carl two-putted for his seven, John sunk his for birdie and Web Miter made his par.

The next hole was a 500-yard dogleg right par five. The drives followed the pattern of the first hole. John Rollings cut the corner and put his ball in the left center of the fairway 200 yards from the green. Jason's drive sailed 280 yards to the corner of the dogleg. Web hit his on the left side of the fairway 260, but far enough to get around the dogleg and go for the green. Carl put his drive in jail, another slice into the right rough and with no chance of hitting his next shot toward the green. Carl pitched his second shot to the corner of the dogleg where he was still away. His third shot found the right rough again, about 40 yards from the green.

Web Miter hit a solid 2-iron between the two sand traps that guarded the right and left sides of the entrance to the green. Jason hit a 3-iron on the front edge of the green and John Rollings cozied a 4-iron about 25 feet from the cup. Both of them marked their balls and acknowledged the polite applause from the a few spectators standing around the back of the green. In John's experience there were never very large crowds in Pro-Ams, with the exception of the fans who followed the big-name players like Tiger or Arnie or Jack, or some celebrity amateurs. On some holes the number of volunteers in their broad-brimmed white hats and yellow shirts seemed to outnumber the spectators. Mostly the crowd watching any particular group was composed of the friends and relatives of the amateurs, and John hadn't yet noticed any fans rooting for the amateurs in his group. No wives, no girl friends. It was strange, John thought. Usually there were at least a few fans trailing along watching their man struggle through his round of golf.

As was becoming the custom, Carl was away once more. He hit a pitching wedge over a sand trap and ended up about 40 feet from the cup. Then Web, with no obstacles between him and the green, took a 5-iron and ran another pitch and run to within ten feet of the cup. Carl sent the putt ten feet past the cup. He two-putted from there for his seven. Jason putted next and left his ball four feet short of the hole and marked it. John lipped out for his eagle from 25 feet and tapped in for his second birdie in two holes. Web Miter rammed his birdie putt into the back of the hole. Finally, Jason, who seemed aggravated by something, missed his four-foot birdie putt and had to settle for par.

After two holes, John was two under, Web was one under, Jason was even par, and Carl was five over.

John took Jason aside on the third tee. "You seemed to get a little steamed about something, Jason," John said. "What gives?"

"Nothing. Just a few spike marks that started to look as big as pebbles when I stood over that last putt. The guy should have marked his ball," Jason said as he gestured toward Carl Buffsky.

"He has the right to putt out," John said. "Spike marks are just the rub of the green. You have to learn to ignore them."

They were still waiting for the group ahead of them to finish putting on the third green. John walked over to Web and Carl. He had seen more than one fine young player shoot a poor round because he couldn't get a bad break out of his mind.

"Web, the way you hit those pitch and run shots, you ought to go over to Britain and play some of those courses over there," John said.

"Oh, Web's big on anything foreign. Isn't that right, Web?" Carl said.

"I don't follow you," Web said.

"Didn't they call you the 'Father of Off Shoring' when you were CEO of United Eastern?"

"What's off shoring?" Jason asked.

"A company off shores when it ships work that had been done in the USA over to some foreign country. Web's corporation was a pioneer in off shoring, especially computer programming jobs to India and China. I own a small manufacturing company and we can barely compete against the Chinese."

"We live in a global economy. It has to do with cost and competition. Look at the PGA Tour. Now there are players on it from Korea, Japan, South America, South Africa and Europe," Web said. "Don't you think that makes the Tour more competitive, John?"

"Don't forget Australia," John said. "I guess you're right, Web."

"But what about Americans who have lost their jobs?" Carl asked. "How many thousands have lost their jobs because of off shoring?" Carl was almost yelling.

John waved Chump over to him. "Tell them to keep it down," John said. "They can save the world economy on the 19ᵗʰ hole. I've got a good round going here, and I don't want it interrupted by their arguments."

Chump walked over to the other side of the tee to Web and Carl. "Hey men, let's talk golf if you're going to talk anything. My man's off to a great start. He wants to stay in the zone, you know?"

The third hole was a 190-yard par 3. John hit a five-iron right on line, eight feet below the hole. Jason put his twenty feet left of the cup. Web ended up five yards short of the green. Carl played his slice this time and rolled across the green 40 feet from the pin on the right side. Web hit a pitch and run again three feet from the cup and putted out for par. Carl three-putted for bogey, Jason two-putted for par and John sunk his eight-footer for birdie.

After three holes John was a phenomenal three under par, Web was one under, Jason was even par, and Carl was eight over. Although John's was the best score against par, Web was shooting the best score against his ten handicap.

John slowed down over the next six holes, although he still ended up his front nine at a respectable three under. Web continued to get up and down with his pitching game, and was only one over on the front nine. The wheels fell off Jason's game. He bogied the fourth, fifth and sixth holes and double bogied the eighth. Carl continued with his wicked slice and ended up 16 over par for his front nine.

Meanwhile, 50 miles east of the Hartford Open a short man wearing a white cowboy hat was ushered into the upstairs office of the Foxwoods Casino by one of the plainclothes security men. After being buzzed in, he faced a man sitting behind an ornate mahogany desk. The man was known as the Chief throughout Connecticut. In twenty years his reservation had grown from little more than a roadside stand selling untaxed cigarettes to Foxwoods, the most profitable gaming casino in America. And now anybody who was serious about running for political office in Connecticut first visited the Chief.

When the Chief was jockeying for federal recognition a quarter of a century earlier he used a local pizza parlor as his office, always sitting in the same booth. Back then he wore beaded bracelets, the type a Girl Scout might make for a crafts project. People who frequented the pizza place thought him a rather pathetic figure. Now he wore diamond-studded bracelets, to go with his diamond rings and $5000 Rolex watch. His tribe was one of the wealthiest in the nation, and he was not above distributing some of that wealth to politicians who would do his tribe some good.

Butch Tyler held his cowboy hat in his hands and carefully thought out what he was going to say before he spoke. He knew he would probably never have another chance.

"There is an establishment in Las Vegas where you can bet on anything. They will give you odds on whether or not the sun will come up tomorrow and you can place a wager on it."

"I know the place," the Chief said. "What is it you want from me?"

"I need a loan of $100,000. They gave me 50 to 1 odds against my bet. But it would be a sure thing. Five million dollars that I would be willing to split with you."

"A sure thing?" the Chief asked. "What is this sure thing?"

"I will bet that an M.I.A., a man missing in action in the Vietnam War, shows up alive in the USA in the next 90 days."

"Why is that a sure thing?"

"Because he's been living in the U.S. for the past thirty years. We served together in Vietnam. I've kept in touch with him most of those years."

"And why is he going to surface after all these years?"

"I've convinced him he could run for office right here in Connecticut. As long as he is introduced to the public in the right way, he would be treated as a hero."

"Why would he be treated as a hero?" the Chief asked. "I'm listening."

"Do you remember the Japanese soldier who turned up in the early seventies? A Japanese soldier named Yokoi was discovered in the jungles on the island of Guam in 1973, twenty-eight years after Japan surrendered in World War II. Half of Japan thought he was nuts for living in the jungle all those years. The other half of Japan thought he was a hero, living up to the ancient code of Bushido, a code that said a Japanese soldier never surrenders. When he returned to Japan he was greeted by Emperor Hirohito, and was showered with cash gifts and marriage proposals, mostly from teenage girls. Within a couple months of coming home he married one of them."

"But our hero is different," the Chief said. "He wasn't holed up in the jungles of Vietnam for the past thirty years. He wasn't upholding any code. He was a deserter. He walked away from a combat unit."

"That's why we are doing it the way we are," Tyler said. "If he just turned himself in to the local police station and said, 'My name's William Robinson. I deserted from the Marine Corps in Vietnam 30 years ago,' what's the American public going to think of him? But if we videotape him rescuing a driver from a burning truck cab, the public will discover him. The videotape will be shown on every news station in the country. Then he's not a deserter, he's a hero."

"Will girls be flooding him with marriage proposals?" The Chief laughed.

"Who knows?"

"Your proposition interests me," the Chief said. "Sometimes, those who have been missing can return with more insight than those who have been here all the time. What makes you think he can get elected?"

"Celebrity," the cowboy said. "Celebrity translates into popularity, which translates into votes. And besides he's not saddled with a past, like other politicians are."

"How do I know I'm not backing an ax murderer?"

"Would it matter? Nobody will know of your connection. There's no record of his fingerprints on file for any crime. He has an impeccable work record for the past thirty years. He was married for fifteen years before his wife died ten years ago. He's worked in different parts of the country. As I said, his work record is impeccable."

"What does he do for a living?"

"He's a computer programmer."

The Chief laughed again. "At least you are not bringing me another lawyer. I've had enough of lawyers to last me a lifetime." He paused before he spoke.

"You know, the Indian understands defeat in war, because he has experienced defeat. He understands it much better than the white man. Perhaps that's why the Native American veterans came to terms with the Vietnam War much easier than white veterans." The Chief paused. "He may make a good congressman. But first I must ask you, what is he going to do for my tribe?"

"There are two other tribes vying for recognition in Connecticut. If they are recognized their casinos will cut into your profits at least fifty percent. If elected, Robinson will do everything he can to prevent their recognition."

"The man with no past. They tried to claim my tribe had no past, which is the excuse they used to delay federal recognition of my tribe. Just as we must prevent other tribes from getting official recognition by showing they don't have enough of a past to be an official tribe. He may be the right man for the job. My accountant's office is downstairs. The security man will take you down. I'm taking a chance on this

William Robinson, but then I've taken chances all my life. Good-bye."

"And one other thing," the Chief said. Tyler turned back toward him. "Colonel George Armstrong Custer was a celebrity and a hero when he rode into the Little Big Horn." Both of them laughed.

There were sodas and sandwiches on a table in front of the clubhouse behind the tenth tee. Carl and Web had not spoken to each other since the third tee and Jason had been sulking about his round.

Before John scooped a sandwich off the table Carl and Web were at it again.

"Don't tell me about the cost of labor being cheaper overseas," Carl said. "What about all the Americans who are losing their jobs? What about American jobs? How can you or any of the corporate weasels who off shore jobs overseas even call yourselves Americans?"

"What was your battalion in Vietnam, Buffsky? Don't you ever question my loyalty to this country! I got a Purple Heart fighting for the USA when I was a Marine company commander in Vietnam in 1969. Where did you serve during the Vietnam War?"

Carl seemed flustered. "I got a high lottery number in the draft," Carl said sheepishly.

"That lottery means nothing. If you were a patriot you could have volunteered for service. I volunteered for the Marines when I got out of college. Draft dodgers have no right to question anybody's loyalty to America."

"I wasn't a draft dodger. Like I said, I had a high lottery number."

John walked over to Chump. "Now we're going to re-fight the Vietnam War. See if you can calm these two down before we start the back nine." Then John walked over to talk with Jason and his kid brother, who was caddying for him.

Chump walked over to Carl and Web.

"Look, John's shooting a great round of golf. Can you two wait until we get to the 19th hole to solve the world's economy and re-fight the Vietnam War. I'd hate to see my man lose out on first place money because a couple of his amateur playing partners were distracting him. What do you say?"

"Fine with me," Web said.

"You got it," Carl said.

The order of tee-off on the tenth was John, Web, Jason and Carl. The tenth was a 570-yard straightaway par-5 with a slight wind to the golfer's back. It was reachable for most of the pros who put their drives in play. John hit his driver 310-yards between the two traps which guarded the fairway on both sides. Web hit it 280 yards on the left edge of the fairway, and Jason put it over 300 yards down the middle. As they had all come to expect, Carl sliced his drive into the right rough.

By the time the group reached the green, John and Jason were putting for an eagle, Web was putting for par, and Carl was on in five. Both John and Jason ended up making their birdies, Web made bogey and Carl made an eight.

John cruised through the next several holes at even par, Web made a birdie on a par three, and Jason traded two birdies with two bogies. Carl was shooting what Chump called an 'infinity' round, a round so high it wasn't even worth it to keep score any more. Though it was somewhat distracting to John, he rationalized that Carl was by no means the worst golfer he'd ever played with in a Pro-Am.

By the time they reached the par-3 17th hole, John was four under par, Web was a very respectable three over considering his ten handicap, Jason was frustrated at five over and Carl was just playing along at 27 over. The 17th tee was about 30 feet above the green, which was 167 yards away in a kind of bowl open at the front with bunkers to the right and behind the green. Because of its shape the hole was called the Teacup Hole. As usual John teed off first. He hit an 8-iron 15 feet behind the cup. There was polite applause from the small gallery of spectators who sat on the mounds that formed the natural amphitheater behind and on each side of the green.

Web hit a 7-iron onto the green 30 feet to the left of the pin.

"This is the best round of golf I've ever played," he said to John.

"I wanted to ask you if it was," John said. "But just like ballplayers never mention when a pitcher has a no-hitter going in the seventh inning, it's bad luck to talk to a golfer about his round when he's got a great round going. But with a ten handicap, three over is the equivalent to shooting a 65. I'm really happy for you, Web. This is no easy course for the average golfer." Then in a low voice only the two of them could hear, he gestured toward Carl. "We've got the best round one of us ever shot and the worst round. Now make this putt, Web, and finish it off with a bird on eighteen."

Jason put his 8-iron 20 feet right of the pin. Carl sliced his drive into the right hand bunker. As the group walked down the hill toward the green John and Web continued to chat. Jason and his brother had also stayed together for most of the round. John thought it was probably because Jason was so much younger than his playing partners that Jason had a hard time making conversation. John wondered how Jason got into the Pro-Am in the first place. He didn't seem to have a company behind him to foot the $6000 entrance fee, and he hadn't mentioned that his father was a big shot who would pay his way. He seemed like he was a pretty good golfer who played on some mediocre college golf team.

John saw Carl as a lost cause. Carl had hardly talked to anybody, including his caddy, since Chump had warned him about being disruptive during a match in which a pro was playing. He hadn't even hit that one shot that John was waiting for, that shot about which John could say, "Way to go, Carl. That shot will keep you coming back again."

The group was silent as they walked down the hill toward the green. Carl plodded into the sand trap and hit a decent shot out twenty feet from the cup. Web was next to putt. Sanjay held the pin and Web snaked it two feet from the hole. Sanjay lifted the pin from the cup as the ball settled, then moved off the green. Web tapped in for his par, made a hesitant wave to the crowd and bent down to retrieve the ball from the cup. The rest of the group was positioned around the green lining up their putts. Web's last thought on earth was, "One more par and I shoot a 75, my best score ever."

As Web touched his ball the cup exploded.

Meanwhile, in the clubhouse behind the eighteenth green, 43-year-old Detective Richard Geany of the Lordship, Connecticut, Police Department, manned the police communications station. In a larger police department a detective wouldn't be doing such work but small-town Lordship only had a 15-member force, and since the annual PGA Hartford Open was held at the Lordship Country Club, every man in the department worked the day shift at the golf course.

Geany heard the explosion and and could see a plume of black smoke rising from the 17th green some 400 yards away.

"This is Geany," he called over his walkie-talkie. "There's been some kind of explosion at the 17th hole. I'm going there now."

He commandeered one of the nearby golf carts and drove down the edge of the eighteenth fairway toward seventeen.

The other players and the caddies instinctively dropped to the ground and turned away from the blast. Web's caddy, Sanjay Gupta, ran up to his boss first. The metal cup had shot straight up, mangled Web's right arm, and caught him flush in the neck. He was lying on his back bouncing up and down spastically like a fish just pulled out of a lake. He was desperately trying to breathe, but his windpipe was crushed.

All Sanjay could do was kneel next to Web Miter and say, "Are you all right, Boss?"

Carl was the first to recover. "Does anybody have a cell phone?" he yelled toward the two-dozen spectators. One fan came forward with one. "Call 911," Carl said. "Lordship Country Club. 17th hole. There's been an explosion! A man's been injured!" John wondered why Carl was explaining it to the fan, who was only a few feet further away from the explosion than Carl was.

Within a minute an ambulance was racing from the clubhouse to the 17th hole. What none of the players realized was that a television tower just behind the 17th green had a camera on it. The cameraman had been testing angles for the next day's tournament. When the cup exploded on the green he called back to the production trailer. The director in the trailer told him focus on the green and keep rolling, and then the director had called the ambulance. There was a group of fans milling around the 17th hole, some running toward it and some running away from it.

By the time the ambulance had arrived Web lay still. His face was first blue, then ashen white, and Carl assumed he was dead. One of the EMTs tried to cut a hole in his tracheal tube but his neck was crushed so severely he was not successful.

The television announcers took over once the camera was rolling on the 17th hole tower.

"This is Josh Parrow and Bill Wyner reporting from the 17th hole at the Lordship Country Club in beautiful Lordship, Connecticut. There's been a major accident on seventeen. Apparently there was an explosion at the hole which seriously injured one of the amateurs who was putting out there. Bill, do you have any more information about the incident?"

"Josh, I can see the hole, or what used to be the hole, on our television monitor. The explosion made a small crater about a foot in diameter."

"The question in my mind is, Bill, will they be able to repair the damage before tee time tomorrow morning. For that matter, will they be able to finish up play today? A Pro- Am doesn't mean that much dollar wise to the amateurs, but the pros make a few bucks here."

"Josh, it won't take much to fill in the crater and tamp it down smooth. But I doubt if even that super bent Bermuda grass could grow by tomorrow morning. They could place the hole away from the damaged area for the next four days so it doesn't come into play where the pros are putting. I've just gotten word over my headset that play will not continue today. This 17th hole is a crime scene now and that won't change for quite a while. They've got that yellow crime scene tape all around it and the ambulance is here."

"Speaking of ambulance, Bill, they're wheeling a gurney right across the green. Won't that have an effect on putts tomorrow, leaving those tracks on the green like that?"

"It sure will. The ball will just skip over those gurney tracks, deflecting the ball's line ever so slightly. I see they are lifting the body onto the gurney now. There is a sheet over the body. I hope that doesn't mean the worst. Getting back to those gurney tracks. It's a real shame. Obviously those ambulance drivers are not golfers."

"At least they didn't drive the ambulance up over the green. I see now more and more police are arriving on golf carts. There is an ATF person taking scoops of soil from the crater and putting them into cellophane bags. He's wearing a black windbreaker that says 'ATF' in yellow letters. I believe that stands for Alcohol, Tobacco and Firearms."

"Josh, any idea exactly what happened?"

"The word is one of the amateurs was bending down to pick up his ball out of the cup after putting out, when the cup exploded. The metal cup flew up in the air and caught him in the throat. The pro in that group, by the way, was John Rollings. I understand both John and the amateur were shooting great rounds. John was

four under at the 17th and the amateur, a ten handicap, was only three over. A real shame. The guy's shooting the round of his life and something like this has to happen."

"You can bet tomorrow they'll have guards guarding those greens."

"You can bet tomorrow the pros will have their caddies retrieving the balls after they putt out. There's no rule that says the man who putts it has to be the one who takes it out of the cup."

Detective Geany arrived at the 17th hole five minutes after the explosion. Two uniformed policemen had already arrived on the scene. He assigned one to secure the crime scene and the other to start questioning spectators to find witnesses to the explosion. Geany then notified headquarters that he would need help from the ATF, as Alcohol, Tobacco and Firearms units were also experts in explosives. Then Geany located the remaining members of the group that was playing number seventeen when the hole exploded. John Rollings and his caddy Chump left immediately for the locker room after the explosion. Carl Buffsky argued with John that they should all stay until the authorities arrived, but the journeyman pro would have none of it.

"They can get in touch with me in the clubhouse," John yelled over his shoulder as he and Chump walked quickly toward the 18th fairway on the way in.

So when Detective Geany arrived he gathered up Carl and his caddy, Jason Sombery and his brother, and Sanjay Gupta, who was in shock after seeing his longtime employer die so horribly.

After recording all their names and phone numbers, Geany asked Carl, "What happened, Mr. Buffsky?"

"We were all on the green," Carl said. "The other three had put their drives on the green. I drove into the right bunker and blasted out onto the green. Web Miter putted about two feet short of the hole. Then he walked up and tapped it in. He reached down to get his ball out of the hole and – Boom! His body shot up in the air like a rag doll. A few minutes later he was dead."

"How did you see it, Mr. Sombery?"

"That's the way I saw it too," Jason said. "Except I never saw the body fly up. I was talking with John Rollings when Mr. Miter was tapping his ball in. So when the explosion went off I just went down on the ground. But I did see Mr. Miter wave to somebody in the crowd after he tapped it in."

"Did you see who he was waving to?"

"No. I didn't bother to look up and notice. It didn't seem like a big deal at the time."

Next Geany tried to talk with Sanjay Gupta. It was useless.

"Mr. Gupta, what did you see here today?"

"I worked for Mr. Miter for fifteen years. What now? What's going to happen now? Who's going to tell Mrs. Miter?"

"The police will see that she gets notified, Sanjay. Do you remember what happened here this afternoon?"

"His throat was crushed and his arm was mangled. And he was all black from the waist up. Then he choked to death. I remember him telling me about Marines who died like that in Vietnam. It was terrible…"

Geany gave up interviewing Sanjay Gupta and quizzed the two other caddies. Both gave basically the same account of what happened as Carl and Jason. Neither remembered Web Miter waving to anybody in the crowd. Then Geany asked each member of the group if they remembered whether Miter's hand was down inside the cup or not. None of them could recall exactly whether Web Miter hand was down inside the cup when it exploded. Geany asked the officer who was interviewing the spectators to ask each one the same question. One of the three spectators who witnessed the explosion said Miter was reaching into the cup when it exploded, while the other two said they weren't sure.

Geany walked behind the television tower, showed the cameraman his badge and yelled up to him.

"Were you filming when the explosion happened?"

"I was here in the tower, but the camera wasn't on when the hole blew up. Then they told me from the trailer to get it running."

"What's your name?" Geany yelled up at him.

"Tad Reincke. Spelled R-E-I-N-C-K-E."

Geany wrote it down in his notebook and moved back toward the green. He spotted a Hartford Open volunteer with the broad-brimmed white hat, yellow shirt and white slacks standing near the television tower.

"I'm Detective Geany of the Lordship Police Department. Were you working the seventeenth hole here when the explosion happened?"

"Yes, I was," the volunteer said. "I was standing like this when the hole exploded." He raised both arms up in the air, a 'QUIET' sign held in his right hand.

"What's your name please?" Geany asked him.

"Jim Wallace."

"Where were you standing, Jim?"

"Just about right here, behind the green on this rise. Almost underneath the television tower."

"Tell me, Jim. Did you see the man who was killed wave to anybody in the crowd just after he made his putt?"

"I think he gave a little wave," Wallace said. "But it was just to acknowledge the applause from the crowd. A lot of the golfers did that as they came through. It was just like a reflex reaction."

"Did you notice anything unusual about the spectators around the green? Did you notice any of them carrying what might look like a cell phone?"

"No, I'm sorry, Detective. I didn't notice anything like that."

"All right. Who is your employer?"

"I work for Aetna Insurance Company."

"Will you be volunteering here at seventeen for the rest of the tournament in case I want to get hold of you?"

"Will they be having the rest of the tournament after this?" Wallace asked. "Yes, I'll be here if it continues."

By this time a police photographer was taking photos of every angle of the green. Miter's body had been removed by the EMT ambulance. Geany laid down adhesive tape at the spot where the group said Miter's body had ended up after the explosion. By now an agent from the ATF had arrived. He introduced himself as Bob Corsino. After several photos of the crater were taken he took soil samples to be analyzed back in the lab. A crowd of spectators circled the green. What a circus! Geany thought. When there were no more spectators to interview, Geany called up headquarters and asked that they contact the pro shop. He asked that the pro shop sound the siren signifying there was lightning in the area and that all spectators leave immediately. After the siren sounded he had the officers who had recently arrived shoo the crowd away. They were like the rubber-neckers passing by a grisly accident. None of them wanted to leave. They'd rather gawk at the crater and the stark outline of a recently dead golfer. But finally, after much urging by the uniformed cops, the crowd dispersed and headed up the 18th fairway.

A policeman retrieved the mangled cup, which a souvenir-hungry fan was in the process of carrying away. Before Geany was two hours into the investigation he got a request from Lordship Police Headquarters. News crews were requesting permission to broadcast from the 17th hole. ABC Sports was asking if the investigation at the murder scene would be over in time for the regular tournament to begin at seven o'clock the next morning.

"Ridiculous," Geany responded in his cell phone. "There's been a murder here. We can't give up our crime scene so they can play golf tomorrow. Besides that, how do we know other holes haven't been booby-trapped. Do you think those golfers will want to play here?"

Within ten minutes police headquarters relayed a message from the governor's office. The governor was concerned about the drastic economic consequences if the tournament was canceled. The governor assured Geany that his office would provide every possible assistance, including bomb-sniffing dogs now stationed at Bradley International Airport. He also wanted Geany to estimate how many National Guard troops it would take to guard all 18 holes to make sure nobody tampered with them.

Chapter 2 – The Explosive

$$\blacktriangledown$$

The next day was the opening day of the regular PGA Tour Hartford Open tournament at Lordship Country Club. Instead of the fewer than usual spectators expected, there were more than ever before. It was like an air show crowd the day after a plane had crashed. Much of the crowd congregated around the 17th hole. Dick Geany arrived early and walked down the side of the 18th fairway to the 17th. They had filled in the crater, tamped it down and spray painted it green. Probably for TV, Geany thought.

A National Guard corporal stood just to the left of the green. He held a German Shepherd on a short leash.

When Geany identified himself as the Lordship detective in charge of the investigation, the young trooper dug out a small piece of blue-colored wire that was burnt on one end.

"One of the spectators found this on the other side of the green this morning," he said. "He gave it to me."

Geany put it into a cellophane baggie. "I'll get it to the ATF lab."

Geany walked behind the television tower and yelled up to the cameraman, Tad Reincke.

"Did you get much of the crowd right after the explosion?"

"I wasn't shooting the crowd. I had the camera zoomed in to what was happening on the green. But I might have got part of the crowd. You'll have to go to the trailer. They have the tapes."

"Thanks." Geany was hoping the bomber might act like some pyromaniacs do – they stay around to see the fire. Maybe the bomber stuck around to see what his explosive had done. Maybe he was caught on tape. At least Geany hoped so.

He nodded to the volunteer on the hole, James Wallace. He watched Wallace as each group came through to putt. Wallace held both hands high with his 'QUIET' sign in his right hand. At least he could never have triggered a remote control device in that position, Geany thought. He noted that the large crowd burst out in applause whenever one of the PGA touring pros retrieved his own golf ball from the bottom of the cup after putting out. Most of the pros had their caddy retrieve their ball from the cup.

Geany trudged back along the 18ᵗʰ fairway to the clubhouse. The governor was on the putting green with a putter in his hands, shooting a commercial. A young man held a huge reflector to the side and a young woman held up cue cards. When the director yelled "Action!" the governor spoke:

"Golf is safe. Let's not allow golf terrorists deter us from playing this great game. You know, about 350 years ago just to the north of us, the Native American Chief King Philip led a band who terrorized the first Connecticut settlers. Legend has it that King Philip himself peered down at the burning settlements from King Philip's cave. But those brave settlers rebuilt their towns, and if they were alive today they would be out this weekend playing golf.

"Take advantage of the dozens of fine public golf courses in our great state. Don't let the golf terrorists win. Call your local pro and get a starting time. And come on out to the Lordship Country Club these next four days to watch the best golfers in the world play."

The governor then bent down and stroked a five-foot putt four feet past the cup.

"Cut!" the director said.

"Can we do another take on that putt?" the governor asked.

"We'll have somebody else putt it and splice it in, Sir. Don't worry. You'll make that putt when the spot runs for keeps."

Geany had arrived an hour before John Rollings's starting time to interview him and his caddy, 'Chump Change' Williams. He didn't expect much from either one of them, and he was right. He waved John off the putting green and spoke with the pro and his caddy. He apologized for interviewing him an hour before John was scheduled to tee off, but Rollings dismissed his apology.

"Don't worry about it," John said. "The only time I'd be upset about you talking to me was if I was 4-under on the front nine, and you wanted to talk to me on the 10th tee. It was the worst thing I've ever seen in almost twenty years on the PGA Tour."

"Can I ask either of you," Geany addressed both John and Chump, "if you remember exactly where Web Miter was in relation to the hole when it blew up?"

"He was reaching in to take his ball out of the cup," Chump said.

"I really wasn't paying attention," John said. "I've learned over the years not to watch other people putt, especially the amateurs. You pick up too many bad habits."

"Chump, you're sure he had his hand down inside the cup."

"Absolutely positive."

"One more question. One of your playing partners said just before Miter tapped in his last putt, he seemed to recognize somebody in the crowd and gave a kind of wave. Did either of you see that?"

Neither John nor Chump remembered Miter waving to the crowd. Geany thanked them for their time, then entered the pro shop. The head pro, Clark Hersey, was behind the counter. Geany knew Clark to say hello to after working at the Hartford Open so many years, but he flashed his detective shield anyway.

Hersey introduced Geany to a man standing at the counter.

"Dick, I want you to meet Wayne Sedlock. Wayne is an insurance investigator with the Alco Insurance Company. Wayne, this is Detective Dick Geany of the Lordship Police Department."

"Hello, Dick. We knew each other in another life. I was an officer in the Lordship Police Department about a dozen years ago."

"Sure, I knew you from somewhere. You were only with the department for a year or two, right? This case is a far cry from somebody getting beaned with a golf ball."

"Alco covers the Lordship Country Club in all its liability cases," Sedlock said. "And this case is certainly a liability case."

Clark Hersey broke in, "The worst that's ever happened in the 17 years I've been here is somebody flipped over a golf cart and sued us for not putting Velcro on the golf cart paths."

"Detective Geany, do you subscribe to the governor's theory that Miter was killed by golf terrorists?" Sedlock asked.

"We'll find out who killed Miter. You just stick to investigating phony worker's comp cases. Let the police solve the murder cases."

Sedlock forced a laugh.

"Clark, tell me how the groups for the Pro-Am are determined," Geany said.

"There are several ways," Hersey said. "Some of them are groups that have played together for years. Often they ask to get paired up with a particular pro who they may have played with before. Then there are the local celebrities who might want to pair up with some of the better-known pros. Then there are others who enter as singles and it's just pot-luck. They get paired up with whatever pro has an opening in his group."

"Would it be possible for you to tell me how the John Rollings group got put together?"

"Yes, we keep a book of all the groups."

Hersey brought out a large 3-ring binder from behind the counter and leafed through it until he got to the Rollings page. There were copies of checks for entry fees stapled to each page.

"Do you mind if I look?" Geany asked. He took out his notebook and took notes as he scanned through the stapled sheets. Copies of $6000 checks made out to the Hartford Open were stapled together on the Rollings page. Carl Buffsky had signed one of his company checks, and Web Miter had used his consulting company as the sponsor for his entry. What was especially curious to Geany was Jason Sombery's entry. Rebecca Miter had written out the entry fee check for Jason. Geany never thought to ask Jason if he was related to Web Miter or a friend of the family. He knew from reading the newspapers a couple years earlier than the present Mrs. Miter was Web Miter's second wife, decades younger than her husband. He was thinking she might be Jason Sombery's older sister, and made a note to check it out. He couldn't figure out any other plausible reason for the second Mrs. Miter to write out a check for Jason to play in the Pro-Am with her husband.

As Geany thumbed through the binder, Clark turned to Sedlock.

"What's our liability, Wayne? Miter's family will sue, right? They'll go for the deep pockets. Are we liable for what happened yesterday?"

"This is a new one on us, Clark. Our lawyers have read over your policy a hundred times. What it boils down to is it depends who did the crime. If it really was terrorists, as the governor said, the federal government will be the ones with the deep pockets. If it was a murder done for some other reason its possible the Lordship Country Club could be liable. The thing is this type of crime hasn't been done before. It's breaking new ground, if you'll pardon the pun. We just won't know until we catch the perpetrator."

"Damn it, Wayne, I'm just a few years short of retirement. If this golf course is sued and goes into bankruptcy, or if the board of directors lets me go because of this, where am I going to get another golf course professional job at my age?"

"What do these words 'REQUEST' mean on some of these entries?" Geany asked Hersey.

"That means that person requested to play in that group," Hersey said. The word 'REQUEST' was written on Jason Sombery's entry. He requested to play with John Rollings. Or did he request to play with Web Miter? Geany made a note to check that out too.

"One more question," Geany said. "Yesterday we talked with the fellow who changed the pin position on the 17ᵗʰ hole before the Pro-Am round. He said it takes about five minutes to make a new hole and he finished seventeen about 6:45, fifteen minutes before they teed off on the 1ˢᵗ and 10ᵗʰ tees. How do you go about making a new hole and does that time sound right to you?"

"It sounds right," Hersey said. "For a tournament like this we have two guys changing pin positions, one does the front nine holes while the other does the back. They have a schematic for each hole. The drawing shows how many feet from which edge the hole will be. They use a measuring tape to measure the distances. They use a kind of post-hole digger that we call a cookie cutter that augurs out a hole four and a half inches in diameter, just large enough to hold the cup, but it goes about an inch deeper than the cup. This is so the ball never actually touches the metal part of the cup until it has actually rolled in. If the cup is too high inside the hole the ball could bounce off the cup's metal wall, and bounce out of the hole. Once the cookie cutter has taken the dirt out of that spot in the green, the guy takes the cup out of wherever it had been before and puts it into the new hole. Then he takes the dirt plug he just pulled out of the green and deposits it into the old hole with the grass on top and tamps it down. He has the pins in the back of his cart. He puts one in the new hole and that's it. Our guys here have been doing this for years. I'd say it would only take them two-three minutes tops."

"Did any of the pros from the groups before the Rollings group mention anything about the cup at the 17th hole being too high or too low?" Geany asked.

"No, nobody said anything, and believe me, these guys notice anything out of the ordinary."

"OK. Thanks, Clark. I'll be taking the Rollings entry from the book. Wayne, can I talk with you a minute outside?"

Geany and Sedlock stepped outside the pro shop.

"Look, Wayne, I didn't mean to come down hard on you inside like that. I just had to let Hersey know that the police were in charge of this case, not the insurance companies."

"No, I understand, Dick. No hard feelings."

"Here, let me give you my card," Geany said. He took a business card out of his wallet and gave it to Sedlock. Wayne did the same. "I'll have my twenty years three months from now," Geany said. "Then I'm going to pull the pin – retire."

"Good for you, Dick. Going down South, or any particular plans?"

"No, my wife's family is around here. She'd never move. I'll only be 43, too young to be out fishing every day and the wife doesn't want me hanging around the house." Both men laughed. "I was thinking about a job like yours. They take a lot of ex-cops in your business, don't they?"

"They sure do, Dick. Most of the investigators I know were in some type of law enforcement or security job at some point in their careers."

"Look, maybe I could work with you on this case. Then when I retire maybe you could put in a good word for me with your boss."

"That sounds o.k. to me, Dick. If we could catch whoever blew up Web Miter, it would certainly be a feather in your cap, a way to get your foot in the door in the insurance investigation business."

"Great. I'm going to talk with the ATF man now. You're welcome to ride up there with me."

Geany and Sedlock headed north twenty miles to the town of Simsbury. The ATF rented time from the lab at the Ensign-Bickford Company which manufactured prima-cord, a kind of explosive rope-like cord. The company had a 600-acre woodland test site and storage facility that the ATF used for testing explosives. The neighbors around the E-B complex were long used to occasional blasting since the company had been there about 200 years. The ATF agent doing the testing at E-B was Bob Corsino.

"Your explosive is C-4," Corsino said when Geany and Sedlock arrived. "We used it extensively in the Marine Corps in Vietnam."

"You were in the Marines before ATF?"

"Yes, that's where I got my introduction to explosives. Seems like a thousand years ago. After I was wounded in Vietnam they stationed me at Camp Lejeune, North Carolina, where I instructed green troops headed overseas how to use explosives, mainly C-4. After I got out of the Marines I got a B.S. in applied chemistry at the University of Massachusetts. My senior year I talked with a recruiter from the Alcohol, Tobacco and Firearms Department and mentioned my experience in the Marines as an explosives instructor. So I've been with the ATF for just over thirty years. Plan to retire in six months."

Geany was anxious to talk about the explosive in the Miter case, but he also realized Bob Corsino seemed to be one of those people who needed to talk and warm up to a person before he got down to business.

"Is this a permanent office for you?" Sedlock asked, gesturing to the cramped space within the surrounding room.

"Ensign-Bickford makes explosive products," Corsino explained. "So several years ago somebody decided it would be a good idea if an ATF agent was stationed permanently on-site to act as an inspector, to make sure nobody blew the town of Simsbury off the map. Of course, this company's been here since before the Revolutionary War, and their people probably know more about manufacturing, testing and transporting explosives than any of the rest of us will ever know, but it's a convenient post where the ATF can send agents who they are just about to put out to pasture. It is mutually beneficial, though. The ATF inspects the E-B operation, and we in turn can use their laboratory to make chemical tests on explosives, as well as a place to store and test-fire explosives. In the vast spaces out West you can drive out into the desert and test-fire, but it's a real problem here in the East where the population is so dense. We're happy to have E-B's facilities available to us."

"What do you plan to do with yourself when you retire?" Geany asked.

"Well, my wife divorced me fifteen years ago, and my two sons are out of college and on their own now. What I'd like to do is live somewhere where it's warm. You can have these New England winters, I can't take them anymore. Actually I'd like to live the way those pro golfers do. They always play in the warm climates. I'd like to get one of those big Winnebego rigs and just follow the sun. As a matter of fact, the reason I was at the murder scene so quickly was because I had just pulled into the Lordship Country Club parking lot to watch the Pro-Am when I heard the call on my radio."

"So what did you find, Bob?" Geany said. "Did you find any evidence of a timer?"

"We found what could have been wire fragments, possibly part of a battery and definitely part of a blasting cap. There could have been a timer or a detonator triggered remotely."

"I almost forgot. The guard at the 17th hole gave this to me this morning." Geany took out the cellophane baggie from his pocket with the small piece of blue wire burned on one end and handed it to Corsino.

"We'll run some tests on it. There are a number of ways the booby trap could have exploded. It could have been what we call a pressure plate device. Somebody touches it and it goes off. It's unlikely it was that."

"Why do you say that?"

"Because dozens of golfers reached into the hole before Miter and it didn't explode. Next, it could have had a timer. Again, unlikely. What are the odds a timer would set off the explosive at the precise second Miter is reaching into the cup? But if it is either a pressure plate or timing device…"

"If it is, the killing was random. We have a golf terrorist, as the governor said today."

"Another possibility is a timer that activates the pressure plate. Then we still have a random killing. Miter was just the next unlucky SOB who came along to trigger it. That would be a very complicated device to make and we probably would have found a lot more hardware at the scene than we did."

"What other possibilities are there?" Sedlock asked.

"A remote detonating device. Like the little remote devices that propel the little toy trucks across the kitchen floor on Christmas morning, or just an automatic garage door opener."

"Are they like the radio controlled model planes?"

"Yes. Somebody in the crowd near the hole or one of the players or caddies might have had some type of device. It might look like a cell phone or one of those remotes to turn the channels on TV. The killer knows electronics. He waited until the precise minute Miter was hovering over the explosive. Boom."

"That would mean it was Miter he wanted all along," Sedlock said. "That would take it out of the realm of a terrorist act."

"The Unabomber was a terrorist bomber," Corsino said. "It took us 18 years to get him. And they had another bomber here in Connecticut they called the Mad Bomber. His name was George Metesky. He planted about 30 explosive devices in the New York City area from 1940 to 1957. It was the first time police used psychological profiling to catch a suspect."

"I want to believe it's not a terrorist situation," Sedlock said. "The Richter Park golf course over in Danbury got a call this morning that there was a bomb in one of its holes. It took them three hours to check it out with bomb sniffing dogs. It turned out it was a golfer who thought he could get a better starting time if other golfers ahead of him in line dropped out and went home. Then we got another nut call that somebody wanted a million dollars or they would booby trap the Hartford Open again. We figured the nuts would start coming out of the woodwork."

"Let's drive over to the test site," Corsino said. "I'll show you what the explosion looked like."

Geany, Sedlock and Corsino drove to the south gate. A guard waved them through when Corsino showed his badge. "Test bang!" Corsino said to the guard as he drove by him. The guard nodded and wrote something on a clipboard. They traveled along a dirt road into the vast woodland behind the E-B complex. Corsino stopped in front of a garage-sized dirt bunker, unlocked a padlock on its door and retrieved a brick of C-4. It looked like a giant stick of butter encased in a clear plastic sheath. He also retrieved a fuse and a couple blasting caps.

"You might notice something different about the trees in these woods," Corsino said, as they drove toward the test site. "They're huge. This company has owned this property since the Revolutionary War. Almost all the rest of the woodland in New England has been logged at least once. That's why the original settlers came here in the first place. But this property never has been logged."

They stopped on the road and walked into the woods about twenty-five yards. Corsino took a trowel out of his back pocket and scooped out a hole approximately the size of a cup on a golf course. Then he sliced off about two inches from the brick of C-4, as if he was slicing a slab of butter. He kneaded the C-4 until he was shaping it in a ball, like a ball of silly putty. He inserted the blasting cap into the C-4, cut off about two feet of fuse, attached them all and dropped the explosive into the hole. Then he looked at his watch.

"Close enough," he said. "Test blasts go off at eleven in the morning and three in the afternoon. The residents nearby are used to that. It's just eleven now." Then he lit the fuse and the two men hurried back behind their car. For such a small amount of explosive there was a very large bang. The men walked over and examined the crater. It was about a foot in diameter.

"C-4 is a powerful explosive," Corsino said. "But one thing I found about the residue of C-4 we took samples from at the Lordship Golf Course. It's an old batch. It has a resin in it that they quit making during the Vietnam War."

"You mean this explosive has been sitting around for 30 years?" Geany asked.

"Yes it has."

Chapter 3 – The Suspects

--- ▼ ---

Detective Geany made arrangements to talk with Jason Sombery at the Lordship Police Headquarters on Friday morning. He invited Wayne Sedlock and asked the Connecticut State Police to bring in a lie detector unit in case Jason was willing to take a lie detector test.

"I'll get right to the point," Geany said once they had settled into the back conference room. "We found the cancelled check for your entry into the Pro-Am Wednesday. It was written by Web Miter's wife, Rebecca Miter. What's your relation to the Miters?"

"I don't know Mr. Miter at all, but I've known Mrs. Miter for about five years. When I was in college I worked part-time at an ice cream shop in Danbury. Mrs. Miter, who wasn't married to Mr. Miter then, worked at United Eastern headquarters in Danbury. She used to stop over for ice cream during the summer. Sometimes she'd stop in at lunch hour and sometimes after work. We just got to know each other. She was five years older than me, but we seemed to hit it off. She had a great sense of humor."

"That doesn't explain why she would write a $6000 check so you could play in the Hartford Pro-Am."

"As time went on Becky found out I was on the golf team at Western Connecticut. I even had aspirations of turning pro some day. I didn't have to work in the morning so I'd get up and play every morning at the Richter Park course. Then I'd be in by noon at One Scoop or Two. I got to be a pretty good golfer during college. My senior year I was the number one seed on Western's golf team. Becky asked me one day if I gave golf lessons. She thought it would really help her career. I had the impression she was very ambitious at United Eastern. She was one of Mr. Miter's executive assistants almost from the day she started there. So we started meeting some nights at a driving range in Danbury."

"How far did this relationship go?"

"What do you mean?"

"Were the two of you having sex?"

"Oh, no. It wasn't like that. I was just a college kid. Becky was dating and eventually married one of the most powerful men in the business world. Mr. Miter used to have his picture in Newsweek. I was just a kid to her. One time we kissed, but I don't count that. Becky had had a couple drinks at an office party after work. Then she came to the driving range for her lesson. She was acting silly, really goofy. I was right behind her trying to straighten out her takeaway and she turned around and kissed me on the lips. But that was the only time anything like that ever happened. I swear."

"Jason, you still haven't explained the $6000 check."

"It was my senior year when she married Web Miter. There had been all that in the tabloids about his divorce just when he retired. They had a field day about what he got. I remember one thing was a hot tub. David Letterman and Jay Leno had great fun with things like that. Then there was a big rhubarb with the ex-wife about who was going to get the hot tub. Then after the divorce Becky marries Web Miter. I thought she was crazy, even though he had all that money. She was about 26 and he was 60. I didn't see her much around that time. Then the next summer she calls me up and asks if I still give lessons. I didn't even know she knew my phone number. I was out of college by then and turning pro was just a pipe dream. I was going down to the City every day on the train. I got a job in the financial district in Lower Manhattan at Paine Webber. Anyway, I agreed to give Becky lessons again. It was hard, too, because sometimes I wouldn't get home from work until seven o'clock. She really didn't seem all that interested in the lessons. She'd drive up to the driving range in her new BMW and mostly we'd just talk. She said she just had to get away from the servants and the cook and the chauffeur and all the domestic help and just talk with somebody her age. She said even Web's two daughters from his first marriage were older than her. She said she felt like the stereotypical trophy wife. I said her husband did a lot of things in his life, but at least I was a better golfer than he was. That's when she told me he was going to play in the Hartford Pro-Am and we came up with the idea of me playing in his group. As it turned out he was beating me by three strokes scratch when…"

"Would you be willing to take a lie detector test to verify what you just said?"

"Yes, I would."

Geany escorted Sombery into the next room and conferred with the state police examiner. They reviewed what questions the examiner would ask. After thirty minutes the examiner told Geany, "According to all my indicators, the kid's telling the truth." Geany took Jason back into the conference room.

"Jason, what course did you play on for your college team?" Wayne Sedlock asked.

"The Richter Park course," Jason said.

"Tough course?"

"A lot of water. It gave you a little variety, anyway."

"What did you major in at college?"

"Economics. I guess it paid off."

"And one last question. Are you absolutely sure that Web Miter waved to somebody in the crowd just before he was killed?"

"Absolutely sure, Sir."

Geany ordered background checks done on everybody in the golf foursome, which included John Rollings and his caddy Philip 'Chump' Williams, Carl Buffsky and his caddy, Jason Sombery and his brother, and Web Miter's caddy Sanjay Gupta. Background checks would also be done on all others known to be at the scene at the time of the explosion, which included three spectators interviewed by the Lordship police and tournament volunteer James Wallace. Geany didn't hold out much hope that the background checks would turn up anything. He felt that the perpetrator of a crime so well planned would never stick around at the scene.

Wayne Sedlock drove back to his office at the Alco Insurance Company in Hartford and spent the afternoon reviewing biographies of Web Miter. Janie Caldwell, a college intern majoring in business and working at Alco for the summer, assembled 48 different newspaper clippings on Miter's dynamic career with United Eastern.

"I could have gotten 100 more," Janie said. "This sure beats processing timesheets. I got a lot of it off the Internet but a lot of it I got off Nexis-Lexis. It took a full day, but like I said, it sure beat what I've been doing for the past four weeks. This is a real case, you know?"

"That's great, Janie. What's Nexis-Lexis?"

"It's computer software that searches newspaper files. Most companies and college libraries subscribe to it. You enter the search key words and it will find any article that has those words. Then you print it out."

"So, what do you have here?"

"I separated the articles into three piles. The first pile is Miter's basic biography. That was fairly easy to get. In fact United Eastern provides his biography on the Internet. The second pile is his business years – what divisions he worked at over the years, what new products he was involved in and what divisions he restructured – in other words, what divisions he cut loose and disbanded. That pile was the toughest, but I did highlight various items on each sheet that I thought might be important. The third pile is more recent information. A lot of it reads like a tabloid newspaper. A couple years ago Miter divorced his wife of thirty years and married his very beautiful 26-year-old executive assistant. At the same time he retired from United Eastern. What he got is all in there, but for example, he got a lifetime membership to a very exclusive Greenwich golf club. His chauffeur who had been driving him for the company for years was to continue driving him at company expense. There's a lot more. All this came out in the divorce. Mrs. Miter Number One wanted to be compensated for all the goodies Web Miter got in his retirement. The newspapers had a ball with all the goodies. Some of those New York Times articles read like the National Enquirer. Pile number three was interesting, to say the least."

"I think I know who that chauffeur is already, Mr. Sanjay Gupta, who was caddying for Web Miter when he was killed. That reminds me, I'm going to have to talk with him. If he's worked for Web Miter a lot of years he may be the one to talk to about who's who in the Miter family."

Sedlock spent the remainder of the afternoon reviewing the information Janie had gathered. Web Miter was born in Bridgeport, Connecticut, in 1941. He was an only child. His father was an engineer with Sikorsky Aircraft and his mother was a schoolteacher. Web showed an early aptitude in science when he won a statewide science fair at age 15. In 1959 he attended M.I.T. Four years later he was a graduate engineer. He attended graduate school at Caltech and received his M.S. in electrical engineering in 1965. After graduation he became a Marine officer serving with distinction in Vietnam in 1968-69. Web joined United Eastern at the end of 1969 and worked there for the next 33 years until retirement in 2002.

Sedlock then read through pile two. Like Janie, he had a difficult time wading through all the assignments Miter took on over his thirty plus year career. He began his career as an engineer in the Rochester, New York, plant. He took on positions of greater and greater responsibility almost from day one. It was clear Web was a natural leader. He met and married his first wife Donna in Rochester and they had two girls soon after. Like many in their generation the Miter family was corporate gypsies. They moved to San Antonio, then Los Angeles, then Minnesota. All the while Web was being groomed for leadership in United Eastern. It was in Minnesota that Web first suggested the corporation scuttle one of the operating groups under him, rather than try to resurrect it. This philosophy ran counter to the paternal attitude United Eastern was known for, but corporate leadership let Web sink or swim with his decision. Within a year it was obvious that it had been the right decision as the rest of the Minnesota operation flourished without its poor sister dragging it down. To counter the argument that employees had to be let go, Web talked of situations in Vietnam where some Marines had to be sacrificed for the greater good of the whole unit. Corporate brought its rising star back to Danbury, Connecticut, and the Miters never were corporate gypsies again.

Web Miter continued his slash and burn philosophy during his entire career, and in his last years after he became CEO of United Eastern he introduced off shoring to the corporate world, especially the off shoring of information technology jobs to India. He became known as the "Father of Off Shoring" and it was not uncommon to see unemployed computer programmers demonstrating with picket signs outside auditoriums when he was speaking. He brought United Eastern back to profitability and he became a model for young managers throughout the corporate world to follow. Off shoring became a way of life in corporations throughout the U.S.A.

Sedlock agreed pile three was more fun to read. At age sixty Miter divorced his wife of thirty years and married a 26-year-old corporate assistant named Rebecca Livingston.

His lawyers had negotiated a deal with United Eastern which provided him with everything from an ornate Roman bath-type hot tub to a herd of half a dozen llamas which were a gift from the president of Peru to season tickets at Yankee Stadium to free postage for the rest of his life to the continued service of his chauffeur. At about the same time Miter exercised his option to buy and sell stock options he had accumulated over three decades with United Eastern, a transaction which newspapers reported netted him a profit of some $25 million dollars. Donna Miter, his ex-wife, had her lawyer contest everything in court for which she would get a share in the divorce settlement. Newspapers and talk shows alike gleefully exposed what looked like the petty greed of corporate CEOs throughout the country.

After he had finished reading, Sedlock asked himself – how many employees had been laid off over the years under Miter's direction? And would any of them hold enough of a grudge to kill him? He thought of the George Metesky case, the Mad Bomber from Waterbury, Connecticut, who was wacko enough to plant bombs throughout New York City for sixteen years, but was sane enough to walk the streets and blend in with millions of other people. One thing Sedlock knew for sure. This wasn't some run of the mill street criminal. For that matter he wasn't even your average hit man. Whoever made this bomb and detonated it was a genius. There are only eighteen spots on a golf course where a golfer is guaranteed to be in the course of playing a round of golf. The location of the bomb was perfect. The timing of the blast was perfect. The planning was perfect. Who was this bomber? Sedlock wondered.

Detective Geany knocked on Chief Livy's door.

"Come in." The chief had an open-door policy for any of Lordship's 15-member police force. For the past two days the chief had been running interference with the media. The Hartford Open was the biggest event all year in tiny Lordship.

Now the chief had to deal with television, radio and newspaper reporters, tournament officials at the Hartford Open, and the governor's office. But Chief Herbert Livy was up to the job. He had been Lordship's police chief longer than most of his men had been on the force, and he wasn't easily impressed by calls from luminaries such as the governor. He knew he had to keep the media away from Dick Geany so Geany could do his job. He admired Dick, who he felt had the best detective's mind he had ever seen in almost forty years in police work. Geany in turn often used the chief to brainstorm ideas in a case. That was the reason he knocked on the chief's door.

"Why a golf course?" Geany asked. "Why not put the bomb in his mailbox? Or underneath Miter's car?"

"Miter is a wealthy man," the Chief responded. "Insulated. A maid may retrieve his mail, if he even has a mailbox. His chauffeur drives him around. Maybe the killer is particular about only getting Web Miter."

"And at the Hartford Open. Why not when Miter is playing with his buddies at the Greenwich Country Club he belongs to? In front of a television camera, yet. The killer couldn't have known that camera behind the 17th hole wasn't going to be running when the bomb went off."

"What else?" Chief Livy asked.

"The big question. Why Web Miter?" Geany asked. "Miter has been retired for two years. He's had nothing to do with United Eastern recently. He's out of the picture."

"Let's back up," the Chief said. "Why explosives? If a disgruntled ex-wife hires a hit man, the contract killer is going to use a method that brings as little attention to himself as possible. Not a killing at a nationally televised PGA golf tournament."

"And the type of explosives," Geany said. "It's called C-4. According to the ATF man it contained a resin that hasn't been used for more than thirty years. Why use an explosive that's been sitting around that long?"

"Because it's what the killer had available?" the Chief asked.

"It keeps going back to the killer is making a statement."

"Dick, do we know the intended victim was Web Miter?"

"We don't know one hundred percent. But the killing points to a remote control triggering device. That means the killer watched Web Miter bend down to pick his golf ball out of the hole. So at that instant the killer intended to kill Miter. I don't even want to think of the killing being random. If it was random we may be in for the long haul."

"How difficult would it be make a remote triggering device?"

"According to Bob Corsino of the ATF it requires a little knowledge of electronics, but all the components are easily available. A hobby store sells remote control kits for model airplanes and cars and a simple automatic garage door opener could be fashioned to detonate an explosive. And of course the Internet could provide any instructions the killer might need. In other words, you don't have to be an MIT graduate to do it."

"Look for some group or person that Miter ran into in his career who might want to make a statement by killing him this way," the Chief said. Both Chief Livy and Geany sat quietly for a full minute. "Wayne, why the 17th hole?"

"The killer only had about fifteen minutes to plant the explosive beneath the cup, from approximately 6:45 to 7:00 o'clock Wednesday morning. The groundskeeper changed pin locations at seventeen just before that. The hole is a 167-yard par three that drops 30 feet from tee to green. The green is open in the front and surrounded by mounds on three sides, with pine trees behind the mounds. The killer would be hidden on three sides when he was planting the explosive. I believe that's why he chose the 17th hole."

"How far away would the killer have to be to trigger a remote detonator? Could he have done it from the tee 167 yards away?"

"Not likely. The killer needed line-of-sight to see Miter taking his golf ball out of the cup. He would have that from the tee, but the effectiveness of a remote device from that range would be very unreliable. Think of an automatic garage door opener. What are the odds it would work from 500 feet away? If the foursome and the caddies check out, I think the killer was on one of the mounds surrounding the green. He could have been standing right underneath the television tower, so he would never be photographed by the TV camera. According to the players, they remember there being ten to fifteen spectators at that hole. And at least one of the players and a spectator we interviewed remembers Web Miter waving to somebody just after he made his putt."

"Did the television cameraman get anything worth seeing at the 17ᵗʰ hole?"

"I went to the production trailer to view the videotape last night. There was nothing to speak of. The cameraman was just lining up shots during the Pro-Am. There were a couple shots of other groups for just a few seconds. There were no shots of any spectators around the 17ᵗʰ green. Then the cameraman started filming for real after the explosion. By that time the 17ᵗʰ was a madhouse, with hundreds of spectators gawking to see what happened."

"Have you checked out the cameraman?"

Geany took out his notebook. "Cameraman's name is Tad Reincke. Thirty-five years old. Has worked for ABC Sports for ten years. According to his employer he's been doing the golf tournament tour for five years. We'll do a background check on him as well as the Hartford Open volunteer working the seventeenth. His name is James Wallace, works as a computer programmer at Aetna Insurance. He was holding both arms up with a 'QUIET' sign in one hand when the foursome was putting. He didn't notice anybody with a remote device among the spectators."

"Are you going to use the state police lie detector on the foursome and their caddies?"

"Yes. We already checked out Jason Sombery, the recent college grad who was playing in the foursome. He was a friend of the latest Mrs. Miter, but nothing out of the ordinary showed up on the lie detector test. John Rollings has a morning tee time today, so he and his caddy Chump Williams have agreed to show up at the Meriden state police facility about four this afternoon. In fact, we're taking them over there in a Lordship cruiser. Carl Buffsky, the manufacturer from New Britain, gave us a lot of static and threatened to bring his lawyer, but finally agreed to be over at Meriden about noon today. We delivered the caddies this morning and they all checked out. We delivered all except Web Miter's caddy, Sanjay Gupta. I tried interviewing him right after the explosion, but talking with a cop was hopeless. I've asked Wayne Sedlock, the Alco insurance investigator, to meet Gupta at the Miter funeral, then see that he gets to the Meriden state police building for a lie detector test."

"It sounds like you've got things pretty much under control. Let me know if you need anything."

Chapter 4 - Eleanor North

---▼---

Eleanor North squinted at the computer screen in the Petaluma Public Library. Generally she did genealogical searches in the San Francisco area, but every once in a while she got a contract from a police department for a background check. This one was for a James Joseph Wallace, born October 6, 1946 in Petaluma. She found him in the birth file almost instantly. Thank God for the project in 1988 when interns were hired to key birth and death records into the computer for most of the towns in the San Francisco area, Eleanor thought. It was so much easier now with the computer. Eleanor remembered the days of poring through microfilm. Sometimes her arm was ready to drop off at the end of the day from turning the crank on the microfilm reader.

She selected the name and clicked her cursor on Deceased File. Immediately the name appeared again, this time with the date July 2, 1950. Eleanor's heart raced. She rarely got subcontracts for background work and she had never discovered a name on the Deceased File before while doing a background check. She had used the Deceased File many times in her genealogical searches, but background checks were supposed to be on living persons. Could it be? Could she have uncovered somebody who had stolen somebody else's identity? She screen-printed the full name and July date and out of habit copied them down in her pocket notebook. Then she gathered up her things and hurried to the microfilm drawers which held the past 75 years' issues of the Petaluma *Chronicle*. She had to be sure.

On the obituary page of the July 7, 1950 issue: *James Joseph Wallace, age 3, died suddenly on July 2 after being hit by a car. He is the beloved son of Thomas and Emily Wallace, and brother of Candice Wallace. He also leaves his maternal grandparents Victor and Ruth Smith of Colorado Springs, Colorado, and his paternal grandparents Joseph and Mary Wallace of San Francisco. The Welty Funeral Home is in charge of arrangements. There will be no calling hours. Burial will be Thursday at St. Catherine Cemetery. "Jimmy will live with us forever."*

Eleanor printed two copies of the obituary, then gathered her things once more, drove home and got her Kodak Sure Shot camera. She drove out to St. Catherine's Cemetery. After conferring with the groundskeeper she found the gravestone of James Joseph Wallace and his parents, snapped several pictures, then drove home to write her report. By now she was beyond excitement. Now she was sure. Somebody had stolen little Jimmy's identity, used his date of birth and given Petaluma as his place of birth. She wrote up her report quickly and precisely. She would drive into the Petaluma Police Department with it. There, they would fax it to the police department that made the request. And she was determined to stay long enough to know who requested it. Her heart beat rapidly. This was one of the most exciting days of her life.

"You're sure?" the Petaluma police sergeant asked her for the second time.

"I checked it over a dozen times," Eleanor said, slightly exasperated that the sergeant might doubt her.

"Do you want a copy of this?" the sergeant asked her.

"I have a copy, thank you."

"Fax Miss North's report to Connecticut," he said to his secretary. "The number's on my desk."

Connecticut, Eleanor thought. Where in Connecticut?

"You mean this one, Lordship Police Department, Detective Geany?" the secretary asked.

"That's the one. Miss North, send in your invoice at the end of the month."

Eleanor drove to the 1-Hour Photo Stop and picked up her photos of the gravesite. She stared at the pictures for several minutes, then re-read the obituary. "Jimmy will live with us forever." How appropriate, she thought. According to the gravestone James's father passed away January 10, 1977. His mother died July 17, 1993. She headed back to the Petaluma Public Library, determined to locate the sister, Candice Wallace.

The microfilm of the mother's obituary showed that funeral arrangements were handled by the Welty Funeral Home, the same funeral home that had buried James forty-three years earlier. She looked up their number and called.

"Welty Funeral Home," a woman's voice answered.

"Hello, my name is Eleanor North, I'd like to make an inquiry about a funeral that took place on July 21, 1993. The name of the deceased was Emily Wallace. I'm trying to locate her daughter, Candice Wallace."

"Just a minute. I'll put you through to Mr. Welty."

A minute later a man's voice said, "Hello. This is George Welty. Yes, I have the file here for that funeral. Arrangements were made by the daughter, Dr. Candice Simpson."

"Can you tell me how I can get a hold of the daughter? Do you have an address or a phone number?"

"I have her phone number at the time of the funeral."

"Do you know what she did for a living?"

"Sure. She taught psychiatry at Berkeley. She was a very smart woman. A Ph.D. Can I ask you why you're trying to locate Dr. Simpson?"

Eleanor paused. "It has to do with the estate. Her father owned a small piece of land north of here."

"I see."

"Mr. Welty, one more thing. This is just my curiosity. On the gravestone is a son, James Joseph Wallace, who died in 1950 at the age of three. Would you have any records of his funeral?"

"Sure, I have it right here in front of me. These are my grandfather's notes. We keep all the records of a single family together. What would you like to know?"

"Has anybody made any inquiries about the boy in the past fifty years?"

"Well, I doubt if we kept any notes on that. No, I don't see anything here."

"All right, I'll take that phone number of Candice Simpson if you don't mind."

After she copied down the number and hung up, Eleanor realized she was breathing hard. For the first time she realized she had lied about the estate, and she didn't know why. She dialed Candice Simpson's number. What would she say? That somebody may have taken her little dead brother's identity? After four rings, a voice message said, "Hello, this is Dr. Simpson. I am on sabbatical. Please contact the head of the UC Berkeley Psychiatry Department, Dr. James Rubin. Thank you." At the beep Eleanor hung up.

Chapter 5 - The Two Mrs. Miters

Sedlock had asked Sanjay Gupta if they could ride together to Web Miter's funeral. He figured since Gupta had been Web Miter's driver for the past fifteen years he could point out who's who in the procession. Sedlock wasn't as concerned with the captains of industry who he was sure would be there as he was with Miter's family and friends. He wanted to know what they looked like as he planned to call on both Mrs. Miters. There was also that remote possibility that the killer might attend the funeral to view his handiwork.

"I still can't believe this is happening," Gupta said as he and Sedlock sat in Sedlock's 5-year-old Saturn outside the church. They found a spot where they could view everybody going in and out. "I've known Mr. Miter for twenty-five years. This is so terrible."

"I thought you said you were his driver for fifteen years," Sedlock said.

"But I knew him before. We both worked together for United Eastern as engineers in San Antonio."

"That's quite a step to go from engineer to driver."

"But I like to think I am more like his assistant. It was my job to see that Mr. Miter was ready for his next stop, wherever that might be. Mrs. Miter, I mean Donna Miter his first wife, used to pack his bags when he went to Peru or China or India. But I would have to check them to see that he had everything he needed. For instance if he was going to Europe he needed adapters for wall sockets because their electrical circuits are wired differently than ours. If he was going to Peru I might have to come up with a greeting in Spanish to greet the president of Peru. I guess you would call me his handy man."

"Sanjay, who is that getting out of the limo and walking into the church now?"

"That is Donna Miter and her two daughters Tiffany and Lisa." A stout woman about sixty years old hurried in front of the daughters, who were 33 and 31. The younger daughter, Lisa, was three years older than Becky Miter, Web's second wife. Just then a model-thin Becky Miter appeared out of her limo, along with her parents. Even though Sedlock expected as much, he was stunned by the difference in ages between the two women. He thought the beautiful Becky looked even several years younger than her 28 years. The two women hesitated for a second at the church door, then Mrs. Miter Number One led her daughters into the church and Becky's parents supported the young widow as they walked into the church.

"It's such a shame," Sanjay said. "I've known Donna for twenty years or more. She was so supportive of Web's career. I remember Web locked himself out of his car once. He was at a conference 120 miles from home. Here was the managerial guru locking himself out of his car. So he called Donna and she brought an extra key. You see, he didn't want anybody to know, even me, that he had done such a dumb thing. But Donna was always there for him. Then just when they should be retiring and enjoying life Web leaves her for that young girl Rebecca. Then all the divorce scandal in the newspapers."

For the next half hour Sanjay Gupta pointed out the who's who of industry who appeared for Web Miter's funeral. Some were Web's peers, CEOs from other corporations. But many of them were younger - the young Turks who imitated Web's slash and burn methods of managing. Just then Sedlock noticed a lone picketer in front of the church. He carried a sign which read "Bury Him In Bangalore" with the inscription SOJ underneath it.

"What's that all about?" Sedlock asked.

"There's an organization called 'Save Our Jobs' that is against off shoring computer programming jobs overseas. They've appeared almost everywhere Web has gone in the past two years. But they hadn't bothered him for the past six months or so. This is the first picketer I've seen in several months. It's sacrilegious to show up at his funeral!"

"O.K. Sanjay. I know you're going to meet Detective Geany and drive up to the state police barracks in Meriden now. I'll want to speak to Donna Miter tomorrow, then to Rebecca Miter." As they drove north on I-95 Sedlock asked Gupta, "Were you supposed to drive one of the limos in the funeral procession?"

"No, I'm in limbo now. My contract was for as long as Web Miter needed my services. Since he is dead now, I will drive for Rebecca Miter until United Eastern tells me my services are no longer needed."

"What will you do now?"

"I am retired now. I will go back to India to live."

"You never became an American citizen?"

"No. My home is India."

"How did you come to America in the first place?"

"When I was twelve years old there was a terrible explosion of a chemical plant in my home town. United Eastern owned the plant. Both my parents were killed. Mr. Miter came to India to assess the damage and negotiate compensation for the victims and their families. He decided to bring all the orphans who wanted to come to America back to the States and educate them. I ended up getting an engineering degree from the

University of Texas and going to work for United Eastern in San Antonio with Mr. Miter. I've been with him ever since."

"That's a great story, Sanjay. Good luck to you. Will you be around for the next couple weeks?"

"Yes, I will give you my cell phone number."

The next day Sedlock drove to Danbury to visit Mrs. Donna Miter, Web Miter's first wife. She owned their Danbury residence after the divorce. He referred to her as Mrs. Miter Number One.

"Mrs. Miter. You have my condolences," Sedlock said to Donna Miter when she answered her door. "I called. I'm Wayne Sedlock of Alco Insurance Company."

"Come in, Mr. Sedlock. I assume you are trying to find out what happened. How can I help you?"

"Is there anybody you can think of who could possibly want to kill Web Miter? You certainly knew him better than anybody."

"I didn't know him as well as I thought. But there were no particular individuals I can think of. There were those damn anti-outsourcing types who were always picketing him. But they didn't strike me as the types who would do something like this. Did you see that sign in front of the church? Horrible."

"Mrs. Miter, as part of our investigation we traced any large sums of money from people we thought were close to Mr. Miter. We saw this crime as almost a professional hit, which probably would have cost a lot to finance. We found a $5,000 check that you wrote recently to the organization 'Save Our Jobs,' one of those anti-outsourcing groups you just talked about. Can you explain that?"

"I can try to explain. I was trying to buy them off. Trying to get them to stop harassing Web. I guess I was trying to get Web back. Obviously it didn't work."

"Who did you send the check to?"

"I sent it to the post office box listed in the web site. I got a call shortly afterward from the president of the organization.

His name was Merriwether. He seemed to be running for office. He talked so excitedly about the laws that were going to be passed to stop off-shoring. And the congressmen who didn't go along with it were going to be booted out of office. He got very excited indeed. I remember thinking at the time how naïve this man was. He had been a computer programmer and had lost his job. And he was going to show the world what outsourcing had done to him."

"Thank you very much, Mrs. Miter. I think that's all I have for now."

"Can I show you something about Web that not many people know? You know we have two daughters? Web's father is also living. He's 90 years old and stays in a convalescent home near here. I have to go over there and tell his father Web is dead. Would you mind going with me?"

"Certainly," Sedlock said. He felt uncomfortable but he felt Donna Miter could be an invaluable ally in solving the case.

They arrived at the Valley View Convalescent Home in five minutes. Steven Miter was sleeping when they entered his room. Donna gently shook him.

"Donna. How are you? What's Web up to? Haven't seen him in quite a while."

"Dad, this is Mr. Sedlock. He's an insurance investigator with the Alco Insurance Company."

"What's the problem? Is Web all right?"

Donna and Sedlock remained quiet.

"What happened?" the old man asked.

"Web is dead, Dad. There was an explosion…"

"Web's dead?" Tears welled up in the old man's eyes. "You never expect to see your children die before you. What happened?"

"There was some kind of explosion, Sir," Sedlock said. "It happened when your son was playing golf. It happened on the 17th hole of the Lordship Country Club."

"Playing golf? Web seemed to be enjoying playing golf so much after he retired. He talked about it."

"Sir, did Web ever talk about anybody who he felt might want to harm him?"

"No, never. But then he never would. Web was strong. People forget Web was a Marine in Vietnam. He didn't have to go over there. He could have stayed out of the Marines. He had his engineering degree from MIT and a master's degree from Caltech. He could have gone to work for any company in the country. He could have gotten a defense deferment and stayed out of the war. But he ups and joins the Marine Corps. I couldn't talk him out of it. He was so strong and determined. When he set his mind to do something, he did it."

"Mr. Miter," Sedlock said, "did Web ever mention anybody from the Marines who might want to do something like this? Did he ever mention anything about an explosive in the Marines they called C-4?"

"Web didn't talk much about the war. He told us a couple times about the mines. The horrible deaths some of his Marines suffered after stepping on a mine set by the enemy. He told a story once about C-4. One Marine was carrying some in his pack when he stepped on a mine. The explosion was so great they couldn't find anything to send home to his family."

Steven Miter began weeping. "He was such a good son. Even though he achieved so much in his life he always visited his mother and me. He always asked what he could do and took care of us." He got himself under control. "Web always wanted to be an engineer. I was an engineer at Sikorsky for forty years. I guess many sons want to do what their father did. But he was so good with people. He found out in Vietnam he was a born leader." The old man stared off into space.

"Dad, the funeral was yesterday," Donna said. "Tiffany and Lisa will be over to see you later in the week. They aren't feeling too well now. We're going to go now."

Donna Miter and Sedlock left in Donna's car.

"I just wanted you to see the other side of Web. The tabloids had a field day with our divorce but you can't be married to a man for more than thirty years and not still love him. I hope you find who did this, Mr. Sedlock."

When Sedlock got in his car he phoned into his office number a message so he wouldn't forget Monday morning. "Check a Merriwether, president of the anti-outsourcing organization 'Save Our Jobs.'"

Sedlock made it back from Danbury to his condo in Lordship in under an hour. It being a Sunday afternoon the main chore was laundry. Sedlock was used to the bachelor's life. He had only been married two years when his wife Nancy divorced him almost a dozen years earlier less than a year after his son was born. He'd had a breakdown which the doctors called a psychotic episode, but whatever it was, Nancy left him because of it. He had been working at a small town weekly newspaper just over the Massachusetts border then, but after the breakdown he didn't feel he could do journalism work anymore. For six months after he got out of the hospital he didn't do anything at all. Then the medication gradually brought him back to reality and he joined the Lordship Police Department. The department fired him less than two years later when it found out he hadn't mentioned his mental illness on his job application.

Sedlock hooked up with Alco and buried himself in his work, and as a result he thought less and less about those terrible days a dozen years earlier. He never knew what caused the breakdown. He asked every psychiatrist he ever talked to, and every one had the same reply, "Nobody knows for sure."

As he waited for the washing machine's spin cycle to stop Sedlock opened the bottom drawer of his bureau. Tucked neatly in a pile were several medals and ribbons he had won in high school and college at different golf tournaments. Yet he hadn't played golf in the dozen years since the breakdown. Once golf meant almost everything to him. He dreamed of becoming a golf professional. But those dreams, Sedlock thought, slipped away, just like his marriage and his journalism and police careers. All he had left was his insurance investigative work and he was determined not to lose that. He was driven in his work and he was determined to find Web Miter's killer.

Sedlock thought about his son Justin. He was twelve now and Sedlock was trying his best to stay a part of his life. Nancy had mellowed over the past few years in her attitude toward allowing Sedlock to see Justin. They saw each other some weekends now, and were getting to know each other. Nancy trusted Sedlock as long as he stayed on his medication. Sedlock watched some of Justin's Little League games. Justin was quite an athlete, a good hitter for his age. Sedlock thought about taking him to a driving range and teaching him what he knew about golf.

But he knew Justin's first love was baseball. He logged on to his computer and brought up the Ebay screen. He read: *"This is possibly the hottest card in the 1950's – the scarce 1952 high number rookie card of Ed Mathews. We grade this card VG-EX – very well centered, great color and visual appeal. Moderate surface wear. It's got 3 thin light surface wrinkles in the bottom third of the card. Full guide is $10,000. See our other vintage and graded items for auction on Ebay."*

Sedlock was wavering between the 1952 Eddie Mathews rookie baseball card and a 1955 Roberto Clemente rookie card. He kicked himself again for throwing away all the baseball cards he had collected as a kid. He remembered how all the kids in his neighborhood used to clip baseball cards to their bicycle wheels with clothespins to simulate an engine revving as the cards flapped against the spokes. How many Mickey Mantle rookie cards were destroyed that way? Sedlock thought. Those were the days, he mused. Buying more Topps bubble gum than he could possibly chew just to thumb through a half a dozen brand new baseball cards. And how many of those cards would be 'keepers,' ones you didn't have yet? It was the anticipation as much as anything, getting a whole generation primed for the state lottery, Sedlock thought.

Then a summer day golfing with his buddies, sometimes playing as many as 54 holes. Top it off with an ice-cold twenty-five cent bottle of soda.

Sedlock thought a lot about his 12-year-old son, Justin. In just six years he would be going to college. He looked at the baseball cards not only as gifts, but as investments toward college. Often Sedlock wondered if Justin was having the pleasures growing up that he had. Was sitting in front of a computer screen playing computer games anywhere near as fulfilling as his own upbringing had been, Sedlock wondered?

Sedlock had arranged a meeting with Rebecca Miter on Monday morning. She lived in Greenwich, so he made arrangements with "Becky" Miter to meet her at the Miter estate. He jockeyed his Saturn into the passing lane on I-91 South, unsure what kind of traffic he would run into at eight o'clock in the morning. Traffic was horrendous. After he turned west onto I-95 at New Haven it was stop and go until he reached the Greenwich exit at 9:30. Sedlock was glad he didn't have to commute downstate every morning. His trip from his condominium to the Alco Insurance building in Hartford took about twenty-five minutes. The Miter estate was about ten minutes off the exit.

Web Miter's estate was six acres and had a buzzer at the high steel gate. Six acres in Greenwich was not six acres in rural Maine. The land alone would run into the millions. On top of that land sat a mansion which, according to the tabloids, Miter bought for close to ten million. As he drove through the gates Sedlock remembered reading that Miter received $25 million in stock options and other severance goodies when he retired from United Eastern.

A gardener was pruning the rose bushes out front. A maid answered the door when Sedlock rang the doorbell and led him into a waiting room where Rebecca Miter, Mrs. Miter Number Two, sat. They shook hands. Mrs. Miter's face was red and puffy. Obviously, she had been crying.

"I'm Wayne Sedlock. I'm so sorry, Mrs. Miter," Sedlock began. "Let me assure you we are working twenty-four hours a day to try to find out who killed your husband."

"I appreciate it, Mr. Sedlock."

Sedlock noted her voice was a young girl's voice. For a second he wondered what the attraction could have been between Web Miter and her. She was young, and certainly beautiful, with long raven-black hair and a light complexion. But he thought there had to be something more to it than that. All this went through his mind in just a few seconds as he stood in front of Becky Miter, unsure exactly where to go next. He decided to get right to the point.

"Mrs. Miter, do you know Jason Sombery?"

"Yes, I know Jason. He worked in an ice cream store I used to go to when I worked at United Eastern. For the past few years he's been my golf instructor. He was a great golfer at Western Connecticut State. We hit golf balls together at a driving range in Danbury."

"Can you explain why you wrote out a $6000 entry fee check so Jason could play in the Hartford Pro-Am with your husband?"

"I did it as a kind of payment for Jason, for all the time he spent trying to teach me how to golf. He mentioned how my husband had done just about everything in his career, yet Jason had accomplished nothing so far. I told him he was a better golfer than Web, and he could prove it by beating him in the Pro-Am. As it turned out Web was winning even in golf when he died."

"Mrs. Miter, do you know of anybody who might have had a grudge against your husband?"

"You mean enough of a grudge to kill him? No. I don't know of any individual. But there are organizations that have been formed in the past year or two that are against outsourcing work overseas. They showed up where he was to give a speech. They tried to embarrass him. Once they threw an egg at his car. Web wasn't afraid of them, but he was worried about what they might do in the future. Their tactics were getting more and more radical. Many of them were out of work, so they had the time to picket and whatever. I know it's quite a step from picketing to setting off an explosion and murdering somebody, but I think you should check them out."

"We will check them out. But you know of no particular individual who might be capable of doing this? Any disgruntled employee who might have sent Web threatening letters in the past?"

"Before I met Web he was involved, or should I say instigated, many corporate reorganizations at United Eastern. Some people lost their jobs. Whether there is any who still hold a grudge after all these years, Web never told me about any such person."

"I was thinking of somebody who perhaps was mentally ill. In several past bomber cases the perpetrator was mentally ill and often wanted to boast about his grievances to either the newspapers, the police or to letters to the intended victim. Since the police and newspapers haven't heard from the murderer I was thinking he might have sent letters directly to your husband."

"If he has, I don't know anything about it. Web kept a good-sized room full of boxes of papers from his years at United Eastern. He was going to write his memoirs soon. In fact he had just received an advance from a publisher to do it and was about to hire a researcher to sort through all his papers. The publisher was lining him up with a ghost writer."

"One other thing, Mrs. Miter. The explosive that killed Mr. Miter was a type that was used forty or so years ago, during the Vietnam War. I understand Mr. Miter was in the Marine infantry in Vietnam. It may be just a coincidence but we want to check everything out. Did he ever tell you anything about his experiences in Vietnam?"

"He told me a couple stories, but nothing about explosives. But Web did intend to attend his battalion's reunion next week in Washington, D.C. He thought it would not only be great to see the men again, but it would also jog his memory for his memoirs."

"I would like to attend that get together," Sedlock said. "Could I get a copy of the schedule and itinerary?"

Rebecca Miter gave him a brochure which contained the information.

"Since he retired two years ago, what did Mr. Miter do? What were his interests and hobbies?"

"Web loved golf. He's what I'd call a natural athlete but he never had time to play golf much when he was working. He held a membership at the Greenwich Club and he played every chance he got. But he also ran a consulting company. He'd make presentations at various companies about effective leadership in management. I mentioned he was working on his memoirs. He was on the board of directors for a half dozen companies. Occasionally he traveled for them. And of course he was director of the committee that was doing work for the B.I.A."

"What's the B.I.A.?"

"The Bureau of Indian Affairs. As you may have read in the papers the Mashicoke tribe will probably be recognized by the B.I.A. sometime next year. They announced they wanted to open a casino in the Danbury area. United Eastern is dead set against this. The traffic and all on I-84. It's a quality of life issue for the United Eastern employees who live in that area. So United Eastern asked Web if he could chair a study group that might convince the B.I.A. to overturn its decision."

"Has there been any opposition to Mr. Miter doing this?"

"Web did say he saw a sign being held by one protester as he left a hotel after a speech in New York City. The sign said 'Custer Died For Your Sins.'"

"Just one more question. Mrs. Miter, would you mind telling me if Mr. Miter had any life insurance on himself, and who the beneficiaries would be?"

"United Eastern insured Web's life while he worked there because he was such a valuable asset to the corporation. The corporation itself was the beneficiary. Since he retired I don't know if they kept him insured."

"I'm sorry. I had to ask the question. Good-bye Mrs. Miter."

"Good-bye, Mr. Sedlock."

Chapter 6 – Golf Lesson

———————————— ▼ ————————————

Back at Alco Insurance headquarters Sedlock knocked on his boss Bill Walthrup's door.

"Bill, I'd like to run a few things by you," Sedlock said. "First of all, I'd like to get advance expenses for a trip to Washington, D.C. this Friday. There's a reunion of the Marine Vietnam battalion Web Miter served in 35 years ago."

"What's the purpose of going down there?" Bill asked.

"The type of explosives bothers me, Bill. According to the ATF lab it's a type of C-4 that hasn't been made since early in the Vietnam War. In other words it's not something that could be bought or stolen off some construction site today."

"What do you think? Somebody's been hiding this C-4 away for the past 30 years?"

"It's a possibility. And I just wonder if there's a Vietnam vet who was in Web Miter's unit who might harbor a grudge about something that happened that many years ago. Anyway, I'd like to go down there for a day or two."

"I think it's a long shot but I'm going to give you the advance. What else have you got?"

"There's a group called 'Save Our Jobs.' It started up about two years ago. It's a bunch of out-of-work computer programmers who are upset because computer work is being sent overseas, mainly to India. According to their website its president is a fellow named Stu Merriwether with a post office box in Meriden. I don't think this group is very radical. They carried signs and picketed wherever Web Miter went. One even threw an egg at his car. I don't put them in the same category as that tree-hugger group out west that burns down any new house being built in the wilderness. But you never know. There may be one nut among them who is clever enough to make a bomb, and has the guts to set it off. Anyway I sent an email to this Stu Merriwether through their website saying that I am a reporter with the Technology *Times*, and that I'd like to interview him concerning the outsourcing situation in Connecticut."

"OK," Bill said, "and the next move after you talk with him is to see if you can attend some of the group's meetings. The president of the organization might not voice the same party line that the rank and file does. See how upset they are. See how desperate they are financially. Try to get a feeling whether any of them are desperate enough or angry enough to do something like this. What's next?"

"This morning Rebecca Miter told me Web Miter was for the past year involved in some group of influential Connecticut citizens which opposed the Mashicoke tribe starting up a casino near Danbury. United Eastern has their headquarters there so the corporation asked Miter if he could do what he could. Again, at this point we have no evidence that the Indians planned to do anything radical, but the Indians have a lot of money backing them and it's possible it was a contract killing."

"Why would anybody do a hit on a golf course?"

"Maybe it was meant as a warning to the others on that committee. Who knows?"

"Wayne, you haven't yet mentioned either the family or the other playing partners in that golf match. What other motives are there for this murder?"

"Bill, I checked them out. His current wife, Rebecca Miter, was set for life no matter how long Web Miter lived. Also, Donna Miter, the ex-wife, was awarded a several million-dollar divorce settlement. She didn't seem particularly bitter over the divorce. She has two daughters in their mid-thirties. Both are married, both are career women. Neither would stand to gain by their father's sudden death."

"What about the playing partners?"

"According to Dick Geany the foursome and their caddies all took lie detector tests and they all came out clean. He's waiting on background checks on the others we know were around the green when the explosion happened."

"Have you thought of a possible suicide?"

"There was no indication Web Miter was depressed. He was a very fit 62-years-old, no indication he suffered from any disease. And I don't know how he would have pulled it off. We recovered all his clothing and golfing equipment. He had no detonating device. He would have to have placed the bomb in the cup in a 15-minute span between 6:45 and 7:00 a.m. He didn't show up to the golf course until 9:30, an hour before his tee time. Several people verified this. I don't see how it could have been a suicide, Bill."

"What about the golf terrorist the Governor talked about on television the other day? Could it have been a random killing?"

"If it was we may be in for a long wait before we get the murderer. But I would say no simply because of the way it was planned and executed. Somebody wanted to kill Web Miter, for whatever reason. Terrorists like to make their demands known to the media or the police. We've had none of that."

"What bothers me most about this whole thing is the planning and execution of it," Bill said. "If it was a remote detonating device, which it seems at this point that it was, this was a very sophisticated man or men. And it seems almost like a military operation in its planning. Setting up the explosive device within a fifteen-minute window. Being within sight of the victim when he was killed. And the location. A hole on the golf course the victim is playing on – it's brilliant in its simplicity. What do you think, Wayne?"

"I think if the operation was well funded we have a better chance of finding him or them because more people will know about it. If the bomb was made secretly in somebody's garage workshop by somebody who was mentally ill but who had a grudge for whatever reason against Web Miter, then we may be in for a long hunt. Unless we can get lucky and turn up that one person in Miter's 40-year career. That's what I'm trying to do now."

"All right. Keep me informed, and if you need help, let me know. I've shifted all other cases you were working on to the other staff. We'll keep you on this one alone until you start running out of leads. You're doing good work, Wayne. By the way, the Big Man called today." Sedlock knew this meant Jeremy Fondsworth, the CEO of Alco Insurance. "He wants daily status reports on the Miter case. I'll tell him we are making progress but no suspects yet. Keep up the good work."

When Sedlock returned to his desk he had a message from Stu Merriwether, who left a phone number to call him. Sedlock called the number.

"Hello, Stu. This is Wayne Sedlock of the Alco Insurance Technology *Times*. I'd like to talk to you about your organization, 'Save Our Jobs.' I'm interested in what your organization has done in Connecticut in the past year. What I was thinking was I'd like to attend your next meeting and talk with a couple members who have been displaced by outsourcing. Would that be all right?"

"Tell you what. Do you play golf?" Stu asked.

"I've hit that little white pill around the pasture a few times. I'm not very good at it, why do you ask?"

"Three of us are playing tomorrow at the Avon Old Farms course. You're welcome to join us to make it a foursome. All three of us are out-of-work computer programmers. And don't worry about it, we aren't very good golfers either. The course is at the base of Avon Mountain off Route 44. Our starting time is 10:30."

"OK. I'll dust off my clubs and will see you at 10:30 tomorrow morning."

"OK. See you then. Bye."

"Good-bye."

Sedlock hung up then dialed Jason Sombery's work number.

"Jason, this is Wayne Sedlock of Alco Insurance. I know this is short notice but could you meet me this evening about eight o'clock at the driving range in Danbury where you used to give Rebecca Miter golf lessons?"

"Sure, I guess I could be there," Jason said. "Anything new about the case?"

"In a way it's about the case. I need a golf lesson. I'm supposed to play a round tomorrow and I haven't swung a golf club in twelve years. Can you help me out?"

"Sure thing, Wayne." Jason laughed.

"Thanks a lot, Jason. And I'll pay you for your time. What do golf lessons go for these days?"

"Don't worry about it, Wayne. I'm just glad you didn't pin the Web Miter killing on me. I'll see you at eight o'clock."

At seven that evening Sedlock took I-91 north from Lordship ten miles to Hartford then turned west onto I-84. It was about a 45-minute drive on I-84 to Danbury. Commuter traffic had thinned out in half an hour as Sedlock passed by Waterbury. As he noticed the hundreds of houses up on the hillsides around the city Sedlock couldn't help thinking about George P. Metesky, the 'Mad Bomber' of the 1940s and 1950s who lived a life of anonymity for sixteen years in one of those

Waterbury houses. During those years he planted 30 explosive devices in the New York City area. Curious as to exactly why, Sedlock had Janie look up Metesky on the Internet. *'He worked for United Electric and Power Company (which merged with Con Edison), and had suffered an on site accident at the plant where he worked. He blamed his subsequent tuberculosis on that accident – a claim that could not be proven. After his disability claim was denied, Metesky had written several angry letters to the company – one promising revenge for the firm's "dastardly deeds."'*

At eight o'clock Sedlock pulled off the Danbury exit ramp and drove two miles to the driving range where Jason was waiting for him.

"I don't think I can make you another Tiger Woods with one lesson," Jason said as Sedlock bought a bucket of range balls and lugged his golf bag over to one of the driving range stalls.

"That's all right," Sedlock said. As he teed up a ball he asked Jason, "Have you thought any more about Web Miter waving at that spectator? Does anything else come to mind on that?"

"One thing. It was as if Web stopped and recognized the person first. He sort of did a double take. Then he broke out into a smile and waved."

"All right, tell me what I'm doing wrong." Sedlock took a couple practice swings, then he made a decent pass at the ball with his driver. The golf ball sailed in a high arc out past the 250-yard sign.

"For somebody who hasn't swung a golf club in twelve years, you did great. When did you start playing golf?"

"There was a nine-hole course near where I grew up. All of us kids played baseball. That was the big sport. You know, collecting baseball cards and all. If I'd kept those cards today I'd be well off now. Anyway, during the summer we used to sneak on to the course and play five or six holes. We didn't know anything about how to grip the club. We used a baseball grip. I was a pretty fair hitter in baseball, so I guess I had pretty good hand and eye coordination and could hit a golf ball a long way. I played a little in high school and college. Then after college, you know, you move to a strange town where you don't know anybody so you go over to the local public golf course on a Saturday morning and put your bag in line to join up with a threesome. But since I took this job I haven't played at all."

"I'm not going to fool with your grip. You're better off using the one you use. But I'll give you a couple hints. The average golfer gets tired legs during his round. That's why he hits a great drive off number one but by thirteen he's slicing or hooking the ball. That's because he's not using his legs like he was at the start of the round. So let's practice a fade and a draw. I didn't say a slice and a hook. You might need to compensate in the later holes. What is this, a big money match tomorrow in the annual Alco golf tournament?"

"No, nothing like that." Sedlock teed up another ball and took out his three-wood. "I can usually turn the ball one way or another with this club."

"Let's see you hit a draw."

Sedlock shifted his feet and turned his right hand underneath the grip. His swing looked awkward but the ball sailed 200 yards, hooking far left.

"This is the mistake so many weekend golfers make," Jason said. "You don't have to shift your feet so much and you don't have to turn your right hand underneath so much. You can draw the ball with a very slight change to you regular swing. Same with a fade. You don't want to slice the ball, just fade it. Now try the fade."

Sedlock shifted his feet slightly and put the right hand on top. He swung slightly outside in and hit a very high fade that moved slightly from left to right.

"That's beautiful, Wayne. Use the fade and the draw when you feel you're losing your drives to the right or the left. Just a little hint for the weekend golfer. It won't cost you anything."

They continued until Sedlock finished the bucket of balls. Sedlock felt invigorated with every swing, like he was 15-years-old again. Then it was time to go.

"Thanks a lot, Jason. That was the best golf lesson I've ever had. In fact, I think it was the only golf lesson I've ever had. I'll keep in touch about the case."

"OK, Wayne. And I hope you catch him soon." Jason got in his car and left the parking lot. Sedlock loaded his clubs into his trunk then walked over to the shed where he bought his bucket of range balls.

"Was that him?" Sedlock asked the attendant.

"It sure was," said the old man behind the counter. "That's the first time I've seen him this summer, but he used to come out here quite a bit. He was on the Western golf team if I remember. The last couple summers he was giving lessons to the most beautiful young lady you ever saw. She used to drive up in a brand new BMW."

"Did they drive up together?"

"No, they came in separate cars and left in separate cars. She turned into a pretty good golfer, at least from what I could see on the range. Sometimes she'd come alone and hit a bucket. She really worked at what he taught her."

Sedlock took out a copy of a photo of Rebecca Miter that had been in the society section of the Danbury *Times*.

"Is this her?"

"Sure looks like her. Yes, that's her."

"What would you say the relationship of the two was?"

"I never saw any hanky panky, if that's what you mean. They used to kid around a little, but like I said, they always left in separate cars."

"OK, thanks a lot. I've got to play some golf tomorrow."

Sedlock drove his Saturn north on I-91 to Hartford then took I-84 west one exit to Asylum Street. Eventually he ended up on Route 44 west, through West Hartford, then up over Avon Mountain. At the base of the Avon side of the mountain he turned north a half mile to the entrance of Avon Old Farms Golf Course. A tall man with salt and pepper hair was waiting for him in the parking lot.

He offered his hand in greeting. "I'm Stu Merriwether."

"I'm Wayne Sedlock," Sedlock said.

"'Save Our Jobs' has grown leaps and bounds since it was started last year," Merriwether said. "I guess that says something about how much outsourcing overseas has taken root in our state in both manufacturing and information technology. Let me introduce you to the other two in our foursome."

Merriwether escorted Sedlock into the snack bar. Two men, about mid-fifties, sat at a far table.

"Wayne, this Bob Rosa and Steve Wilson. This is Wayne Sedlock. He's a reporter with the Alco Insurance Technology *Times*. I've been out of work a year, Bob's been out about eighteen months and Steve's been out two years. Off shoring is just ruining the middle class."

Sedlock asked, "How do you guys get by financially? The unemployment checks must have run out by now."

"I'm lucky," Bob said. "I've got a little pension and my wife works."

"I've got a part-time driver's job," Steve said. "My wife works too."

"Let's get out to the first tee," Stu said. "Our starting time is in fifteen minutes."

When they were next on the tee swinging their clubs to loosen up Sedlock said, "I'm sure you all heard of Web Miter's demise at the Lordship Country Club. As you know he was the 'Father of Off Shoring.' What did you all think of his death?"

"Couldn't have happened to a more deserving person," Rosa said.

"I second that," Steve Wilson said. "The trouble with a guy like that is he spent most of his life riding around in the back of a limousine. He has no idea how the middle class lives."

"Amen," Merriwether said. "We're up." He flipped a tee three times. "Steve, you're up first, then me, then Wayne and Bob bats cleanup."

Each of the four hit their drives in the first fairway. Sedlock and Stu motored off in one cart and Bob and Steve in another. Sedlock wanted to turn the conversation back to outsourcing.

"Stu, what's your definition of outsourcing? And how angry are the out of work computer programmers in Connecticut?"

"Outsourcing, and I'm really talking about off shoring, is when a company ships its jobs overseas where the labor is cheaper. This produces a surplus of unemployed workers in the USA which drives the compensation for what jobs are left in the States down. Are programmers angry? You're damn right they are. Some of them are losing their homes. There's been one suicide that we know of."

"Have you talked to companies that are outsourcing?"

"Yes. A company will tell you they're outsourcing, but they're not outsourcing as much as the other companies. Just the other day the Information Officer of a bank told me they only outsource jobs where they can't find anybody in the USA that has the computer skills to do that job. Are you trying to tell me there are computer skills in India that you can't find in the USA? Then she tells me they haven't displaced any employees, just contractors. Don't you think contractors are part of the American middle class also? So we want to encourage people to take their money out of that bank. The trouble is, it's hard to find a bank to move your money into because just about all of them are outsourcing overseas."

The foursome stopped short of their golf balls and hit toward the par-4 first green. Stu flew it over the green, Sedlock left his thirty yards short and Bob and Steve both put theirs on.

"One thing about being out of work," Bob said, "you have plenty of time to work on your golf game."

Stu and Sedlock chipped on and the four men putted out. They picked up any putt within three feet. As they waited to hit on the second tee Stu pointed out a large tower on top of Avon Mountain.

"Wayne, I don't know if you know what that building is. It's called Heublein Tower, built by the Heubleins of whiskey fame. You can see forever up there – the Farmington Valley to the west, Hartford and beyond to the east, and up to Bradley Field and Springfield north. Legend has it during World War I Heublein was evicted from the tower. The locals suspected he was sending signals to German U-boats in Long Island Sound. He was German, you know. I don't think you can see quite to the Sound from there. I think it was a little bit of panic in the population."

The four men teed off on the short par-4 second hole. Sedlock wanted to steer the conversation back to outsourcing and how it might be related to Web Miter's murder. As they waited to hit onto the green Sedlock spoke to Stu.

"Stu, let me play the devil's advocate. If Mr. Heublein lived and worked four years before World War I he paid no income tax. The income tax didn't start until 1913. So he and other robber barons had the money to build gaudy palaces like that tower up on the mountain. Computer programmers are complaining that foreigners are in the USA on special visas taking their jobs. Yet Heublein probably hired stonemasons from Italy and carpenters from England. You could make a case that this country was built on foreign labor. Now we live in the era of large corporations. Why can't these corporations do everything possible to pay the lowest possible cost? Why shouldn't they get the cheapest labor? Why shouldn't somebody like Web Miter be held up as a hero to the American public instead of vilified by organizations such as 'Save Our Jobs'?"

Merriwether paused about five seconds to gather his thoughts before answering.

"But in the days of the robber barons there was a shortage of skilled labor in the U.S. There's no shortage of skilled computer programmers in this country today. Look at the unemployment rate in this area among IT professionals. It's around 30 percent. That's the difference. There are those in this country who want a one-world economy. Call it globalization, call it whatever you want. But these large American corporations wouldn't exist if it weren't for the infrastructure of this country. If this was some third rate banana republic would IBM be as large and successful as it is? The corporations use our roads, our communication systems, and our mail systems. And don't forget our military. Our Armed Forces has been able to project America's might throughout the world. We have a society of domestic tranquility because the American middle class makes all this possible. The American middle class pays the taxes which makes this infrastructure possible. Countries like India and China are bleeding us dry when they take our jobs. They're giving nothing back in return. Don't you see it? When you pay Americans for their work you are contributing to the tax base. You are maintaining the infrastructure. What happens when there is no middle class in the USA ten years from now? We'll be just another third rate banana republic. As far as Web Miter goes they should build a monument to him. Just like the monument they built in Groton memorializing when Benedict Arnold sailed into the harbor with British warships during the Revolutionary War and burned Fort Griswold, butchering the Americans who defended it. In my opinion Web Miter, the 'Father of Off Shoring', was just as much a traitor to the United States as Benedict Arnold was."

"So your argument against off shoring is patriotic as well as economic?"

"Off shoring hurts the individual worker. But the argument that it hurts the individual has no effect on corporations. Perhaps they will understand that in the long run what they are doing is destroying the corporations as well. I just hope they don't realize it too late."

The foursome played the next couple holes without any talk of anything serious. Then when they were on the fifth tee waiting to hit onto the par-3 Bob said, "You know I don't want to sound prejudiced, but I've heard those Indian programmers aren't worth a damn when it comes to testing their programs. A friend of mine who worked in partnership with an Indian company said they were a sorry group when it came to testing. We were brought up to test. It's second nature to us Americans. Maybe it's because we live in the same areas as the companies we work for. The Indians move all over the country from job to job. They're just there to put in as many hours as possible. They don't give a damn about what the company makes or what kind of business they are in. Americans take pride in their work because the people who work in those companies are our neighbors. That's why we test every program thoroughly."

"That reminds me of something that happened in a company I worked for," Steve said. "A group of us coded this dispatch system, which allowed you to send out customer engineers to fix computer equipment like keyboards and such. The whole thing was dependent on date and time. Anyway, the system was running fine for three years until it came to a leap year, February 29th. Couldn't bring up the system. Instead of dividing the year by four and checking the remainder, the programmer had divided four by the year, which always had a remainder. So the system never recognized a leap year and never allowed February 29th. Just shows you that even when you think a system is tested and debugged something might crop up years later."

Steve hit first off the fifth tee. His ball bounded onto the front edge of the green 180 yards away. Bob hit a 5-iron short and right of the green. Stu hit a 5-wood to the left of the green. Then Sedlock set up for a draw and smacked a 4-iron, the sweetest feeling shot of the day. He barely felt the club hit the ball because it was hit so solidly. The ball sailed high and moved just a little from right to left.

"All over that pin!" Bob yelled.

The ball landed just short and right of the pin, bounced twice and settled three feet away from the cup.

"That's a 'come back tomorrow' shot if I've ever seen one," Stu said. "Great shot, Wayne."

"Thanks a lot. It really felt good," Sedlock said. For the first time during the match Sedlock forgot he was conducting a murder investigation.

Sedlock got his birdie. They continued on to the long par-5 sixth, then the seventh and eighth. The three programmers played conservatively. All had obviously played the course many times before. Sedlock started to stray with his drives and wasn't able to correct them using Jason's lesson of the night before. He tried cutting corners of doglegs to make up for his errant drives and found himself in more and more trouble. He realized that even though he was about twenty years younger than his playing companions they scored much better with their conservative play. At the ninth tee, a 165-yard par-3, they again were held up from teeing off by the group in front of them.

Bob said, "Wayne, there's one more aspect of outsourcing you should know about. The pay rates for contract work dropped considerably. Recently a buddy of mine was offered $15 an hour for a job. After taxes that's barely more than you get on unemployment. Again, this goes back to the destruction of the middle class."

"What does that compare to what you were used to making?" Sedlock asked.

"Five years ago contractors like him were making four times that in Connecticut."

"What about your skills. Is it possible the demand for the type of computer programming just isn't there any more?"

"The demand for Americans isn't there any more. That's the excuse corporations use. That the skills can only be found in India and China."

"Is it possible you guys aren't being hired because you are members of groups like 'Save Our Jobs'? Maybe the corporations are afraid to bring you into their premises. Afraid of sabotage or whatever?"

"It's possible," Stu said. "But don't we have rights as Americans to point out to the public what's happening to us? We aren't a bunch of right wing gun nuts plotting like some Timothy McVeigh to blow up some federal building. We aren't the Posse Comitatis or some group like that. We're a group of computer programmers who want to make a living in our profession."

"I'm not questioning your rights," Sedlock said. "I'm just playing the devil's advocate again. Look fellows, I'm going to drop out after the front nine. I think I've got enough for my article and I have to transcribe what you said to my notebook. If it's all right with you I'd like to attend your August meeting to talk to more of your members."

"Sure," Stu said. "You're leaving us with the only birdie of the day. We meet the first Wednesday of the month at 6:30 pm at the Elks Club in Meriden. We'd be glad to have you at the meeting."

Sedlock said his good-byes after playing out the ninth hole and headed for his car in the parking lot. He put away his clubs then sat in the front seat scribbling all the conversation he could remember from the golf match.

He saw the three members of 'Save Our Jobs' as conservative and relatively well off financially. They played golf right down the middle. And they couldn't be particularly destitute if they were able to spend $24 for a round of golf several times a week. Yes, they were angry. Who wouldn't be if after a 30-year career he were no longer able to find work in his profession? They might hold picket signs at one of Web Miter's seminars. But

Sedlock doubted they were capable of murder, especially the savage bombing that occurred at Lordship Country Club.

As he was writing what he remembered about their conversation about testing it dawned on him.

"Testing!" he said aloud. "Whoever made that bomb would have tested the remote detonator beforehand. Where do you test a bomb with that kind of explosive capacity?"

Sedlock started his car and turned left on the road that paralleled the Farmington River. The ridgeline on his right was crowned by the Hueblein Tower. He turned right up Simsbury Mountain and pulled in to the entrance of the Talcott Mountain State Park. He parked his car and walked quickly up the mountain trail toward the tower. It took him twenty minutes to reach the tower after a brisk walk. When he reached it he was greeted by an off duty state policemen who lived there during the summer. Sedlock introduced himself and showed him his Alco identification.

"I'd like to climb to the top of the tower and look west toward the Ensign-Bickford property," Sedlock said to the state trooper. "Do you hear the explosions from the tests they do down there?"

The state trooper led Sedlock up the winding staircase. "We sure do," he said. "Let me point it out to you."

On the top floor massive windows circled the room.

The trooper pointed slightly north of west. "The E-B Powder Woods start just on the other side of that bridge. That road that runs south to north eventually becomes the main street of Simsbury. From the bridge all the way to the center of Simsbury, everything west of that are the Powder Woods. It runs straight back west for about a mile and a half. It's bounded by roads but you can barely see them through the trees."

Sedlock stared at the huge woodland. For two hundred years the residents of Simsbury had been used to the Ensign-Bickford Company testing its explosives. If the bomber tested his remote detonating device in the Powder Woods, who would even notice it? He thanked the state trooper for his help and hurried down the staircase. As he walked down the mountain toward his car he thought it might be a long shot but it was worth looking into. He drove the two miles toward the Ensign-Bickford gate.

"Do you remember me?" he asked the security guard at the gate. He took out his Alco identification card and showed it to him. "I was here three days ago with Bob Corsino of the ATF. We set off a test explosive back in the test area."

"Yes, I remember you now," said Mel, the guard.

"Do you remember any explosions back in the woods that were not cleared with the company? They might have happened in late July."

"Yes, there was one day in late July. Two explosions, one right after the other. They went off right at eleven o'clock, which is the time test explosions are scheduled to go off. But nobody notified me there would be a test that day. I drove back there as quick as I could. Saw a car driving off. Had two fellows in it but I couldn't get much of a description. One was tall with light hair, the other short and dark. I can show you the blast holes if you want. I wrote it all up in the log book."

"You can show me the craters? That's great. Let me call Bob Corsino."

Sedlock took out his cell phone and called Corsino. "Bob, can you come out to the main gate? And bring whatever you need to take a soil sample from a blast crater."

Corsino showed up in five minutes and the guard showed them the way to the mysterious bomb craters that were made the day before the Pro-Am, on July 23rd. When they arrived at the back road spot Sedlock noticed immediately that both craters were approximately the same size as the one on the 17th green of the Lordship Country Club. Corsino took out a folding measuring stick and laid it across the first crater. It measured nineteen inches in diameter, just two inches wider than the golf course explosion. Then he took several pictures of the crater from different angles with the measuring stick both across the diameter and sticking straight up from the bottom of the hole. The depth was exactly the same as the depth of a regulation golf cup. The measurements of the other crater were almost exactly the same as the first. Then Bob took a small trowel and scooped out dirt from the bottom of each crater and placed the samples in cellophane bags. Then he did the same with samples from the wall of each hole.

"I don't see any hardware, wires and such. They may have policed it up before they left," Corsino said.

Sedlock asked the guard "Do you remember anything about the car? You said there were two men leaving the scene when you got here? Do you remember anything more about them? You said one was tall and one short."

"No," the old man said. "My eyesight's not all that good at a distance. It was a light car, a sedan. But they were driving away so I was looking at the car from the back. One fellow was lighter, one fellow was darker than the other."

"I suppose it's too much to ask if you got a license plate number."

"I was hoping you'd get to that, Son," Mel said. "They installed a contraption about a year ago that takes a picture of every license plate of every car that goes in or out of the three gates on the property. We kept a copy of that plate. It's up at the Security Building now."

"Can we get a copy? Did you trace the plate number?"

"No, we didn't. We didn't find any damage done. Thought it was a couple kids with a pipe bomb."

"How close together in time were the explosions?" Sedlock asked.

"Very close. Just a minute apart."

"Let's get over to the lab," Corsino said. "I can test these samples right away. I'll compare them with the sample I have from the Lordship explosion. We can have the results within an hour."

They drove back through the dark forest, land that had never been logged since the first settlers arrived in New England in the 1600s. Sedlock thought that if the samples were from the same batch of C-4 the killer must have been familiar with this woodland.

The two explosions happened right at eleven o'clock, the time Ensign-Bickford always set off test explosions. Perhaps the killer hiked in these woods, or played in them when he was young. Perhaps he lived nearby or grew up nearby. Within ten minutes they were at the lab.

Corsino took a pinch of each sample from the cellophane bags and dropped it into a solution. Then he spun the solution in a small centrifuge for five minutes. Then he poured the liquid which had been separated from the dirt sludge. After allowing a tiny drop of the liquid to dry he examined it under a microscope.

"Bingo!" he exclaimed. "This sample is almost positively the same batch of C-4 as the sample from the golf course explosion."

"When you say almost, what degree of probability is that?"

"I'd say ninety percent."

"So they were right here on July 23rd testing out the detonators. The day before the Lordship bombing. And there were two of them. And the C-4 was almost forty years old."

"You're getting there, Wayne. You're starting to fill in the pieces of the puzzle."

Sedlock got a copy of the license plate from the guard at the main security building. He checked with Motor Vehicles at the Wethersfield office. The car was a rental car.

A check with the rental agency uncovered an identity theft. Whoever rented the car used a false drivers license and credit card. The car rental was the only purchase made on that credit card. According to the Motor Vehicle Department the drivers license was re-issued just a week before the car rental.

The identity theft bothered Sedlock. He ran the identity of the proper owner of the drivers license through the Alco computer system. The person whose identiy was stolen, a Mr. Charles Howell, was an Alco client. He was covered by Alco's auto and homeowners policies.

"It's too bad this didn't happen a month later," Janie said. "Robby from the computer department was telling me today at lunch that Alco is offering Identity Fraud insurance coverage for Connecticut starting next week. If Charles Howell had that protection he wouldn't have any out-of-pocket losses for somebody using his credit card. And Robby said, coincidentally, Charles Howell was used as a test case for the new system."

Sedlock called up Robby that afternoon. "Robby, this is Wayne Sedlock. Janie Caldwell works for me. She mentioned you might know something about one of our clients whose identity was stolen recently."

"Well, if he's the same Charles Howell who we used as a test case for our new Connecticut Identity Fraud coverage, I do. We needed a male test case which had two identities. Apparently Howell is an Indian, a Native American. He had a pseudonym on the master file of Little Coyote. I haven't been involved since the system design six months ago, but I remember his name because it was so unique."

"Who picked out Charles Howell's name as a test case?" Sedlock asked.

"No idea. The test cases were determined before I got involved with the project."

"Who would have access to the information associated with the test cases? Social security number, drivers license number, birth date, etcetera."

"Anybody making coding changes to our software. A firm from India took over after we did the initial design. And the business analysts and the consultants who copied the test cases over from production in the first place. And system design people like me. I must have seen that data because I remember that name specifically."

"Damn, Rob, you need a dispensation from above in this company to view just about any type of confidential data we own. Isn't there some sort of protection against everybody seeing these test cases?"

"It funny, Mr. Sedlock. This is the third insurance company I've worked in, and all of them have the same attitude toward test data. Information that is called production is sacrosanct. You need permission from on high to see it. But once something is labeled test data, even if it had once been production data, there are no protections on it at all. Just about anybody who knows how to access it can access it."

"Who would most likely know how to access it?"

"The Indian programmers for sure. They are the ones who would be using it on a daily basis. The business analysts might see glimpses of it on some of the screens they were testing. The designers if they were looking for it. And the consultants who created it."

"How do you know they were consultants who created those test cases?"

"Because an American consulting company was originally going to do the project. Then when the project got to the design phase Alco decided to give it to an Indian company. Booted the American company right out the door and brought over a dozen Indian programmers on work visas."

"What was the name of the American firm that was let go?"

"American Systems Corporation – ASC."

"Thanks, Rob. You've been a big help."

CHAPTER 7 – MORE CLUES

$$\blacktriangledown$$

As part of the investigation of the Web Miter murder case Sedlock had requested any reference to Miter in any past FBI reports. There were two files, the online file of more recent years' information and the archived file which went back some fifty years and which took longer to retrieve. The online files were retrieved the day after the murder. There was nothing out of the ordinary, just security clearances for Miter when he worked at various divisions of United Eastern, mostly from requests to visit different foreign countries. But on Tuesday the archives arrived in the mail. There was one relevant item to do with Miter's Marine Corps service in Vietnam.

Sedlock read the following: *9 JUN 68: Capt. W.L. Miter, company commander of Bravo Company, Greatest Groundpounders Battalion, was a character witness for one of his men, Lcpl. C.T. Howell a.k.a. Little Coyote, who was apprehended attempting to send C-4 explosives home through the mail. Subject was arrested and court-martialed. Explosives package was addressed to his father in Kent, Connecticut. All FBI offices should be aware that military personnel in sympathy with such radical groups as the Weathermen and the Black Panthers may be supplying them with weapons, ammunition and/or explosives.*

"This is it!" Sedlock said. "This is a tie-in to C-4 explosives almost 40 years ago."

This was the biggest break in the case so far. Could this Howell have held a grudge against Web Miter all these years? Sedlock tried not to think about the case one way or the other. But did he send C-4 through the mail to somebody in 1968? There were radical groups back then who were bombing buildings.

Sedlock then picked up a fax off his desk which Dick Geany of the Lordship Police Department has sent him. It was a copy of a fax from the Petaluma, California, Police Department.

He whistled softly. "James Wallace, the tournament volunteer who works at Aetna, is using a stolen identity." Janie Caldwell was the only one close enough to hear him.

"Janie. Can you get me the phone number of an Eleanor North in Petaluma, California?"

Janie got the phone number off the Internet and gave it to Sedlock. Wayne looked at his watch and guessed he could dial the California number all right without waking anybody. Eleanor North answered.

"Eleanor, this is Wayne Sedlock. I'm an insurance investigator with Alco Insurance Company. Detective Geany of the Lordship, Connecticut, Police Department sent me a copy of the fax you sent him concerning the identity of James Joseph Wallace. That was a great job you did. I just wanted to give you a call to congratulate you."

"Thank you, Mr. Sedlock was it? I've been doing background checks for police departments on and off for about fifteen years, and that's the first time I ever discovered anybody who had stolen somebody else's identity. I'm trying to locate the surviving member of the family of the little boy whose identity was stolen, but I haven't found her yet. She's a sister named Candice Simpson. She'd be about fifty years old now."

"Candice Simpson?" Sedlock wrote the name on a scratch pad on his desk. "Eleanor, will you do me a favor? If you locate this woman will you call me so I can talk with her? I'll give you my phone number at work. You can call collect."

Sedlock gave Eleanor his phone number.

"I don't suppose you can tell me what this is all about. You're with an insurance company. Is it insurance fraud?"

"We really can't discuss our cases, Eleanor. But let me congratulate you again. That was great piece of detective work. Good-bye."

Sedlock took the report from Petaluma and leafed through his notebook until he reached the copy of the brief interview Dick Geany had had with James Joseph Wallace. According to Geany's notes Wallace, or whoever he was, worked at Aetna Insurance's Middletown facility. Sedlock called the Aetna Security Department. Indicating it was part of the Miter investigation, he asked that Aetna fax Wallace's personnel records. Sedlock also asked if security could monitor Wallace's email.

When the personnel records arrived later that morning Sedlock was somewhat disappointed. They didn't give much more information than the report from the Petaluma Police and Geany's interview. Wallace claimed to be born on October 6, 1946, in Petaluma, California. He gave a condominium complex about three miles from the Aetna headquarters as his current address. Sedlock noted Wallace was a widower. A copy of the resume Wallace submitted to Aetna when he applied for the job revealed an extensive job history with consulting assignments all over the country. Wallace's personnel records also noted he was a volunteer for both the United Way and the Hartford Open. Other than that the records just gave financial information, such as past pay raises and insurance deductions. Sedlock noted all the bosses Wallace had in his seven years with the company rated him very highly.

Then Aetna Security Department called about the trace of James Wallace's email at work. They faxed a message from a John "Butch" Tyler. It read as follows:

Jim - Just a reminder. The reunion starts August 1 at the Dupont Hotel in DC. Don't worry about anybody recognizing you. There's practically nobody left from Bravo anyway. We don't have to worry about the Madman being there, anyway. We'll go visit the Wall on the anniversary - Two August. All those names, especially yours.

Will meet you at the Dupont 8/1. Register as Jim Wallace. That's all for now. Semper Fi – Butch

Sedlock thought of the Vietnam War. He needed help deciphering the email and immediately thought of Bob Corsino. He called the ATF agent who agreed to be at the Alco building in 45 minutes.

When Bob Corsino arrived, Sedlock filled him in.

"Bob, I'm investigating a stolen identity case. It's part of the Miter investigation. Aetna Insurance security department intercepted an email sent to our suspect at work. I think the note has to do with a Vietnam veteran reunion. And the Semper Fi at the end refers to Marines. That's why I thought of you. You're just about the only ex-Marine Vietnam veteran I know."

"There's no such thing as an ex-Marine, or so say ex-Marines," Corsino said as he read the email.

"Looks like a note from one Marine to another."

"Why do you say that?" Sedlock asked.

"Semper Fi is a greeting used between Marines," Corsino said.

"That's interesting. There was no indication on any of James Wallace's records that he served in the military," said Sedlock.

"Tyler definitely did," Corsino said. "I would guess he's talking about a reunion of his Vietnam unit. Bravo probably refers to the company he served in. That means his battalion was the 1ˢᵗ Battalion of some regiment. First Battalion always has Alpha, Bravo, Charlie, and Delta companies. Visiting the Wall refers to the Vietnam Memorial Wall. All those names may mean seeing the names on the Wall of those killed. I don't know what he means by 'your name.' That's strange. He couldn't mean seeing Wallace's name on the Wall. He must mean seeing Wallace at the reunion."

"Two other things seem strange to me," Sedlock said. "'Don't worry about anybody recognizing you' and 'Register as Jim Wallace.' Why would he register as anybody else?"

"Who knows?" Bob asked. "I'm sure some of these veterans who go to reunions fool around on their wives. Perhaps they don't want any record in the hotel registry that they were there."

Sedlock spoke up. "According to his file James Wallace is a widower."

"Maybe he has a girlfriend he fools around on."

"Thanks, Bob. You really were a big help," Sedlock said. "This is a real coincidence. Web Miter's Vietnam Marine unit's reunion is tomorrow, August 1ˢᵗ. Do you suppose Tyler was in that unit? I planned on going."

As Corsino stood up to leave he said, "I subscribe to a couple veterans' magazines. They list upcoming reunions. I'll check to see what reunion is scheduled for August 1ˢᵗ. And I wouldn't read too much into what Butch Tyler says about nobody recognizing the other fellow. Maybe they're gay and they don't want to be seen together. Maybe Wallace had a run-in with one of the other vets in the battalion at a previous reunion. Who knows? The trip to the Wall has become almost a sacred pilgrimage to Vietnam vets, especially grunts who saw heavy combat, which Tyler apparently did. Just reading those names on the Wall can bring it all back. Believe me, I know. But Vietnam vets still don't have it all together yet.

Especially the frontline combat vets. Just don't read too much into Wallace not wanting to be seen."

"Thanks. Bob? Were you a frontline combat vet?"

"I was a rifleman with Alpha Company, First Battalion, Fifth Marines in February, 1968 when we took back Hue City from the North Vietnamese during the Tet Offensive. We lost 142 Marines killed and 900 wounded to get that city back. I was one of the wounded. That was the end of the war for me."

Late that afternoon Bob Corsino sent Wayne Sedlock a fax confirming the Greatest Groundpounders battalion was scheduled to have a reunion at the Dupont Hotel in Washington, D.C. from August 1st through the 5th. Corsino also faxed a copy of a page from a recent veterans' magazine which listed the 20 deadliest battles of the Vietnam War. He underlined the battle listed seventh. It was Two August 1968. Corsino noted that it was the bloodiest single day battle of the war, as the other six battles listed above it lasted several days. Eighty-four were killed in that one-day battle. Corsino wrote that every Marine who was in Vietnam at that time had heard of the Two August battle. The company commander, Web "Madman" Miter, had called in artillery on his own position and had eventually been awarded a Navy Cross, the second highest medal awarded by the Marine Corps, for doing so. In the meantime a copy of John "Butch" Tyler's military records arrived from the Military Records Center in St. Louis. He served in Bravo Company in 1968 under Captain Miter. The "Madman" from the note, Sedlock thought. Tyler was wounded on Two August and was back in the field by August 15th.

The way Sedlock read it, Butch Tyler wrote, "Don't worry, Jim, nobody from Bravo Company will recognize you at the Vietnam reunion on August 1st at the Dupont Hotel in Washington, D.C." But why would anybody from Butch's unit in Vietnam recognize Jim Wallace anyway? According to the resume that accompanied his personnel records, Jim Wallace was working as a waiter and going to a computer technical school in San Francisco when John "Butch" Tyler was in Bravo Company in Vietnam in 1968. And "the Madman" wouldn't be there, anyway. The Madman, Sedlock thought, must be referring to Web "Madman" Miter, the company commander of Bravo Company on August 2nd 1968. Where would James Wallace know Miter from? And the phrase, "All those names, especially yours." Tyler was referring to the Vietnam Wall in the previous sentence. Was he talking about the names on the Wall? The names of those killed on Two August? The whole thing didn't make sense to Sedlock.

The pieces started to fall together. Sedlock searched through his desk drawer for the itinerary of Web Miter's Vietnam reunion that Rebecca Miter had given him. It was scheduled from August 1st through the 5th at the Dupont Hotel in Washington, D.C. Tyler and Miter were in the same unit in Vietnam. Sedlock called information to get the number of the Dupont Hotel. He didn't understand where James Joseph Wallace fit in the picture. Sedlock made reservations for August 1st and 2nd. Then he had half dozen copies of James Wallace's Aetna badge photo made. He wanted a photo he could show around to other vets if he had to.

Lastly, Sedlock ordered a background check on John "Butch" Tyler, who enlisted into the Marine Corps in 1966 from Coffeyville, Kansas.

CHAPTER 8 -
THE BATTALION REUNION

▼

Wayne Sedlock and Bob Corsino drove south on I-95 in Sedlock's car. Sedlock asked Corsino to attend the reunion with him because he felt Corsino could blend in with the other veterans, and Corsino readily agreed. They took turns driving, so by the time they reached the Silver Spring, Maryland, Metro garage at 10 o'clock the night of July 31st Sedlock was still fresh. They then took the Metro into D.C. and arrived at the Dupont Hotel before midnight. After they checked in to their rooms Sedlock asked the desk clerk if James Wallace had checked in yet and where the sign-in for the reunion was. Wallace had not checked in. The clerk pointed to a table in the far corner of the lobby manned by a bearded man of about sixty. Corsino told Sedlock he was turning in for the night and asked the desk clerk for a six A.M. wakeup call. Sedlock approached the bearded veteran, who said, "You're too young to have been in the battalion during Vietnam. What can I do for you, Son?"

"You're right," Sedlock said, flashing the best smile he could muster. "My name's Wayne Sedlock. I'm a writer for a magazine called Technology *Times*. I'm doing a piece on Web Miter, who was a captain in your battalion in 1968.

You may have read about it. He was killed by an explosion on a golf course about a week ago. I'm here to try to get some background material on him for my article. I'm not sure what company he was in or whatever. Can you help me out and point me in the right direction?"

"It's a shame about Miter," the bearded veteran said. "He was signed up to be here at the reunion. He's probably one of the biggest success stories to come out of the battalion. A Navy Cross winner, then after a career like he had in business he retires and gets blown up by a mine. And after all the minefields he walked through in Vietnam where he didn't get a scratch. Ironic and a damn shame. To answer your question he was company commander of Bravo Company in the second half of 1968. We don't break out by companies anymore at the reunions. We did in the early years, but not anymore. So your best bet is to take this unit directory here up to the hospitality suite and just ask around for any of these guys who were in that unit at that time."

The directory, which was several sheets stapled together, listed the men of the battalion by company and platoon and what years they were in Vietnam.

Sedlock took the elevator up to the hospitality suite. He was twenty years younger than the Vietnam veterans but that didn't seem to matter. The vets were absorbed in conversation in their little groups, some relaxing with a can of beer in one hand. Some had brought their sons to the reunion and Sedlock observed he wasn't that much older than that younger generation.

The walls of the suite were covered with photos and posters, which defined the battalion's history. Many vets donated their photo scrapbooks which lay on the fold-out card tables. The scrapbooks were a tribute to the then 19-year-old Marines who fought in a jungle war almost forty years earlier. There was also a box which contained charcoal rubbings from the Wall, the names of all the young men in the battalion who were killed in that war. The Vietnam Memorial Wall, built mostly from donations from Vietnam veterans, had taken on such a symbolic meaning for all Vietnam vets, that many shed tears at the very sight of it. The battalion reunion group planned a wreath laying ceremony at the base of Panel 94W of the Vietnam Memorial Wall the morning of August 2nd in memory of the Two August 1968 battle, in which more Americans died than in any other single day battle in the Vietnam War.

In one corner of the suite a veteran hawked paraphernalia such as souvenir tee shirts, ball caps, pins and medals – all with the battalion logo on them. Sedlock figured that vet might know some Bravo Company veterans, so he walked up to him.

"Hi. My name is Wayne Sedlock. I'm a reporter with the Technology *Times*. I'm doing a story on Captain Web Miter. He was killed a week ago and I wonder if you know any of the men from Bravo Company who served with him."

"Everybody calls me Waldo. I read about Captain Miter's death. Terrible thing. I was in Alpha Company myself, but about two years before Miter was a company commander. Take a walk across the room with me. I'll introduce you to a couple of his men."

Waldo led Sedlock to the other side of the room where he approached a group of three ex-Marines who were discussing the pros and cons of the M-16 rifle.

"Let me interrupt you fellows for just a minute," Waldo said. "This is Wayne, and he's a reporter doing a story on Captain Web Miter. Wayne, two of these guys served in the captain's company in 1968. Guy Walker and Larry Wertzer. Can you two help him out? I've got to get back to my table."

Waldo went back to sell his gear.

Sedlock asked, "Could you tell me what kind of a leader Web Miter was in Vietnam? The whole world has learned what kind of a manager and business leader he was in the corporate world. I just wonder if he developed those leadership skills in the Marine Corps."

"America didn't allow us Vietnam veterans to have many heroes," Larry Wertzer said. "But Captain Miter was a hero to all the men in his company. He was up front when he could have stayed back surrounded by his men. I remember he dragged one man out of a minefield under fire. He didn't have to do that. He was a great leader."

"What about non-combat situations?" Sedlock asked. "Did he stand up for his men if a man was being court-martialed, for example? I heard a story of one man who was caught sending C-4 home through the mail. Do you know anything about that story? Did Web Miter stick up for the man, or what?"

"I remember it," Guy Walker said. "The man was an Indian. We called him Little Coyote, but that wasn't his real name. I can't remember his name but the excuse he gave for sending the explosives home was that his father was getting old and had to remove a lot of stumps to clear a field for planting. So Little Coyote figures he'll save his father this back-breaking work. He'll send the C-4 home and when he gets home he'll help his father by blowing out the stumps with the C-4. Little Coyote wasn't any 1960s radical. He just wanted to help out his father."

"Could Little Coyote's real name have been Howell?"

"That was him. Howell. I think he was from New England. Didn't know they had any Indian tribes from there until I met him. Anyway, Captain Miter really went to bat for Little Coyote in his court-martial. Little Coyote, in spite of his sending explosives through the mail, was a very good Marine. Very gutsy under fire. But the judge didn't want to hear any of it. I guess they were afraid of radicals back in the States getting hold of explosives back then. Little Coyote had the F.B.I. and the U.S. Postal Service, as well as the Marine Corps, stacked against him. They sent him to prison at Fort Leavenworth for two years, then gave him a dishonorable discharge. None of the men from Bravo Company ever saw him again after they marched him off from his court-martial. I was kind of hoping we'd see him at one of these reunions, but I guess not. I don't even know if he's still alive, or if he ever got those stumps cleared for his father."

"How easy was it for somebody like Little Coyote to get hold of C-4 back then? At least enough to send home without it being missed?"

"Very easy. We were issued all kinds of ordinance to carry, or hump, as we called it back then. A rifleman might carry any of the following: rifle ammo, machine gun ammo, a LAAW (Light Anti-tank Assault Weapon, which was like a compressed bazooka), a 60 millimeter mortar round, a claymore mine and a stick of C-4. So Little Coyote stashed his C-4 in his pack. When he got back to the rear area base he put what sticks he had in a cookie tin and mailed it at the base post office. I heard they used to x-ray every third package. I guess Little Coyote's number came up."

Sedlock said, "Miter tried to take care of the good Marines like Little Coyote at his court-martial. What about the Marines who screwed up? How did he treat them?"

Larry Wertzer laughed. "Wayne. You should know better than that. Marines never screw up. But seriously, if you remember that incident I told you about earlier. There was one Marine who froze in a minefield. He wouldn't move. We were under fire. So Captain Miter goes out and gets him. When it was over the captain read that Marine the riot act. The Marine jeopardized the whole company. Shortly after that the captain had the man transferred to a battalion rear area job. Last I heard he was ordering meat for the battalion PX. Contrary to what a lot of people think it wasn't the dolts that were put in the Marine infantry. A rifleman had to be on the ball. He even had to have a little bit of guts. Those that couldn't hack it were transferred out."

"Thank you, fellows. I've got good background material here. I've got to get back to my room to write up my notes. Do you know the name of that Marine who Miter dragged out of the minefield?"

"No, it was a long time ago," Wertzer said. "I just don't remember." Guy Walker drifted away to talk with some other ex-Marines. "Wayne, remember what I said about riflemen having to be on the ball. That goes for ex-riflemen too. You're no reporter. What gives? Why all the questions about C-4? Was Web Miter killed by C-4? Are you a cop?"

Sedlock thought of maintaining his impersonation, but then he thought Wertzer too sharp to continue the ruse. He took a card out of his wallet which identified him as an insurance investigator with Alco Insurance Company.

"I'd appreciate it if you'd keep this between the two of us. I'm investigating the murder of Web Miter. My company wrote an insurance policy for the golf course where Miter was killed. And yes, the explosive was C-4. If there's any help you can give me, anything you think of in Web Miter's Vietnam tour to do with C-4, let me know. Also, if you can think of any Marines who might hold a grudge against Miter give me a call. Thanks."

"Look, Wayne. I forgot to bring it with me, but I have a company photograph they took of us when we were in Okinawa. I wrote down everybody's name under each face picture. When I get home I'll try to find it. Maybe the names will jog my memory."

"My email address is on my card. Can you scan the photo and send it to me?"

"Yes, I can. I've got to find it first. Are you going to the wreath laying ceremony day after tomorrow? I think they're going to say a few words about Captain Miter there."

"I'll be there. And I appreciate everything you've done, Larry."

"It's the least I can do for the captain."

Sedlock retreated up to his room and jotted notes in his notebook. Web Miter may very well have learned many of his leadership principles in Vietnam, Sedlock thought. He tried to aid good Marines like Little Coyote even though the young Marine broke the rules by sending C-4 home to his father. And he eliminated Marines from the company who posed a danger to the group, like the Marine he dragged out of the minefield. But what Web "Madman" Miter was most famous for in the Marine Corps was calling in artillery on top of his own position in order to save his company. This was similar to his winnowing weak profit centers to make the larger corporation more financially robust. Some employees lost their jobs for the greater good of the parent corporation. Miter may have looked at outsourcing overseas in the same light. Less expensive products even though it meant the loss of some jobs in the U.S.A.

After he finished with his notes Sedlock scribbled what he knew about the murder so far. First was the explosive C-4. It was almost forty years old. That meant it may have been brought home by a Vietnam veteran. Howell, a.k.a. Little Coyote, was caught sending C-4 home through the mail in 1968. Had he successfully sent home some of the explosive before he was caught? Did Howell belong to the Mashicoke tribe in Kent, Connecticut? Could he have held a grudge for almost forty years against Web Miter for his two-year imprisonment and dishonorable discharge? But Guy Walker maintained Miter was supportive of Howell in his court-martial. All these thoughts went through Sedlock's mind.

Second, the ATF was almost positive the explosive which killed Web Miter was detonated by a remote controlled device. Did Howell have the skills necessary to make such a device?

Third, Jason Sombery swore Web Miter waved to a spectator who stood next to the 17th green just before the explosion. Could that spectator have been Howell? Would

Miter have recognized him after all these years? Did he only recognize him after being a few feet away on the green?

At 6:30 the next morning Sedlock and Bob Corsino met for breakfast in the hotel restaurant.

"Tyler and Wallace are to meet today at the Vietnam Memorial Wall," Bob Corsino said. "My guess they will be in front of Panel 94W. That's where the names of those killed on August 2nd, 1968, are from Miter's and Tyler's Bravo Company."

"If Wallace doesn't want to be seen by other vets they will probably meet this morning," Sedlock said. "I checked with the front desk. Both Wallace and Tyler checked in late last night. I also got a schedule of events for the reunion." Sedlock read from a brochure. "It lists a wreath laying ceremony at the Vietnam Wall tomorrow on August 2nd at 11 A.M. The other big events are a visit to the Marine Corps Museum on Friday and the dinner on Saturday night. The rest of the time is devoted to sightseeing and telling war stories in the hospitality suite. Sunday everybody goes home."

"I think we ought to stake out the Wall," Corsino said.

"I was thinking the same thing. Bob, I don't want Wallace to see me. You stay up near the Wall in front of Panel 94W. Mingle with the other tourists. When Wallace and Tyler show up try to get close enough to them to hear what they are saying. Sound like a plan?"

"Sounds like as good a plan as any, Wayne," Corsino said. "We can keep in touch by cell phone. You keep a low profile here at the hotel. There's a little park just outside the front entrance. If you sit on one of those benches out there reading a newspaper you can keep track of the veterans as they leave the hotel. When you spot Wallace and Tyler, call me on your cell. OK, I'm heading over to the Wall now. There are a couple dozen names I want to look up myself. Take care." With that Corsino got up and left.

Sedlock bought a USA Today at the front desk, walked across the street to the small park and sat down on one of its benches. In the next forty-five minutes veterans left the hotel, some singly, some in groups, others with their families. Sedlock casually checked them all out. Just at 7:30 he saw Wallace leaving with a much shorter man. The shorter man, who wore a white cowboy hat, was gesturing excitedly with both hands and arms. Sedlock called Bob Corsino on his cell phone. "Here they come, Bob. Wallace is six foot or more, wearing a dark blue shirt and light trousers. A shorter man with him, I assume it's Tyler, is about five foot six, and is wearing a light yellow shirt and blue jeans, and has a white cowboy hat on his head. Good luck."

Just after 8:00 Bob Corsino positioned himself in front of Panel 94W. There were very few visitors at the Wall that early in the morning. A few minutes later Jim Wallace and Butch Tyler walked up to the panel. Corsino tried to stay within earshot of both of them and at the same time stay as unobtrusive as possible.

"You remember Hector Ortiz, don't you?" Jim Wallace asked. "Once he had to stay back in the rear area while we went out on an operation. So I asked him if he would go to the post office for me and send some souvenir copper plates to my folks. He did it, only I had a defused chi-com grenade I was sending home. They x-rayed the package at the post office and were damn near ready to court-martial him. The Madman had to smooth things over with the brass. Hector would do anything for you. He was a great guy."

"Remember Clark. He was a Mormon. Got in trouble with the Madman once for staying too long in Danang after his R&R. Told some cock and bull story about meeting up with some other Mormon Marine and they held religious services or something." Butch Tyler laughed. "I would have come up with something better than that."

"Do you remember Livingston?" Wallace asked. "He told me once one of his ancestors signed the Declaration of Independence. He said that was his great whatever grandfather's death warrant if the British ever caught him. I thought he was just putting me on. But after I got settled in the States I looked it up. There was a Philip Livingston, a wealthy businessman from New York, who signed the Declaration of Independence."

"I met Livingston's son," Tyler said.

"You met his son? When? Where?"

"It was right here on this spot about eight or nine years ago. He was staring at Panel 94W, so I asked him if anybody on that panel was a loved one of his. He said Livingston was his father. He never knew him because he was born after Livingston was killed. He asked me if I knew his father and I told him I knew him pretty well. Then he asked me how he died. I told him about Captain Miter calling in artillery on top of us. He asked if Captain Miter was the same Web Miter who was the big shot CEO of United Eastern."

"How did he take it all?"

"He didn't say anything. After he asked all his questions he just walked away."

Both men remained quiet for a moment.

"All these names. Smith. Williams. Kosecki. Johnson. Hughes. We knew damn near every one on this panel from Bravo Company. And there's you, Buddy." Butch touched one of the names. Corsino noted the name. William W. Robinson. He also noticed it had a cross next to it.

"When are you going to come home?" Butch asked the Wall. Or was he asking James Wallace? Corsino thought. James Wallace and Butch Tyler hung their heads for a minute, then turned and left.

Corsino took out his notebook and wrote all the names Wallace and Tyler mentioned. In his notebook next to William W. Robinson he put a cross and a question mark. He walked to the far end of the Wall where the park ranger sat at a card table with a large computer printout to help people find names.

"Excuse me. What does it mean when there is a cross next to a name?" Corsino asked him.

"Each name on the Vietnam Memorial Wall is preceded by a symbol. A diamond signifies a confirmed death, while a cross signifies Missing In Action/Prisoner Of War. If an MIA/POW's death is confirmed, lines are etched over the cross to make it a diamond. If he returns alive, a circle is etched around the cross to signify life."

When he arrived back at the hotel Bob Corsino immediately knocked on Sedlock's door.

"Wayne, I don't know where to start. I overheard Wallace and Butch Tyler at the Vietnam Wall. I think Wallace was in Tyler's unit in Vietnam. They were talking about some of the Marines that were killed in the Marine battle called Two August. Wallace seemed to know every Marine Tyler was talking about."

"So you think Wallace was in that unit and he switched identities after he got home. Why would he change identities?"

"I think I know why, Wayne. You're not going to believe this. Tyler said 'Your name on the Wall' to Wallace. Then he pointed to one of the names. It had a cross chiseled next to it. After they left I asked the park ranger what the cross meant…M.I.A. Missing in action!"

"What was the name next to the cross?"

"William W. Robinson."

Sedlock was silent.

"Wayne, we should stay in Washington until the reunion is over on Sunday. We can mingle with the veterans from the battalion and see what we can find out about William W. Robinson. If he was an M.I.A. on Two August there should be somebody here who knew him or knew of him. M.I.A.s were rare in the infantry. Most of them were downed flyers. There should be some scuttlebutt about him."

"OK. I'll call my boss and fill him in," Sedlock said. "I have to get an advance for two more days here. Maybe he can get Robinson's military records Federal Expressed here. Let's try to find out what happened with Robinson, how he turned up missing. And if there's any explanation of how he got back to the States. And Bob…"

"Yes?"

"If Wallace is really Robinson, this story will be big. Let's keep it to ourselves for now. What story do I use with the Marines at the reunion?"

"Tell them in your research of Web Miter's company you're interested in an M.I.A. from the Two August battle."

As he dialed Bill Walthrup's number, Sedlock thought, 'Big' isn't the word for it.

He also called Detective Dick Geany. Sedlock and Geany had been sharing information about the investigation since its onset and Wayne didn't want Geany to find out Wallace's real identity from somebody else. He figured this big a story wouldn't stay a secret for long.

After he hung up with Geany Sedlock hit the palm of his hand against his forehead. "Damn it!" he exclaimed.

"What's the matter?" Corsino asked.

"I was supposed to see my son Justin play in his Little League playoffs Saturday. There's no way I can make it now."

"I guess I was lucky. My wife and I split up after my two boys were out of high school. You're just going to have to explain it to him, Wayne. Sometimes the job comes first in this business."

"A full-time Dad can say that and get away with it," Sedlock said. "But Nancy, my ex-wife, only lets me see Justin about twice a month as it is. Little League baseball means just about everything to a 12-year-old. And if they lose this playoff game, that's the end of his Little League career."

"Call him, and explain it to him. That's all you can do."

"It's better if I don't call. That way he'll think I'm sitting in the stands rooting for him. If he knows I'm not going to be there it might affect the way he plays. It's better if he found out after the game that I wasn't there."

"Look at it like this," Corsino said. "There's a fifty percent chance they'll win the game and you can always be there for the next playoff game."

"I hope so, Bob. I've asked myself a lot over the years whether the job should come before spending what little time I get with Justin."

After listening to two ex-lifers in the hospitality suite Butch and Jim both came to the conclusion that career Marines, those who had made a career of the Corps, did not understand what civilians endured when they returned home from Vietnam. The lifers' peers had also most likely served in Nam. The civilians went their separate ways. Some, James Wallace thought, were better off than others. Many from the infantry went into law enforcement, where there was a fairly large Vietnam veteran population. But in his field of computer programming, Wallace reflected, he could count the number of combat veterans he had met on one finger. Of course it didn't matter to James Wallace anyway. He couldn't reveal his combat experience to anybody.

"Don't I know you?" a heavyset, balding vet asked James Wallace.

"No, I wasn't in the battalion," Wallace said. "I'm just visiting with my buddy, Butch. Maybe you know him. Butch Tyler."

"I'm Butch Tyler, Bravo Company," Butch said. He offered his hand to the other ex-Marine.

"I'm Henry Baily. Charlie Company. You aren't one of those Bravo survivors, are you? That battle in August '68? I was over there in '69."

"I sure am a survivor all right."

"Hell, let me buy you a beer. What're you drinking, Marine?"

"Not right now, Henry. My buddy and I just want to take all this in. We'll see you later at the bar."

Tyler and Wallace walked around the hospitality suite. There were only a half dozen battalion veterans there this early in the afternoon. There was a bulletin board with newspaper articles and pictures tacked up on it. Some were hard to read, some were out of focus. There was a table with battalion memorabilia. Two veterans were debating the finer points of Hollywood Marines versus Parris Island Marines. There were maps of Vietnam and rubbings from the Vietnam Wall. There were colorful yellow and red t-shirts with the battalion emblem on them. There were pins, Purple Heart medals, Vietnam medals, USMC bush hats, ball caps, and emblems. James thought, you could overdose on the experience. He knew he wouldn't be back, at least for a long time.

"Hope it's what you expected," Tyler said. "I once said we could hold our battalion reunion in a phone booth."

One vet, slightly drunk, said to Butch and Jim, "If you want to know what happened in Vietnam, just ask a pogue."

"We're going to have a meeting of Bravo Company in two hours," Butch said. "You're welcome to come, Jim."

"You take care of it, Buddy. I'm not ready to come out of my bunker just yet."

"If the colonel is there, do you want me to talk to him?"

"Feel him out. See what he says. Ask his advice. Hell, he's an ex-colonel. He must know something."

"All right, stay in the room. He might want to talk to you. If for no other reason, to check you out, see if you're the real McCoy."

"By the way, how do I prove who I am? What's he going to do, check my phony social security card?"

"Oh, he can check you out, all right. All he has to do is go back to that day in August of 1968. Both of you remember that day as if it was yesterday."

"I heard one of the Jarheads say Two August was the deadliest single day battle of the Vietnam War. Butch, you had a long time to think about it. Was it worth it? The war, I mean."

Butch thought for a moment. "If you look around here, the war is all around us. The memories are here, and they'll always be with us. So if you mean - was the war worth it to us, on a personal level, I think it's what you make of it. I'm sure there are guys who went right on with their lives – they never skipped a beat. But look at how it affected you. You've been living underground for thirty years."

"You think it affected any of these other guys that way?"

"I think a lot more than we'll ever know. The Marine infantry was so different than what even most other Vietnam vets experienced. But how we are viewed by the American public, that's another story. Talking to the guys here about the war is like preaching to the choir. But what about all those civilians? And I'm not just talking about the draft dodgers. What about all the urban legends the younger generation believes? They believe those stories. They watched 'Apocalypse Now' and the 'Deer Hunter' and 'Platoon' so they think they know what Vietnam vets went though. Atrocities, drugs, a bunch of psychos in an immoral war. The shame of it is all those Marines who died on Two August made just as big a sacrifice as the troops who died at Normandy. But to the average American their sacrifice didn't amount to anything. That's only true of the Vietnam War though. In World War II before us and in the Gulf War after us, none of those guys died in vain. But you can change that, Bill."

"You better call me Jim. We're taking a big enough chance here as it is. I've been lucky nobody has recognized me."

"How many survivors were there from our platoon? A couple. And chances are they wouldn't show up at the reunion. Besides we all changed so much in 30 years."

"You think they died in vain on Two August, Butch? You really think my coming back from the dead would have an effect?"

"You'd be a hero, Jim. I guarantee it. We just have to introduce you to the American public the right way. And as a hero you would have celebrity. And celebrity can mean power in the United States. Political power. Votes."

"After what we went through, why aren't there more Vietnam veteran leaders, Congressmen, even a President?"

"It's just not in the cards, Jim. First of all there just aren't that many of us compared to World War II veterans. And then you've got that stigma about Vietnam vets that exists in the eyes of Americans. That's a big hurdle to get over. And I think a lot of Vietnam vets have given up. Not quit on life, but quit on the idea of ever being a leader."

That afternoon Colonel Gray Standard held court with other survivors of Bravo Company. Besides the colonel there were seven ex-Marines present in the Gilded Room.

The colonel spoke: "We survived a once in a lifetime experience together. Why we survived, and why all those others died, we will never know. I was just a private first class then. The toughest job I ever had in my 35 years in the Marine Corps was identifying the bodies of those Bravo Company Marines killed on Two August 1968."

Butch raised his hand. "And don't forget Corporal William Robinson, who was M.I.A. that day."

Standard paused, searching for his next words. "I retired from the Marine Corps this past spring," he said. "I've been offered the job of chief executive officer of Jusen Firearms in Hartford, Connecticut. Jusen, as you know, made the AR-15 rifles that performed so poorly on Two August. I've thought all these years about what I could do to make it up to our brothers who lost their lives that August day 35 years ago. One thing we can all do is make sure it never happens again to any other men under arms. That's one of the reasons I'm taking this job. I just wanted to tell you about it first before you read about it in the newspapers." Standard paused again. "If you know of any of our brothers who we can help, either those here tonight, or those who for whatever reason don't attend reunions – let me know. We'll see what we can do for them."

As the meeting broke up Butch approached Standard. "Sir, I'm Butch Tyler. I was a rifleman in 2nd Platoon. There's one man I believe we should help. But I have to talk with you in private." The others had left the room. The two veterans of Two August sat down, and Butch Tyler told Colonel Gray Standard one of the most fantastic tales the colonel had ever heard.

CHAPTER 9 – WAR STORY

▼

By mid-1968 the U.S. Marine Corps had established a number of bases just south of the Demilitarized Zone that separated North and South Vietnam. The Marines' mission was to prevent the infiltration of North Vietnamese troops into South Vietnam. Although the borders of South Vietnam from the South China Sea on the east to Laos on the west were only about twenty miles wide near the DMZ, the Marines had to patrol relatively flat jungle-covered terrain to the east and mountains to the west. The Marines bulldozed a 500-yard wide strip through the jungle six miles east to west between the Con Thien and Gio Linh artillery bases, and then east to the South China Sea, which newspapers called MacNamara's Wall (after Defense Secretary Robert MacNamara), but which the Marines simply called the Strip. There were about a half dozen artillery bases across the DMZ which provided interlocking fields of fire for the Marine infantry operations in that area.

A network of what the Marines called MSRs, or main supply routes, crossed each other in this area. They were no more than paths that had once connected several villages that had been relocated earlier in the war. Although Marines could move in single file fairly rapidly on these MSRs, many commanders would rather have their men hack through vines and elephant grass to avoid possible mines and ambushes along the well-traveled paths. There were also level-graded roads running from north to south above which bamboo trees were tied together to hide them from aircraft. NVA (North Vietnamese Army) troops could jog from staging areas in the North down these roads four abreast at night, attack any of the Marine bases, and disperse before dawn. Marine Corps reconnaissance units called these roads the Red Ball Express.

On the morning of August 1, 1968, a Sikorsky UH-34 Marine helicopter landed among the troops of a battalion known as the 'Greatest Groundpounders' in the jungle about two miles northeast of the Con Thien firebase. It was the first of the month – payday. The Marines of Bravo Company lined up one platoon at a time, displayed their military identification cards to the paymaster who was sitting at a small folding table in front of the helicopter, and signed for their MPC, military payment certificate script. The MPC was used in place of U.S. dollars to try to defeat the black market in Vietnam. Corporal Bill Robinson, who usually left all but ten dollars on the books, took $680 in back pay because he was due to go to Bangkok on R&R in fifteen days. After the paymaster had finished with Bravo Company, his helicopter made a quick hop over the treetops to Alpha Company. Several NVA scouts from the 320B Division noted where the helicopter had landed. Thus was set in motion not only the deadliest single-day battle of the Vietnam War, but also a convoluted saga of deception that had not yet ended more than 35 years later.

There was a bright red sun that morning of August 2, 1968. As Bravo Company saddled up and moved out in column to hunt for the North Vietnamese Army, Corporal Bill Robinson, who was in the middle of the lead platoon, thought of the sailor's ditty, "Red sky at night, Sailor's delight, Red sky in the morning, Sailors take warning." Robinson had been 'in country' long enough, about six months now, that he could sense when the enemy was nearby.

On Two August 1968 three companies of his battalion were patrolling just south of the Demilitarized Zone about two miles northeast of the Marine combat base called Con Thien. Approximately nine o'clock that morning one battalion of the North Vietnamese Army waited in ambush along MSR (Main Supply Route) 28. The MSR, misnamed like most things on the Americans' maps, was no more than a path through the jungle. The jungle had grown over what had years earlier been a village that was razed and moved ten miles south when the war started, because it was too close to the Demilitarized Zone, which was also misnamed. The maps the Marines carried called the area the 'Marketplace,' in reference to what had been there years earlier.

Enemy machine guns opened up with deadly accuracy from the front and the western side of the north-south column that was Bravo Company, in what the Marines called an "L" shaped ambush. Twelve Marines went down immediately. From the center of the column company commander Captain Web Miter tried to maneuver his men into some kind of defensive perimeter. He also tried to ascertain what the situation was in the forward half of the column, which seemed to be taking the brunt of fire in the ambush. Small arms fire, meaning AK-47s, immediately opened up on all sides. In Miter's five months in Vietnam this was the most enemy fire than he had ever heard, and he knew his Marines were in serious trouble. Just then 61 and 82-millimeter mortar rounds started marching up and down the column.

In a moment of out-of-body lapse of concentration Miter thought about that old college game his fraternity brothers at M.I.T. used to play called, 'What Could Be Worse?' The object of the game was to think of a bad situation then go around the room, everybody taking a turn coming up with a situation that could be worse. Right now Web Miter couldn't think of a worse situation.

Miter had his artillery forward observer, who was a full-blooded Cherokee Indian named Lance Corporal Laughing Cloud, start calling in fire missions. LC Twice, as he was called, knew he'd have to work outside the ambush and move inward. The NVA were too close to do anything else. The NVA were doing what they called hugging the belt, that is, staying close enough to the Marines so the Marines couldn't call in artillery without calling it onto themselves. Miter was getting nothing over the radio from the lead platoon.

Corporal Bill Robinson and PFC Butch Tyler, who were part of the lead platoon, were sharing a bomb crater. The instant the ambush was sprung they instinctively dove away from the enemy machine gun, and there happened to be a 500-pound bomb crater nearby. Usually there were few targets when they engaged the NVA because the enemy soldiers stayed well camouflaged. But today there were targets, green-clad NVA soldiers popping up and darting all over the place. Robinson tried to keep his breathing under control as he fired his AR-15. He fired east and Tyler fired west. Each had several enemy kills. Within a couple minutes Tyler's AR-15 jammed. He knew he needed a cleaning rod to go through the barrel and punch the jammed round out of the chamber. He also knew he had lost his in the jungle a couple days earlier.

Tyler could barely be heard over the din and chaos of the battle when he yelled to Robinson, "I need your cleaning rod!"

Robinson reached down to the cleaning rod pouch that hung from his web belt. He fished out two pieces of the rod but the third piece was missing. He noticed the bottom of the cleaning rod pouch had a hole worn in it. The missing piece must have fallen along the trail somewhere, Robinson thought. They couldn't clear Tyler's weapon because two pieces of the rod screwed together weren't long enough to reach the jammed round. Tyler felt that "Oh shit!" feeling in the pit of his stomach and took out all five fragmentation grenades from his grenade pouches and lined them up along the rim of the crater.

About twenty minutes into the fight Captain Miter also experienced a sickening feeling in his stomach. His radioman had just informed him that Alpha Company had been ambushed in its attempt to rescue Bravo. He could hear the M60 machine guns giving a good account of themselves but the AR-15 rifle fire had slackened appreciably in the past five minutes. And he thought he knew why. His battalion had been having problems with the new AR-15 rifles. They had been jamming. Until now they had lived with it but they had never been in a fight like this before. They were in a desperate situation. He told his artillery forward observer to put a white phosphorous round at the center of each side of the column. The rounds arrived two minutes later.

"That's your bracket, LC," Miter told his forward observer. "On my command I want HE (high explosives) airbursts set to explode 30 feet above the ground walking along the column, but not inside that bracket."

"Sir, you might be bringing it on top of your own men."

"At least this way we have a chance to disengage. If we do nothing we won't have any chance." The captain turned to his radioman. "When I say cease fire, everybody is to pull back south to the Strip."

Captain Miter relayed his plan over the radio to whoever was still alive to listen. Robinson and Tyler had no radio. While Tyler tried to clear his jammed weapon by smashing it butt first against a rock Robinson spotted a target some twenty-five meters to his right front. As he aimed he realized the NVA soldier he was aiming at was aiming an RPG, a rocket propelled grenade, at him. Robinson squeezed the trigger. One round fired then the rifle jammed. Before he even realized what had happened he could see the RPG round coming toward him, as if it was flying in slow motion.

"Down!" he yelled. It was the last word he uttered in what became known to Marines throughout I Corps as the Battle of Two August.

When Corporal Bill Robinson came to Tyler was gone. The jungle was silent. He was covered with dirt from the exploding RPG. His right forearm was bandaged with the first aid bandage from his web belt. Tyler must have done that, he thought. He looked up and down the trail, but he dared not call out.

Suddenly an NVA soldier appeared over the rim of his bomb crater. The green clad enemy soldier had foliage strapped to the back of his pack. He leveled his AK-47 at Bill. Bill felt like crying, but he stood there frozen with no weapon to defend himself. He was ready to die. Then the NVA barked a command in his sing-song language. "Lie die!" he kept shouting, at least that's what Bill heard. Then he reached down and grabbed Bill by his shirt and started dragging him out of the crater. A single artillery round whooshed down and exploded fifty feet from the two of them. A piece of shrapnel entered the NVA soldier's brain, instantly killing him. Bill was untouched in the crater, although he was temporarily deaf from the concussion. The thought occurred to him that he had been a POW for approximately fifteen seconds.

"They left me!" was all he could think of. "My whole platoon left me."

He walked back through the Marketplace, south on MSR 28. Gear and bodies, both Marines and NVA, covered the jungle. He was only a couple miles as the crow flies from the Marine base at Con Thien. The base was south and west of him, and he felt he could make it back there. He knew the area well from patrolling it so many times that summer. He knew the path he was on intersected another east-west path, and that led up to Con Thien. He walked at first, then double-timed. Within an hour he came to the east-west path, and turned west.

After an hour along that road he came upon a wider road that came south from Con Thien. Marines were loading bodies off a tank onto two trucks. They were on the dirt road that was used to re-supply Con Thien during the monsoon months when helicopters could not fly. As Robinson approached the trucks from the jungle a Marine who was standing guard spotted him.

"Get back in the truck!" he shouted at Robinson. "If you have to piss, just piss over the tailgate. Don't you know this is Indian country?"

Robinson peered over the tailgate into the first truck. It was dark inside, covered with a dark green tarpaulin, but he could make out wounded Marines, highlighted by their bloody white and red bandages and white tags tied to their arms and legs. In the second truck body bags were stacked two and three high. There seemed to be more room in that truck so Robinson hoisted himself over the tailgate and settled in with the dead.

The truck driver who was standing guard yelled over at the Marines working around the tank, "What's takin' you guys so long? We gotta get outa here. Don't you know this is Indian country?"

The Marines around the tank were taking dead bodies off of it, zipping them into body bags, and loading the body bags into the back of the truck. Robinson noticed there were about a half dozen empty body bags lying on the bed of the truck. He unzipped one of the empty body bags and climbed into it like he was zipping himself into a sleeping bag. He pulled his bayonet out of its sheath to cut his way out of it if he had to. Then he zipped it over his head. As the trucks moved out of Indian country Corporal Bill Robinson left the jungles of Vietnam behind forever.

There were two Marine Corps in South Vietnam in 1968. There were the front line infantry grunts like Bill Robinson, who slogged through the jungles and rice paddies on patrols to kill Viet Cong and North Vietnamese soldiers. Their jobs were to stop the infiltration of the NVA into South Vietnam and to act as a screening force to protect the huge Marine airbases such as Danang, Chu Lai and Phu Bai from mortar and rocket attacks. The grunts lived like animals, always dirty, always tired, patrolling all day with 70-pounds of gear strapped on their backs, awake much of the night on watch in a hole they dug, often up all night on listening posts or ambushes, at most getting three or four hours sleep on the ground each night. There were no true front lines in Vietnam, so even when the grunts were pulled back to their firebases along the DMZ for a few days they manned the perimeter line on watch day and night. Many front line commanders felt their grunts were corrupted if they spent too much time among the pogues, the rear area troops, at the larger bases near Vietnamese villages where marijuana and other drugs were available.

And then there were the rear area support troops, the pogues as Marines like Robinson called them, who lived on the huge Marine bases that were as large as some cities in the States. The grunts and the pogues each had their own perceptions of each other.

The grunts envied the pogues their clean clothes and showers every day. They envied them their giant post exchanges (PXs), which rivaled some department stores in the States. They envied their clubs with cheap beer and their movies every night and the Vietnamese women who were available just outside the gate of every base. Bill Robinson's unit was rumored to be rationed one beer per Marine per day for every day they were in the rear. But a sergeant major was said to be selling that beer on the Vietnamese black market, so the Marines of Bravo Company never tasted a beer during their tours. There were even rumors that pogues lay on China Beach in Danang sunning themselves on the white sand and swimming in the South China Sea, and that they played volleyball to relieve the boredom, and that they lived in air conditioned Quonset huts.

While pogues watched Bob Hope USO shows, Marine grunts patrolled the jungle nearby to insure the enemy didn't launch rockets and mortars toward the Dallas Cheerleaders.

The pogues believed the grunts to be vicious maniacs, who cut off the ears of dead enemy soldiers and hung them around their necks as trophies. They ran into grunts mostly in places like the Air Force club in Danang, which Marines swore was more luxurious than any Marine enlisted men's club in the States. Marine grunts, who passed through Danang alone away from their unit while going to or from R&R or on the way home, never had to pay for a drink, as long as they gave a red-star NVA belt buckle to a pogue as a souvenir and kept the stories coming. And Marine grunts had a knack for putting on the pogues, adding that little bit of exaggeration or gore to their tale that assured them another cold beer. In return the pogues heard firsthand about the war, and got something to write home to their girls about, other than the usual complaints about the boredom of their jobs as clerks and cooks and supply mules and computer operators. Thus were born the urban legends that defined the Vietnam War to the American people.

"There's just too many of them," the sergeant at the Marine Grave Registration Unit at Dong Ha said. "Our freezer will only fit 100 sleds max. From what I hear we'll get that many from the Groundpounders alone. Then we can expect a dozen or so more from the rest of the 3rd Marine Division. We can't let these bodies cook out in the sun tomorrow. We're going to have to ship 50 of them down to Danang to the 1st MarDiv Graves Unit. Let's get the medevac choppers in and get them shipped down to Danang."

The 3rd MarDiv Graves Unit spent that evening of Two August into the wee hours of the next morning loading body bags into helicopters, which flew them down to the huge Danang Airbase. The Danang Graves personnel unloaded them and lined them in a long row, where they began the tedious task of identifying the corpses. Bill Robinson unzipped himself out of the thirty-second body bag in the row and calmly walked away from the Graves Registration Unit. As he walked along the paved road other Marines he passed seemed startled by his appearance. Then he noticed their cleaned and pressed fatigues and he realized he was caked in dirt and blood. Fatigues were hanging on clotheslines beside the tents on either side of the road. He picked several off the lines and held them up to his body, finally settling on one that fit him. Then he spotted a half of a 55-gallon drum mounted on stilts. He stripped down and stood underneath the makeshift shower, pulled the cord and washed the grime off of him. When he was done he dressed himself, then spotted several pairs of spit-shined jungle boots sitting outside a tent. He found a pair that fit and put them on. The perfectly dressed pogue, Robinson thought to himself as he headed out the North Gate.

"What you looking for, Marine?" the young Vietnamese man asked.

"I want knockout drops."

"What are knockout drops? No understand."

"When a girl wants to put a Marine to sleep so she can take his money out of his wallet, she puts something in his drink. I want what she puts into his drink."

"Now I understand. You going to put your sergeant to sleep?"

"No, I'm going to put Ho Chi Minh to sleep. Do you have it?"

"Ho Chi Minh number 10. Marines number 1. Will cost you $30. Makes ten drops."

"How many drops to make somebody sleep 24 hours?"

"Four drops should do it, Joe."

"And I want a bottle of Jack Daniels."

"That's three dollars more. $33 total."

From there, Robinson headed to the Air Force Enlisted Men's Club.

"Jim Jones. Mind if I join you?" Robinson said to the Marine with his head slumped over one arm on the table.

"Sure. Be my guest," the other Marine said. "Lloyd Duckworth. Everybody calls me Ducky."

"Stationed here in Danang?" Robinson asked.

"I'm in the Cryptology Section. Not supposed to talk about it, though. Unless you have a Top Secret clearance."

"No. I'm just a grunt passing through on R&R to Bangkok."

"I'm on the big bird to Hawaii tomorrow morning myself for R&R. You in the transit tent? I just stacked my gear there."

"No, I don't even know where the transit tent is. Just got here from up north. Why are you staying in the transit tent if you're stationed here at Danang?"

"Well, actually I'm stationed on a mountain outside Danang. Can't talk about it though unless you've got a Top Secret clearance. What unit are you with up north?"

"Ducky, seeing as you've got a Top Secret clearance I guess I can tell you."

They both laughed.

"I'm a fire team leader with 2nd Platoon, Bravo Company, the Greatest Groundpounders," Robinson said.

"The Groundpounders! Holy Shit! They just got their asses kicked. Were you with them when it happened?" Duckworth asked.

"No, they pulled me out for R&R just before it happened."

"You're one lucky S.O.B."

"Could you tell me where the transit tent is?"

"Better than that I'll show you. It's first come, first serve. Got to get a cot early, or you end up sleeping on the ground. Guess you're used to that, though."

Both Marines walked out of the club a quarter of a mile to the transit tent.

"What time does your flight for Hawaii leave tomorrow?" Robinson asked.

"Ten A.M."

"How long a flight is it?"

"It's about eight hours. So I get there about three P.M. today."

"Today?"

"Yes. We will be flying backwards across the International Dateline. So if I leave Vietnam tomorrow I'll arrive the previous day, which is today. So I'll get to live today all over again. It doesn't matter what I do today because I get to live today all over again in Hawaii anyway. When does your flight leave, Jim?"

"In the late afternoon."

"One question, Jim. You said your name is Jones but it reads Ortiz over the pocket flap."

"I had to borrow these utilities from a buddy. I didn't have any clean."

"I got news for you, Jim. You've got to have a khaki Class A uniform to go on R&R. You did bring one, didn't you?"

"Mine got lost way back. I'm going to buy one at the PX tomorrow."

"I've got to get some sleep," Ducky said.

"How about a drink to celebrate?"

"What time is it?"

"One A.M., my friend." Robinson offered Duckworth a canteen cup of Jack Daniels. "Before you drink that, Ducky, tell me, what the hell do you do on that mountain outside Danang?"

"I tear little strips of paper with holes punched in them off one machine and feed them into another machine. We're a computer relay station. Try doing that twelve hours a day. That'll drive you to drink."

"Here's a toast to our R&Rs, and all the pleasures they hold."

Both Marines drank from their cups.

CHAPTER 10 - THE PLAN

▼

When Tyler had finished, the colonel said, "If we're going to do this I have to meet him in person."

"Roger that, Colonel," Tyler said with a broad grin on his face. "He's up in my room now, Sir."

When he walked in the room retired Colonel Gray Standard examined ex-Corporal William Wilson Robinson as if he was viewing the mammoth dinosaur skeleton at the Peabody Museum when he was a kid on a school field trip in Connecticut. He tried to place Robinson in his mind, how he looked back then. Robinson was probably 75 pounds heavier now, and balding. He knew it was no use. The colonel was a PFC then and he'd been in a different platoon and had been in-country less than three weeks when the battle took place. And in truth he only got to know a handful of other Marines very well in Vietnam.

"Why now?" Standard asked. "After all these years why reveal your identity now?"

"The now is because both my parents have passed away, and the parents of the boy whose name I assumed have passed away." He looked at Butch. "And we thought … I thought … we could do something for Vietnam vets … before it's too late."

"Vietnam vets are fifty years old. What are you going to do for them now?"

Butch spoke up. "Sir, earlier this evening you said you would do whatever you could to help ex-Marines from Bravo Company. I believe if Jim, Bill, comes before the American public as a returning M.I.A. he can help all Vietnam vets in this country. He could be somebody the whole country could be proud of. You may not understand. You made a career in the military. You didn't come home to people spitting at you at the airport, or protesters on college campuses. And the urban legends have persisted. Atrocities, drugs, baby killers."

Standard spoke. "How can he help them? Say he turns himself in to a local police station. 'Hi, I'm Corporal Bill Robinson. I'm a deserter from the Vietnam War who was listed as an M.I.A.' So a one-column story appears on page 32 of the New York *Times*. So what?"

"But that's just it, Sir. He has to be discovered by the media. Then they'll make a big deal of it. Then he could be a hero, not a deserter. Then he could run for office. Then he could do something for vets."

"Bill, what have you been doing these past 30 years? How have you supported yourself?"

"I've been a contract computer programmer, Sir. I've worked all over the country. For the past few years I've worked in the insurance industry in Connecticut."

"Do you know I'm from Connecticut and have been offered the job as CEO of Jusen Firearms? I've also been asked to consider running for the Republican Party for the junior Senator seat from Connecticut. What political party are you affiliated with, Bill?"

"I would say I lean more toward the Democratic Party's philosophy."

"My Democratic opponent would most likely be the very popular Attorney General of the state. If a very popular war hero was to run as an Independent, he might draw enough votes away from my opponent so a Republican just might win that seat. Then you would have a Vietnam veteran Senator who was not beholding to special interests and who might be able to do something for Vietnam vets."

Bill said nothing.

"It's a plan," Butch said. "It's not exactly what we were thinking, but it makes sense."

"That means we would be political opponents," Gray Standard said. "If we held a political debate right now in this room, what issues could we debate?"

"Sir, our whole difference of philosophies can be spelled out in the Two August battle. I always believed every Marine was important. No Marine was ever left behind on the battlefield. Why didn't they come back for me?"

Standard looked down at the floor for a few seconds before he spoke. "Bill, Web Miter was in charge of the whole company that day. He had to think about saving as many men as possible. I know there were times when we lost two or three men trying to retrieve a dead or wounded Marine. But those were situations in which we were more or less in control of the battlefield. On Two August he didn't have any idea how many NVAs were out there. What was he supposed to do, turn us all around and march us into an NVA regiment? We were almost out of ammunition and the rifles were jamming. To try to get you would have been suicide. How many Marines would we have lost? Probably damn near all of them. Would you have wanted that on your conscience?"

Tears welled up in Bill's eyes. "But it was his leaving me that was the reason I decided to go home. It was against everything I believed in about the Marine Corps. I always thought one Marine was important. I always thought you go back for him no matter what. That's the reason I've lived undercover all these years."

"And how did you live, Bill? Did you live in a cave foraging for food? You look to me like you ate very well. From all

I've heard the computer profession pays very well. Whatever happened, happened. Now we've got to go on from here. We can do this, Bill. We can get a senator elected who can do things for Vietnam veterans. If you want to use Two August against me in a political debate, that's fine. But in your mind, in your soul, you have to forget what happened to you on Two August 1968. You made it out alive. There are a hundred Marines whose names are on that Wall just a couple miles from here who died there that day. The American people never even heard of that battle. It's up to you, Bill."

"OK, I'll do it."

"The American people are going to hear about that battle now," Butch said.

"All right," Gray Standard said. "We've got to come up with a plan to introduce Bill to America. Like I said, if he walks into a local police station, it's not going to work. Like you said, the ideal situation would be if the media discovers Bill. Both of you think about it. Here's my address and phone number in Connecticut. The senatorial election is 15 months from now. I'd say we have to do this in about three months in order to get Bill's name on the ballot as an Independent. Think. Remember, you want the media to discover Bill. And be careful who you tell about this. OK, Gentlemen, I expect your ideas in writing in a week. Take care."

Standard left the room.

"We've got a plan, Buddy," Butch said.

Sedlock took the elevator up two flights to the Groundpounders hospitality suite. He strolled in, checking out the posters on the walls and memorabilia on the tables. He knew that because he was twenty years younger than the Vietnam vets that he would stick out like a sore thumb. But nobody seemed to notice. Some veterans had their families with them, with teenagers and smaller children. Mellow was the word Sedlock would use to describe the veterans of the Greatest Groundpounders battalion.

He approached a group of veterans sitting at a table drinking beer.

"Excuse me, gentlemen. I'm doing research on Web Miter's company and I'm interested in the one M.I.A. from the Two August battle. Did any of you know William Robinson?"

"Friend," one of the veterans said, "there's hardly anybody alive that knew Robinson. Almost his whole company was wiped out on Two August 1968. There were only twenty survivors."

"Do you think there's anybody at the reunion who knows firsthand what happened to him?"

"I doubt it. Those survivors were scrambling for their lives. They were being overrun by an NVA regiment when Capt. Miter called in arty on the whole thing. They called him "Madman" Miter after that, and he was awarded the Navy Cross for what he did that day. Damn shame what happened to him."

Sedlock took notes in a small notebook he carried.

"Do you know if any survivors of that company are at the reunion?"

"Sully's here. He might be able to help. Dan Sullivan."

Sedlock phoned Sullivan, who invited him to his room.

"I hope you don't mind talking here," Sullivan said. "I don't like to tell war stories in the hospitality suite. Trouble is, as each year goes by, more and more ex-Marines believe they were in the battles. There's probably not more than half a dozen at the whole reunion who were in the Two August battle. Most of the guys talk about Captain Miter calling in arty on top of us. It wasn't that way, at least where I was. They call him Madman Miter, but he saved our asses that day. There was a joke going around for years, if Miter was awarded the Navy Cross when there were only twenty survivors then he would have been awarded the Medal of Honor if there were no survivors at all. I guess you have to be a Marine to get a joke like that. What do you want to talk about?"

"William W. Robinson. Did you know him?"

"I knew him to say hello to. We were in different squads. I was in first, he was in second."

"Would you know him if you saw him?" Sedlock asked.

"What do you mean would I know him if I saw him? He's been M.I.A. since 1968."

Sedlock could have kicked himself.

"What I meant was, do you remember what he looked like?"

"No, I really don't. You've got to understand. You only had two or three good buddies over there, basically your fire team. All the pictures I have today are of only about half a dozen guys."

"Do you know what happened to Robinson on Two August?"

"I don't think anybody knows for sure. Second squad, Robinson's squad, was up at the front of the column that day. They got hit first. Then the captain called in arty, so we were able to disengage and pull back. It was a real Chinese fire drill. NVA popping up all over the place. The AR-15 rifles were jamming. It was a real mess. Not one of the Marine Corps' finest moments. But I remember one thing about Robinson that day. When we finally got back to the Strip - which was a bulldozed cut through the jungle - when we finally got back and got reinforced by another battalion, this little guy kept screaming at Captain Miter that Robinson was still out there, and that we should go back and get him."

"Who was that man, do you remember?" Sedlock asked.

"I can't remember who it was, but he must have been one of the guys in Robinson's fire team. He kept saying Robinson was still alive, just knocked out. The captain kept telling him we couldn't go back out there right now," Sullivan said.

"But they never found Robinson, dead or alive?"

"That's right. As far as I know he's still listed as M.I.A. When they swept through there the next day his body was the only one not accounted for."

"What do you think happened to him?" Sedlock asked.

"One of two things. Either he was captured, and he died in some jungle prison camp. Or an artillery round landed directly on his body. That happened to a Marine back in Danang and all they found was a piece of his canteen cup."

"Do you know anywhere else I can get the whole story of what happened on Two August 1968?"

"You could try the Marine Museum. It has the unit diaries of every battle the Marines were ever in."

"Thanks, Dan. You've been a great help."

"What gives, Man? You're not writing any book," Sullivan said.

"It's for his mother," Sedlock said. "Before she dies she wants to find out what happened to her son. You've been a big help."

The next morning, Thursday, August 2ⁿᵈ, at eleven o'clock the reunion group formed in front of the Vietnam Memorial Wall. They lined up in two ranks, most approaching sixty now, graying hair and balding, eyes and hearing not as keen as when they fought their battles. The park ranger asked the tourists to please stand silent for a few minutes while the battalion placed a wreath at the foot of the Wall. Two old warriors, one missing an arm, walked the wreath up to the base of the Wall. The other man said: "We dedicate this wreath to the Marines of our battalion who were killed in Vietnam, and to the ex-Marines who have died since then. We'd like to note that one of them, Captain Web Miter, Navy Cross winner, was killed by a mine just ten days ago. For some, the war goes on. Let us never forget the sacrifices these men made for us. We will never forget. For many of us would not be here today if it wasn't for these men whose names are on this Wall. Battalion! Hand salute!"

The men in the two ranks saluted, not as crisply as they had some forty years earlier, but never with more reverence for their country and their comrades. There was barely one dry eye among them. Sedlock, standing well back in the crowd lest Jim Wallace see him, noted all of it, and he carried away a little more appreciation of what Vietnam veterans went through.

Chapter 11 - Duckworth

▼

The afternoon of August 2nd the Greatest Groundpounders battalion was given free rein at the Marine Corps Museum. The Marines could travel on their own by the Metro and the museum would make the facility available to them. Sedlock and Bob Corsino decided it would be better if Bob went to the museum alone. For one thing he had been there before to look up his own unit's diary, and for another his being an ex-Marine and a Vietnam vet himself would make it easier for him to pass as a member of the Greatest Groundpounders who was interested in looking up the unit diary of the Two August battle.

The rest of the day Corsino read about the Two August battle in the official unit diary of the Greatest Groundpounders battalion. He wondered - How could half a Marine rifle battalion, with ten other Marine battalions less than 20 minutes away by helicopter, suffer fifty percent casualties in daylight in less than six hours? The diary was written in government-speak, he thought, a far cry from the chaos of battle the Marines who lived through the battle must have experienced.

Corsino reviewed the casualty list. It was typed neatly by fire team within squad within platoon within company. Almost every name in Alpha and Bravo companies had either a WIA for Wounded in Action or KIA for Killed in Action written next to it. Then Corsino remembered the story Sedlock told him about Dan Sullivan remembering the little guy screaming at Capt. Miter about Robinson. He searched for Robinson's name with MIA next to it. The other two members of his fire team were PFC Smith, William and PFC Tyler, John. That's the connection, Corsino thought. They shared the same foxhole in the Two August battle.

On a hunch Corsino leafed through the Military Police logs for both the Dong Ha base, the 3rd Marine Division's headquarters, and Danang, the huge Marine airbase, for the entries just after 2 August 1968. On 4 August a PFC Lloyd Duckworth with the annotation 'orders stolen' appeared in the Marine logbook of the Danang In-Transit unit. There was also a comment that Duckworth was passing through Danang on his way to R&R in Hawaii and reported his orders and plane ticket were stolen. Also, $680 of his U.S. currency had been replaced with $680 in MPC, military payment certificates.

When Corsino returned to the Dupont Hotel with his notes and reviewed them with Sedlock they decided to try to locate PFC Lloyd Duckworth. Sedlock called Janie Caldwell at Alco.

"Janie, this is Wayne Sedlock. Do you think you could do some of your computer magic and try to locate somebody for us? At least get his phone number?"

"That depends," Janie said. "What's his name?"

"Lloyd Duckworth," Sedlock said.

"I might be able to do it," Janie said. "That's an unusual name. If it were Smith or Jones I wouldn't have a chance. I'll get on the Internet and Switchboard Dot Com. I'll call you back when I find something. What's your number?"

A half an hour later Janie called back. "He's in San Antonio. He has a website. It advertises his insurance agency."

Sedlock phoned Lloyd Duckworth in San Antonio. "Hello, Mr. Duckworth. This is Wayne Sedlock of the Alco Insurance

Company in Hartford, Connecticut. Are you the same Marine Vietnam vet whose R&R orders to Hawaii were stolen in August 1968? Somebody boarded the jet impersonating you?"

"That's me. Wow, that was another lifetime ago! I was in the club drinking ten cent beers," Duckworth said. "Another Marine came over to my table. We started to shoot the breeze. He said he had a flight out to Bangkok the next day. I told him I was going to Hawaii."

"Do you remember his name? Could you identify him or give a description?"

"Six feet tall. Average build. Dark hair. Sorry I can't do any better than that. For one thing it was 35 years ago, for another I had been drinking beer. We talked about how the troops in the rear had everything, and how the grunts got nothing. There was one thing out of place about him though."

"What was that?"

"You could tell by the way he talked he was a front line trooper, but he had clean, pressed utilities on. And I noticed the name he introduced himself with, was different that the name stamped above his left breast pocket."

"Do you remember what name he introduced himself with?"

"No, like I said it was a long time ago."

Sedlock thought it could have been Robinson. He might have stolen a set of fatigues somewhere on the Danang Airbase.

"What did he talk about? Did he ever say what unit he was in?"

"He sure did. Said he was with Bravo Company of the Greatest Groundpounders battalion. Everybody was talking about Bravo Company because it was just the day after they got overrun up North. This guy said he missed all that. He said his unit gave him five days R&R to Bangkok and he got pulled out of the field a day before the Greatest Groundpounders got overrun near the DMZ. That's all everybody was talking about."

"How did you lose your plane ticket and orders?"

"We both went back to the In-Transit tent. He had some Jack Daniels we sipped on. Then I passed out on the cot in the tent. When I came to sixteen hours later my orders and plane ticket were missing. And he exchanged my U.S. money for his MPC. He didn't short-change me, I'll give him that. I figure to stay knocked out that long he must have put something in my drink. I reported my plane ticket was stolen. It took a couple days before they got me another ticket to Hawaii. That's about it. End of story."

"If there's nothing else, Lloyd, we appreciate your help."

"You're tracking that Marine who stole my plane ticket, right?"

"We can't discuss that part of our investigation right now. Thanks very much, Mr. Duckworth."

CHAPTER 12 –
THE GREENWICH CLUB

▼

"How many years have you been seeing me, Wayne?" Dr. Alonzo asked Sedlock.

"It's been about 13 years," Sedlock said.

"Is the medication working all right for you?"

"You've asked me that for 13 years, Doc. And my answer still is, it's working great."

"That's good. I consider you one my real success stories. Other than that first year when we were searching for the right combination of meds, it's been strictly maintenance. And I've been real proud of you, Wayne. I watched you move up from a beginner to a top investigator. Now you're working on one of the biggest cases in the state. Do you find it stressful, working on such a big case? There must be a lot of pressure."

"I wouldn't call it stressful," Sedlock said. "I'd call it challenging."

"I've got something to tell you, Wayne. I'm retiring. My wife and I have bought a condo in Florida."

"What does that mean as far as me getting my meds?"

"Well, I'm referring all my patients to another doctor, Dr. Martha Baily. She's very good, has been a psychiatrist for twenty years."

"Will it be the same, Doc? In and out in five minutes. You know, every three- month visit you ask me 'What's new? How's the medication working out for you?' Then you write out the prescription and I'm out of here. That's the way I like it. How much do you get from the insurance company for a visit, Doc -- 80, 90 dollars? That must be some condo you and your wife bought in Florida. But don't get me wrong. That's the way I like it. This new doctor's not going to lay me down on a couch and psycho analyze me, is she, Doc?"

"No, I'm going to recommend she continue maintenance only. You have to see her for a screening interview. She'll want to read through your files first before your visit. I'd like to set up an appointment for this week. Would Wednesday be all right, at two o'clock? You have to sign this form. That gives me permission to transfer your files to Dr. Baily."

"Sure, Doc," Sedlock said as he signed the form. "I remember signing that form thirteen years ago that got me 17 days in a mental hospital. Well, it's been fun, Doc. Enjoy yourself in Florida."

"And just remember, Wayne, take your meds. I know you learned your lesson way back when. Good-bye and good luck."

Rebecca Miter got a two o'clock starting time at the Greenwich Club. Sedlock realized when he arrived at 1:30 that this was the first non-public golf course he had ever played on. Rebecca met him at the snack bar.

"Good afternoon, Wayne. Do you mind if I call you Wayne during our match? The starter will pair us up with another couple and it might be awkward saying 'You're away, Mr. Sedlock' all the time." Rebecca laughed. She certainly doesn't appear to be the grieving widow, Sedlock thought.

"Sure, call me anything but late for dinner. You have a big advantage in that you've probably played this course a hundred times. It's all new to me. And what should I call you, Mrs. Miter?"

"Call me Becky. That's what most people call me. And I haven't played the course that many times. Web and I played it together maybe a half dozen times. He always played with his friends, other corporate hotshots. Oh, and I forgot, I played in a nine-hole ladies league for the past couple of summers. You're right, maybe I have played the course a hundred times. Don't worry, I'll tell you where not to hit it and how the greens break. Would you like to have a coffee, or would you like to go out on the range and warm up?"

"I'd like to do both if we have the time."

Sedlock and Rebecca bought a coffee at the snack bar. When Sedlock offered to pay for it Rebecca said, "We don't pay for anything here, Wayne. I'll just sign the chit. They send a bill every month. I can see you're not used to private country clubs."

"No, as a matter of fact I just realized when I drove into the parking lot that this is the first private country club I have ever played on." They walked over to a table and sat down.

"Saturday night I drove back from your husband's Vietnam battalion reunion in D.C. I spoke to two veterans who were in your husband's company. They both spoke highly of him. In fact they called him a hero. And both offered their condolences."

"Give them my thanks if you talk with them again. Did you find any connection with the explosive that killed Web and anything that happened in Vietnam?"

Sedlock hesitated to tell Rebecca the whole story. After all, his trip to Washington, D.C., was part of a murder investigation. But on the other hand he felt he had to trust her if she was willing to provide information about her deceased husband that only she could. He decided not to mention the M.I.A. William Robinson, but to level with her about what else he found out at the reunion.

"I found a connection between your husband's time in Vietnam and the type of explosive that was used to kill him.

There was a Marine in your husband's company who was caught sending C-4 explosives home in the mail in 1968. The Marine went to prison for two years then was dishonorably discharged from the Marine Corps. He lives right here in Connecticut."

"Could he have had some kind of vendetta against Web after all these years? Is that possible after almost forty years?" Rebecca asked.

"I don't know. According to the two at the reunion who knew this man, your husband did everything he could at the man's court-martial to get him off the hook. We checked him out yesterday. He has an alibi for his whereabouts the afternoon of the Pro- Am. It was a long shot, but we had to check it out. You mentioned you printed a copy of your husband's first draft of his memoir. Did you bring it with you, Becky?"

"Yes, I've got it in the car. I haven't read it. It's about a hundred pages. Some of it is just notes, some of it full text. I'll give it to you after our round. I'm afraid if I give it to you now you'll be sitting on the cart reading it instead of enjoying the game. Is that all right with you, Wayne?"

"That's fine," Sedlock said. "Let's go warm up. Let's hit some practice balls."

Sedlock and Rebecca shared a bucket of practice balls on the driving range. Sedlock noticed Rebecca signed another chit for the golf balls.

"I could get used to that," he said to her as he drilled a 3-wood down the middle of the practice area. Rebecca responded in kind by hitting a crisp 5-iron 150 yards. As they emptied the bucket in the next fifteen minutes they remained quiet. Sedlock was lost in thought – where could all the possibilities of the Web Miter murder investigation lead? He had no idea what Rebecca was thinking. Was she bitter at the loss of her husband? Was she angry at whoever killed him? Was she happy to be inheriting his fortune? Sedlock finally felt he could ask her the one question about the murder that had bothered him from the moment Web Miter was killed.

"Becky, doesn't it seem strange that if somebody wanted to kill your husband they would do it in such a public way? Why not just shoot him with a pistol or a rifle? Why not attach a bomb to his car so it blows up in his driveway? Why do it in a PGA golf tournament where there are 20,000 spectators?"

"You're right, Wayne. I've thought about it myself. It's almost like it's a terrorist act. Somebody wanted to send a message about Web, or about people like him."

"Or somebody wants to make it look like a terrorist act. Make it look like Web was killed because he was the 'Father of Off Shoring.'"

The couple hoisted up their golf bags and walked over to the area where the golf carts were kept.

"You can drive," Rebecca said with a smile. "And try to keep your eyes on the road. What's your handicap, anyway?"

Sedlock slid the scorecard under the clip on the steering wheel. "It's been so long since I played an 18-hole round of golf I couldn't tell you what my handicap is," he said.

"I'll let you off easy then, seeing as you've never played the course before. We'll play one hole at a time, winner takes front, back and match. Loser buys the beer."

"I thought you said the members just sign chits here. What do the guests do?"

"Don't worry about it. We'll just play for the hell of it. Good luck."

Sedlock drove the cart over to the first tee where another couple was waiting for them. The man was middle-aged, graying at the temples and heavyset. The woman was about the same age, slim with dark black hair. Rebecca introduced the couple. "Doug Segall and his wife Ginny, this is Wayne Sedlock." Doug and Ginny shook hands with Sedlock.

"I'm in the brokerage business, work in New York," Doug said. "What's your game, Wayne?"

"I'm a journalist," Sedlock said. "I'm a reporter for the Technology *Times*."

"Technology *Times*? Can't say as I'm familiar with that one. Go ahead and tee it up, my friend. We'll hit then get out of the way so the ladies can show us how it's done from their tee."

Sedlock took a couple practice swings then hit his driver into the right rough 220 yards away. Segall then teed up and with a short, abbreviated back swing hit his driver not very far but straight down the middle of the fairway. Ginny Segall then hit down the middle from the ladies tee. Rebecca Miter pulled her drive left into the rough.

"Looks like we'll be playing golf cart management," Rebecca said. "You in the right rough and me in the left."

As they drove to Rebecca's ball and got out of earshot of the Segalls, Rebecca said, "Why did you tell him you were a reporter? You don't have to be ashamed to say you are an insurance investigator."

"Becky, your husband hasn't been dead two weeks yet. Who knows what they think of you playing golf with another man so soon after the funeral? But on top of that introducing to them somebody who is investigating his murder? Besides, I use the reporter disguise all the time. Remember, I used to be a reporter."

"Wayne, Web was 62-years-old and I am twenty-eight. We talked it over many times. We both knew he would probably die before me. He told me that when it happened I should go on and live my life. I don't give a damn what the Segalls or anybody else thinks."

"OK, Becky. Go ahead and hit."

Rebecca chipped out of the rough into the center of the fairway about 100 yards from the hole. Ginny was inside Rebecca's ball and Doug Segall hit his second shot just short of the green. Sedlock drove the cart to the right rough where Sedlock's ball sat up nicely on a tuft of grass about an inch above the ground. He guessed he was about 190 yards from the hole. He took out a 3-iron and rifled a towering shot that landed on the front edge of the green and rolled to within ten feet of the cup.

"Reporter from the Technology *Times*, my foot," Doug Segall said. "You're a ringer if I ever saw one. Nice shot, Wayne."

"Thanks," Sedlock said. "The ball was sitting up in a beautiful lie. That must be what you call a country club lie. You don't get these kinds of lies in the rough in a public course." Again, he had to remind himself he was on a murder investigation. But the shot felt so crisp, so pure that he was never even conscious of the club striking the ball. His mind wandered for a minute. He remembered what it was like as a teenager. He pictured the nine-hole golf course near where he grew up that was subdivided into acre building lots now. He remembered golfing with his friends who had never taken a golf lesson in their lives. They scrounged up a few golf clubs, none of which matched. And they swung at the golf ball using a baseball grip and literally sometimes tore the cover off the ball. He remembered those times when he didn't seem to have a worry in the world. And after he hit that beautiful 3-iron shot he very briefly remembered that those times twenty years ago were the best times of his life. For just an instant his ball lying ten feet from the cup recaptured those feelings of long ago.

The ladies chipped onto the green but Doug stubbed his chip. By the time it was Sedlock's turn to putt he wished he had spent a few minutes on the putting green. He had no feel for the speed of the green and couldn't read the putt at all. So he decided he had nothing to lose. He aimed dead center at the cup and hit it hard to take out the break. The ball made a beeline for the hole, slammed against the back of the cup, hopped two inches up in the air and dropped into the cup.

"If that cup didn't get in the way your ball would be off the other side of the green," Doug said as he laughed. "Nice putt, Wayne. Nice birdie. As I said, we've got a ringer playing with us."

"Beautiful, Wayne," Rebecca said.

"Nice bird," Ginny said.

"Thanks. Thanks a lot. Next time I'll open my eyes," Sedlock said.

The other three finished putting. Rebecca and Ginny made fives while Doug made six. Sedlock felt exhilarated. For the first time in almost two weeks he wasn't thinking about the Web Miter murder case.

They waited on the second tee for the foursome ahead of them to finish putting on the par-three hole.

"I didn't know you ever had to wait for a shot at a country club," Sedlock said to Rebecca.

"You rarely do," Rebecca said. "Unlike a public course where the object is to get as many foursomes out playing as possible, you'll find most private clubs a lot less crowded. This is unusual. They must have got into trouble with a lost ball on the first hole." Then to the Segalls she said, "This is Wayne's first time out on a private golf course."

"Technology *Times*," Doug Segall said. "I should know that one, but I don't. Is it headquartered in New York?"

"San Francisco," Sedlock said.

"I see. My job at my brokerage house is to study Information Technology and how it affects the stock market. Your husband was a real pioneer in that area, Rebecca. We're so sorry."

"Thank you for your thoughts," Rebecca said. "I'll miss Web so much. He wanted me to move on. Wayne is doing a profile article about Web for his magazine."

"In what sense was Web Miter a pioneer in the IT industry?" Sedlock asked.

"Outsourcing computer work overseas. He kept United Eastern above water at a time when other corporations were sinking because of their exorbitant IT budgets."

"But look at what has resulted from it. American computer programmers are out of work. I interviewed the head of the organization called 'Save Our Jobs.' Contracting rates decreased to half of what they were five years ago. Federal, state and local tax bases have been reduced. A twenty-seven percent unemployment rate among IT professionals in Connecticut alone."

"Whiners and complainers!" Segall exclaimed. "IT professionals were greatly overpaid from 1970 to 2000. That profession raped corporations to fix the Y2K date bug, a fix which had absolutely no value added to the operations of the corporations themselves. Corporations finally woke up and saw what Web recognized years earlier. Web was a prophet when it came to outsourcing computer work overseas. The technology of the personal computer and the Internet allowed it to happen. But Web had the vision to use that technology."

"What about the unemployed American programmers?"

"Connecticut may be an exception but the projection is that there will only be a ten percent loss of computer jobs due to outsourcing. There is always a shakeup in employment when there is a technological change, certainly you must know that. Say computer software was invented that could easily generate other computer software. There would then also be a loss of computer programming jobs. So the unemployed adjust. These aren't the untrainable unemployed. They are smart, clever and reasonably ambitious. Some will retire. Some will retrain within the IT field. Some will drift into other fields."

"What do you see as the mood of these unemployed computer people? Do you think it's possible somebody from 'Save Our Jobs' killed Web Miter?"

"I doubt it. Computer people are very conservative. Most of them might contribute money to an organization like 'Save Our Jobs' but few of them will join. They're afraid their names might get known to the companies who employ programmers and they might be blacklisted. As a group, they aren't much in the way of guts. I doubt if Web's murderer was from that group."

"Would you mind if I quote you in my magazine?"

"Please don't. It's against my company's policy to talk with the press before the company has approved it first."

"In other words you'll donate money but you won't join."

"Touche, Wayne. Go ahead and tee off. Birdie goes first."

Wayne lined up his shot toward the 160-yard par 3 with a wide sand bunker just in front of the green. His took a 5-iron out of his bag and made a half-hearted practice swing. His mind was still on his conversation with Doug when he made his real swing. He yanked his head up early and topped the ball. When he played as a kid they called it a shank. The ball skipped along the ground about halfway to the green.

"Hopefully the wheels aren't falling off already. It's only the second hole," Sedlock said.

"Too bad after that nice birdie," Doug said. Doug chose a 4-iron and punched his shot just left of the green hole high. Both of the ladies then teed off and landed on the green. As Doug and Ginny moved up toward the green in their cart Sedlock parked next to his ball.

"What was your great concern with unemployed programmers that you were discussing with Doug? You made it sound like Web was the pioneer of some diabolical plot," Rebecca said.

"I was trying to get Doug's opinion of whether somebody from one of the anti-outsourcing groups was capable of participating in the murder. I had to paint a sympathetic picture of the unemployed computer programmers. I was just playing the devil's advocate, Becky."

Sedlock took his pitching wedge out of the bag. He estimated he was about 80 yards to the pin and he had to loft his shot over a sand bunker. He concentrated on keeping his head down and sent the ball up over the bunker about twenty feet to the right of the pin. Now everybody was on the green but Doug, who was just a couple feet off the left edge.

"I believe you're away, Wayne, even though I'm off the green," Doug Segall said.

Sedlock lined up his putt. This part of the green had a severe slope from back to front. Sedlock would be putting across the side of the hill. He allowed for a foot and a half of break, asked Rebecca to tend the pin, then gave it his best. The ball broke down the hill toward the pin as if it was guided by radar. Rebecca just managed to yank the pin out of the cup before the ball settled neatly in the bottom of the cup.

"Unbelievable," Doug said. "It's my shot now." He stubbed his 5-iron into the ground. His ball moved three feet. Then he switched to his putter and putted his ball within two feet of the hole. Rebecca and Ginny both two-putted for pars.

"That was a fantastic putt, Wayne," Rebecca said as they walked off the green. "It was as if it had eyes."

"Routine par," Sedlock said and he laughed.

"Unbelievable luck," Doug Segall muttered as he got into his cart.

The foursome played bogey golf for the next four holes. Doug and Ginny played a much more conservative game than did Sedlock and Rebecca. The married couple continued to more or less steer their shots down the center of the fairway. Sedlock and Rebecca let loose much more and hit their shots further, but often ended up in the rough. By the seventh hole Sedlock felt his legs begin to sway when he swung the club, so he used the trick Jason Sombery had taught him. He set up for slight draw on every shot which compensated for his tendency to push the ball to the right.

Doug didn't talk much after the second hole. Sedlock figured Doug might be upset by Sedlock's badgering him about unemployed computer programmers. Then as they waited in their carts in the seventh fairway Sedlock thought he might use a different tact.

"Doug, I have to play the devil's advocate with you. You gather various statistics about Information Technology in corporations which are on the New York Stock Exchange, is that correct?"

"That's more or less my job, yes."

"And I gather you are well-paid. You live in Fairfield County and you belong to the Greenwich Country Club. A person would have to have a good income to do that."

"Yes. They pay me well. What's your point?"

"Now let's say India trained some of its people to do your job - to gather financial information and statistics about IT in American corporations. And let's say they were willing to do it for one-fourth of what they pay you."

"It would never happen, my friend. I have twenty-five years experience in my field. Do you think those Indians could digest and synthesize the information they get and give recommendations to my management. It would never happen."

"But let's say your industry came across a revolutionary computer program. All you had to do was feed this computer program data and it would synthesize the data and make recommendations to management. So they eliminate your job and pay the Indians just to gather the data. You think that could never happen?"

"Maybe it could happen far in the future. Hopefully after I retire."

"But this is exactly what happened to thousands of computer programmers. None of them ever envisioned it happening in their working lifetimes either. But imagine it did happen to you. Do you think if it did you could ever become involved in a conspiracy to kill somebody who you felt was responsible for you not only losing your job, but for eliminating that job from your industry altogether. Remember, you have the mortgage on the house in Fairfield County, the membership at the country club, the children who will be going to college in a couple years and the vacations that you won't be able to afford anymore. Can you imagine yourself under those circumstances?"

"Get involved in something like that? I don't think I would have the stomach for it. Perhaps I'd contribute some money if I had it. Perhaps I'd look the other way if I heard about it. But I'd never get involved no matter how desperate things got. Besides, what would it buy you? In Web's case, the water was already over the damn. Web had been retired, how long? Two, three years already? Killing Web just doesn't make sense. Even killing any particular active CEO wouldn't make sense. They'd just replace him with somebody else who thought just like him, but didn't play golf. It doesn't make any sense to me at all why they killed Web at this point in his life."

"Perhaps as a warning to others. Perhaps solely out of frustration. Who knows? Go ahead, Doug. It's your shot."

They played the rest of the front nine without further mention of Web Miter or outsourcing. The only remarkable shot coming in was a sand blast from a bunker by Sedlock which neatly rolled toward the cup, tapped the pin and dropped in. It was his second birdie on the front side and gave him a score of four over 40.

"That one will keep me coming back," Sedlock said.

"Look folks, we're going to call it a day," Doug Segall said. "It isn't that we can't compete with shots like Wayne's, but Ginny isn't feeling particularly well. Enjoy the rest of your round. Take care."

After they had left, Rebecca said to Sedlock, "Do you want to go on and finish eighteen, or do you want to call it a day? I'm game for whatever you want to do."

"If you don't mind I'd just as soon quit here. I don't want to ruin my 40 by shooting 60 on the back side. Maybe we can finish the other nine some other time."

"All right. I'll get the copy of Web's manuscript out of my car. I'll meet you in the snack bar."

Sedlock and Rebecca set the hundred-page manuscript on a table in the snack bar, sat down, and poured over it. Sedlock was especially interested in reading what Web Miter wrote about Howell's sending C-4 through the mail. When he reached that page he noticed there was nothing about Howell successfully sending C-4 before he was caught. Also, as the two Marines had verified at the reunion, Web wrote that he did everything he could at Howell's court-martial to get the young Marine off from a severe punishment. One new item appeared in the manuscript which the ex-Marines at the reunion didn't mention or didn't know. Web wrote that years after the incident in Vietnam, when Web was chief operating officer at United Eastern's San Antonio division, Howell wrote to Web and thanked him for everything he had done on his behalf during the court-martial. Howell said his life had straightened out after a rocky few years after his dishonorable discharge and that he was married with two teenage daughters. As a postscript in his letter he wrote that he and his father got all those stumps removed from his father's field, and he didn't need C-4 to do it after all. This didn't seem to Sedlock like the letter from anybody who held a grudge against his former company commander.

"This is what I was interested in," Sedlock said. "I'll read the rest of it when I get time. Thanks for letting me have this, Becky. And I really enjoyed our golf match. I think we're making progress, although we don't have a suspect yet. I'll keep you informed if anything new comes up."

"OK, Wayne. Please do keep me informed. I enjoyed the golf match too. Don't you think this Howell might be a suspect?"

"It's too early to tell. From what the two at the reunion tell me, and from what your husband wrote in the manuscript here, Howell would be nothing but thankful to your husband for what he did for him at his court-martial. He certainly wouldn't have any reason to kill him. And there's no indication that Howell ever actually sent any C-4 home. The letter your husband quoted in his manuscript seems to imply that. Before today I would have called him a possible suspect but now I have to wait and see."

"All right. Thanks for staying with it, Wayne. You'll turn up something. Please keep in touch."

"I promise you I will. I meant to ask you. How long have you lived in Greenwich, and how do you like it?"

"I've lived here two years now and I like it fine. It sure beats Syracuse, where I grew up."

"How did you first meet your husband?"

"I went to Syracuse University and got a summer intern job at United Eastern headquarters in Danbury. Then I just stayed with the corporation after I graduated. Before too many months I was one of Web's assistants, and four years later, after his divorce, we got married. I know people see it as a May-December romance but we never thought that way. Web did tell me several times, though, that if he did die before me I should go on with my life."

They walked out together beside each other in the parking lot. Sedlock reminded himself once more that his meeting with Rebecca was part of a murder investigation.

"Can I interest you in a home cooked meal?" Becky asked.

"Somehow I don't see you as the cooking type," Sedlock said.

"Oh, heavens no. I meant I would phone my cook Imelda and she will have something ready for us when we get there."

In cases like this one Sedlock sometimes didn't know where to draw the line. Theoretically, Rebecca Miter was still a suspect in her husband's murder. But Sedlock also realized that if he had dinner with her he might pick up some clue which might help solve the case. Besides, there was only a seven year difference in ages between them, neither one was married any longer, and as much as the logical side of Sedlock's brain said don't – the other part of him said do. He realized he was definitely attracted to the dark-haired beauty.

By the time they reached the Miter estate Imelda had prepared pork chops, beets and applesauce. Becky proposed a toast with the red wine.

"To success, Wayne. Whatever that means to you."

"Success and long life," Wayne said as he tapped Becky's glass with his own.

"Where does the case stand, Wayne?"

"Our biggest lead seems to be the two men who were seen leaving the Ensign-Bickford property the day before Web was killed. They had set off two explosions with the same type of explosive that was used in the murder."

"But you have no idea who these two men were?"

"All we know is one was tall and fair with blond or white hair, and the other was short with dark hair. That's all the guard at E-B saw. Also, the car was a light-colored sedan."

Sedlock thought it better not to reveal that E-B cameras captured the car's license plate number, and that the driver used Charlie Howell's identity to rent the car. He didn't want to name any suspects.

"What about that anti-outsourcing organization, 'Save Our Jobs'? They were dogging Web from the time we got married until a few months ago."

"That's interesting," Sedlock said. "It's curious why they would stop harassing Web. What could have happened that made them change their tactics?"

"Maybe they finally realized Web was retired, and that they should give some other CEO the title 'King of Off Shoring.'" Becky poured herself another glass of wine. "What about the proposed Indian casino in northwest Connecticut? There's a lot of money there. Web's being opposed to it might be a motive for his murder."

"We had a suspect, but it didn't pan out. The whole key to the case that doesn't make sense is the explosive. The explosive is almost 40 years old. We just can't tie it in with our suspects."

"Forty years ago Web was in Vietnam," Becky said. "Could the murder have anything to do with that war? Have any of the clues pointed to Vietnam?"

Sedlock realized Becky was rambling. He kept quiet about James Wallace and his false identity.

"Nothing so far. We've talked to several veterans who served with Web. They all have nothing but the highest praise for him."

"So there's really nothing new. Just two men racing off in a car the day before Web was killed."

"Let me show you the house, Wayne. Web accumulated quite a collection of art and other knick knacks in his thirty plus years of traveling for United Eastern."

Becky and Sedlock toured the huge mansion. Web's taste in art crossed every category, a collection only an engineer would have, thought Sedlock. Web had also collected pieces of sculpture.

"What in the world is this?" Sedlock asked as he stopped to examine a foot-high statue made of brass. Becky was standing behind him.

"You'll have to turn around so I can explain it to you, Wayne."

As Wayne turned Becky put her hands on his shoulders, raised up on her toes and planted a kiss on his lips.

"Do I have to explain it to you again, Wayne?"

Sedlock thought back to the interview with Jason Sombery, one of the Miter group's foursome. Jason said once Rebecca had been drinking at an office party, then showed up for her golf lesson. Jason said as he was instructing her she suddenly kissed him full on the lips. Sedlock's mind told him alcohol must have that effect on Becky.

"I've let all the help go for the night," Becky said.

Suddenly Sedlock remembered.

"Oh, my gosh! What time is it? Almost ten? Do you have a computer where I can get on the Internet, Becky?"

"Sure. Web's office is in the next room. What's the matter?"

Sedlock and Becky hurried into Web's office.

"I want to bid on Ebay for a baseball card for my son, Justin. The auction ends at 10 P.M."

Becky logged onto the Internet. "It's all yours, Wayne."

Wayne tapped the keyboard. "1952 Eddie Mathews rookie card. The auction's ended."

"That's too bad," Becky said. "There'll be more auctions, Wayne. I'm really sorry I messed up your plans."

CHAPTER 13 – ENSIGN-BICKFORD

▼

Thursday morning Sedlock got up early, picked up Justin e's house and drove an hour and a half east on I-95 to meet a fishing boat called the Sparrow Hawk just before it was ready to pull out into Long Island Sound for a full day in pursuit of blue fish and striped bass. Sedlock showed Justin how to bait the hook. Even though neither one of them caught a fish, a day in the brisk salt air together, father and son, was not a loss. By three o'clock the boat was heading back to its dock, and Justin asked his father about the large tower on the Groton hillside.

After they landed they drove to Fort Griswold, the site of the tall monument dedicated to the townspeople who lost their lives against an invading British force during the Revolutionary War.

"The British came from the sea," Sedlock said. "They were led by Benedict Arnold. Here's a plaque listing the names of all the patriots who were killed that day. And the name of a 12-year-old boy, whose life was spared."

"He's the same age as me," Justin said, and he didn't say much more the rest of the way home.

"I found him on the Internet!" Janie Caldwell said excitedly.

"Found who?" Sedlock asked.

"Stuart Merriwether, of course. Who am I responsible for in this investigation, anyway?"

"I'm sorry, Janie. Of course. What did you find?"

"He has his resume on the Internet in one of those job search sites. He's been a computer programmer for twenty-five years. And guess what? He worked as a college intern at that Ensign-Bickford Company during one summer in the early seventies. He also worked one year driving an armored truck."

"College intern? Merriwether might have had access to the explosive C-4 there. Good job, Janie."

Sedlock phoned Ensign-Bickford's Human Resources Department and made arrangements to visit the company. He showed up at the E-B headquarters building in Simsbury promptly at eleven o'clock that morning. Mrs. Mildred McCarthy, the head of personnel, greeted him at the front desk.

"Mr. Sedlock, let me show you our display cases. I think it's important you understand what we make here at E-B. We keep explosives stored in our Powder Woods and occasionally detonate explosives to test our prima-cord. That's our primary product – prima-cord, which looks like rope and is packed with explosives."

Mrs. McCarthy escorted Sedlock around the main lobby where there were several display cases. One case showed the 49ers in California in the middle of the 19th century. Next to that picture was a section of fuse E-B manufactured in that era. The next display was of the Transcontinental Railroad. That picture showed tunnels being blasted through the Sierra Nevada Mountains in California.

"The workers used dynamite to blast through those mountains. One of the big problems was that fuses would be lit, the men would scramble to safety, but nothing would happen. They didn't know if the fuse went out or not. Somebody had to crawl back into the tunnel to see. Sometimes it was just a slow burning fuse and lives would be lost. But the railroad workers found Ensign-Bickford fuses were reliable. E-B built up a tremendous reputation during those times."

The next displays showed sections of E-B prima-cord that were used in various wars, right up to the Vietnam War.

"Applications of our product have included blasting rock for our Eisenhower national highway system and to cut loose boosters from rockets."

"Very impressive," Sedlock said. "Mrs. McCarthy you said the company stores explosives in the woods it owns. Have you ever had any accidental explosions in those woods?"

"About ten years ago a chemist was mixing chemicals in a mixing shed when there was a terrible explosion. The man, who was quite young and recently graduated from college, was killed, unfortunately. But in the twenty-three years I've worked here, that's the only explosion I know about."

"I'd like to talk with the security guard who looks after the Powder Woods. One other question. Did you ever have any employees named Merriwether working here at Ensign-Bickford?"

"That name doesn't ring a bell with me. Let me look it up on our database. This has all our employees going back to the 1960s."

She tapped into her desktop computer.

"Yes, there was a Ralph Merriwether. Retired in 1980. Had thirty-four years service with E-B. Started in 1946. Worked in the Stringer Department. They used to string together fuses like rope. That department has been disbanded for quite a few years now that the operation has been automated."

"Could you give me his address?"

"Sure, he lived in one of our company built houses. 34 Woodland Terrace."

"Is this house on the edge of the Powder Woods?"

"Yes, all our company housing is along the edge of E-B's property."

Mel, the guard who Sedlock had talked to twice in previous visits, showed up in the lobby.

"Mel, could you show me the bunker area where the explosives are kept?" Sedlock asked him.

"Sure. You don't smoke, do you? You aren't allowed to take matches or a lighter into that area."

They drove in a company panel truck out to the Powder Woods. After they had driven about a half-mile they reached a series of bunkers separated by huge dirt mounds. They stopped to inspect one of the bunkers. It had a large metal door with a padlock on it.

"How many years have you worked at Ensign-Bickford?" Sedlock asked Mel.

"Thirty-seven. Hope to retire in a year."

"In your time here have there been any break-ins of these bunkers. Has there been any theft of explosives?"

"Not that I know about, and I would know. We've got a pretty good alarm system they put in during the mid-seventies."

"Mrs. McCarthy mentioned an explosion in one of the chemical mixing sheds about ten years ago."

"Yes, that was a real tragedy. Young engineer was killed. But going back further than that there was an explosion in one bunker in the summer of 1972. That was before we got the alarm system in."

"One of these bunkers exploded? What caused it?"

"They never really found out. They wanted to blame it on lightning, but that's a crock. There would have to be blasting caps or some kind of detonator involved for that type of explosive to go up."

"What type of explosive is that?"

"As I remember it was all C-4 explosives. There wasn't anything left of that bunker after the explosion. One of the guards, a good friend of mine back then, was terribly hurt by that explosion. Completely paralyzed from the neck down. His name was Cleve Jamison."

"Is he still alive?"

"I couldn't tell you that. Mrs. McCarthy might know. The company would still be sending him his pension check if he was alive. I visited him several times during the 1970s. The company let him stay in his E-B house on the other side of the Powder Woods after he was injured. His daughter lived with him. She was about twenty then. I asked him a few times what happened, but Cleve didn't want to talk about it."

"Thanks, Mel. You've been a big help. One more question. Do you remember a Ralph Merriwether who worked here until 1980?"

"Sure, I remember Ralph. We bowled together in the company bowling league. That's when my legs were still spry enough to bowl. As I remember he lived in a company house on the south side of the Powder Woods."

"Do you remember if Ralph had a son?"

"Sure do remember. Last time I saw the boy he showed up at the bowling alley. He had just got back from college. As a matter of fact the boy worked here one summer during college. Ralph was beaming about him graduating from college."

"Would you remember the boy's name? Was it Stuart Merriwether?"

"I just don't remember that, Mr. Sedlock."

"Did you ever see him after that, the boy I mean?"

"No, I don't believe I ever did. We'd ask Ralph about what the boy was doing after he got out of college. I recollect be got into computers. But I haven't seen Ralph since he retired, so I never heard anything more about his boy."

"When you saw Ralph's boy in the bowling ally that time, was that before or after the bunker explosion?"

"That bunker blew up in the summer of 1972. That's the year I bowled the 232. So I would guess I saw the boy before the explosion."

"Thanks for everything, Mel."

Chapter 14 – The Connection

───────── ▼ ─────────

Sedlock leaned back in his chair with his fingers interlaced behind his head. Stu Merriwether had worked as a computer programming consultant for American Systems Corporation. He had worked on the Identity Fraud project at Alco Insurance. Then, as Robby Schroder put it, he had been booted out and programmers from India had replaced him. Was that enough of a motive to murder Web Miter, the 'Father of Off Shoring?'

The two men who had tested the explosives on Ensign-Bickford property prior to Miter's murder stole Charlie Howell's identity to rent a car. Charlie Howell was court-martialed in the Marines 35 years earlier for trying to send the same type of explosive home from Vietnam. The two men who test-fired the explosive knew enough to set it off at exactly eleven o'clock. That was the time the whole town of Simsbury had been conditioned for generations to expect explosives to be detonated at E-B. Stu Merriwether grew up an 'E-B brat.' He would have known that, Sedlock thought. Was there any connection between Merriwether and Charlie Howell, a.k.a. Little Coyote?

Sedlock called Charlie Howell to arrange a meeting.

"I'll be at the state capitol building tomorrow," Charlie said. "Do you know where the Indian fountain is in Bushnell Park?"

Sedlock remembered a large fountain with statues of Indians surrounding it.

"Yes, I know where you mean."

"I'll meet you there at noon. I'm lobbying at the state capitol for our tribe's casino tomorrow."

At 11:45 the next morning Sedlock left his desk. It was only a ten minute walk to Bushnell Park, but he allowed himself another five minutes to catch an elevator. It was hot and muggy in Hartford, but the offices surrounding the park still emptied hundreds of white collar workers into the park by noon. By the time he reached the Indian fountain Sedlock was covered with perspiration. Charlie Howell was sitting on a bench waiting for him.

"Good afternoon, Charlie."

"Afternoon, Wayne. I thought this would be an appropriate meeting place. I like that one in particular." Charlie pointed to one of the Indian statues. It held a tomahawk high in the air, as if ready to scalp somebody.

Sedlock laughed. "Charlie, I need to know if you have any idea who stole your identity, and why."

"No, I don't have any idea, Wayne. As I told the Lordship Police and the FBI, I don't have a clue."

"Another question, Charlie. Do you know a Stu Merriwether?"

Charlie Howell stared back at Sedlock for several seconds. "Brother, that's a name out of the past. I worked with Stu Merriwether years ago. After I was kicked out of the Marines I got a job as an armored truck driver. Stu Merriwether was one of the college kids who worked there summers and holidays. It's strange you mentioned him. I thought I saw him in the capitol building in the lobbyists' area a few months ago. This was thirty years after I worked with him. His hair was grayer and he'd put on a lot of weight. I wasn't sure if it was him or not. I went up to him and asked if he was Merriwether. He said no, and walked away."

"Would Merriwether have known about your trying to send C-4 explosives home in the Marines?"

"Probably. I worked with him a few times. He filled in for whoever was out sick or on vacation. I don't remember talking with him about it, but we were young and all pretty open about everything with each other back then. I didn't try to hide it from anybody."

"That may have been Merriwether you saw lobbying for an organization called 'Save Our Jobs.' It's a group of computer people against outsourcing jobs, especially to India. Would Merriwether have known your Native American name, Little Coyote?"

"I never hid that from anybody, either. Chances are he would have known that."

"That's all I have, Charlie. How's the lobbying going for the new casino?"

"So, so. Some are against us, and some are for us. The major hurdle is getting recognition as a tribe. The wheels move very slowly, but we'll get there."

"I wish you luck, Charlie."

Sedlock and Howell stood up and shook hands.

"And good luck on the Miter case, Wayne. I don't suppose you can fill me in on anything new."

"You just put a big part of the puzzle in place – the fact that you and Stu Merriwether knew each other. Take care, Charlie."

On Saturday morning Sedlock drove south to pick up Justin. His ex-wife Nancy was going to attend a baby shower for her sister in Fairfield that afternoon. She had called Sedlock and had asked him if he could take Justin for the day. Sedlock was feeling almost giddy, since this was the first time Nancy had ever called him to take Justin. He had always had to call her and plead with her to let him have the boy for a Saturday or Sunday. Maybe things were looking up, Sedlock thought.

Wayne and Justin decided to go fishing. Sedlock lamented the fact there were no grandparents to visit. He had fond memories of fishing with his own father, but his father was killed in an automobile accident when Wayne was 17. His mother passed away four years later. Many times he asked Dr. Alonzo if those two early deaths may have been the reason for his breakdown, but he never got a satisfactory answer.

They stopped at a bait store along the way, then drove to an upstate dam.

"Let's drown some worms," Sedlock said.

They each cast their lines some fifty feet out into the lake. A black bird with a long, skinny neck was bobbing on the lake's surface. Suddenly it dove bill first into the water and disappeared. Fifteen seconds later it surfaced again, a fish thrashing in its mouth. The bird shook the fish for a few seconds, then swallowed the fish whole.

"That bird's stealing our fish," Justin said. "That's not fair. He can just dive down and catch a fish anytime he wants. We can cast our lines all day and never catch a fish."

"But we don't need a fish to survive," his father said. "That bird does. There's a difference between fishing for food and fishing for fun."

Father and son sat with their fishing rods cradled in their hands, not talking for several minutes at a time. Something stronger than words was passing between them. After an hour Sedlock asked Justin if he'd like to try something new.

"What is it?" Justin asked.

"You'll see when we get there."

They packed their fishing gear in the car and drove south a few miles. Sedlock stopped at a combination miniature golf course and driving range. He took his golf bag out of the trunk, bought a bucket of range balls and rented a cut-down driver for Justin.

"Let me see you hit one, Jus."

Justin placed a ball on the rubber tee and addressed the ball. He held the club with a baseball grip, took it back and smacked the ball. The golf ball sliced about 150 yards out.

"Great, Justin. You're hitting it just the way I hit a golf ball when I first started. But you need a different type of grip in this game."

Sedlock showed Justin the proper way to grip a golf club. Justin's next swing was more tentative than his first and the ball didn't go as far, but it went straight as an arrow. For the next half hour Sedlock watched his son hit golf balls. By the end of the lesson Justin was consistently hitting the ball straight off the tee.

"Way to go, Justin. Let's try the miniature golf course now."

When Sedlock dropped Justin off at home that night he said to Nancy, "At least for today I was a full-time Dad."

"Justin really looks forward to these days with you," Nancy said. "Maybe I was wrong twelve years ago, Wayne. But can you blame me? The way you were acting I didn't think you'd ever get better, and I thought it best for Justin at the time."

"We can't change what happened in the past, Nancy. But I think it's important Justin has a father close to him during the next few years. I'm up to my eyeballs in this Miter case right now, but I'll make time for him."

"All right. I agree. I can be a mother to him, but I can't be a father, too."

Just then Justin came outside.

"You're investigating a murder case, Dad? That's awesome! Are you going to catch who did it?"

"We're trying, Son. I have to go. See you again next weekend?" Sedlock looked at Nancy, who nodded her head yes. He hugged his son and walked back to the street to his car. Being a full-time Dad was the best undercover assignment he ever had, Sedlock thought.

Chapter 15 — Fired

─────────── ▼ ───────────

When Wayne finished up at Ensign-Bickford Bill Walthrup ushered him into his office. "Please close the door, Wayne."

"Bill, I've been rethinking the Miter case. Our whole focus has been on the type and origin of the explosive – a type of explosive called C-4 that was no longer manufactured after the early 1970s. Because Charlie Howell tried to send this type of C-4 home from Vietnam in 1968 we've been zeroing in on him as our main suspect."

"Do you have another main suspect?" Bill asked.

"There's an organization called 'Save Our Jobs.' It's headed by a man named Stuart Merriwether. Janie found his resume on the Internet. He graduated from Simsbury High School in 1969. And he worked as a college summer intern for Ensign-Bickford, the explosive manufacturer located in Simsbury."

"What are you getting at, Wayne?"

"The ATF does testing of explosives at the Ensign-Bickford Company. E-B makes explosive prima-cord. I visited one of the ATF men there twice. We believe the day before the murder somebody test-fired C-4 which was similar to the explosives that killed Miter. The guard saw two men driving away. The guard is in his sixties and his eyesight is not too good. But he thinks the taller man had a light complexion with blond or white hair, and the shorter one had dark hair. We've been assuming the darker man might be Charlie Howell. But we never thought who the lighter man might be."

"He might have died of old age by now. Will you get to the point, Wayne?"

"I think it might be Stuart Merriwether. He grew up in Simsbury. His father worked for Ensign-Bickford. They lived right next to the Powder Woods, where E-B stores its explosives in bunkers. Stu Merriwether probably played in those woods as a boy. In the summer of 1972 one of those bunkers blew sky high. Nobody ever figured out why. There was no alarm system there then. Suppose he broke into the bunker, scooped up a few sticks of C-4 then stuck a blasting cap in one of the sticks inside the bunker, lit a fuse and ran like hell. The bunker is blown to smithereens and E-B never knows there is any C-4 missing. And don't forget, Stu Merriwether has a motive to kill Web Miter – Miter was the king of off shoring and Merriwether's group has been fighting off shoring for the past two years. Merriwether could be involved. He had access to those explosives in the Ensign-Bickford woods."

"Wayne, I've got to change the subject. Joe Pignitaro is taking over the Miter investigation."

"Bill, I've come this far with it. Let me see it through to the end!"

"Wayne, you're the best investigator this company has ever had. Everything from workers comp fraud to fake automobile accidents to identity theft. Whatever the case, you put your heart and soul into it and came away with a conviction that put bad guys behind bars. But something has come up. I got a rather disturbing phone call from our company psychiatrist, Dr. Menlo. He got a call from a Dr. Martha Baily."

"So much for patient-doctor confidentiality."

"If she feels a there's a problem, she's obligated to talk to us. She was disturbed at how you got with Alco after you had been hospitalized for a mental breakdown."

"For Pete's sake, Bill, that was thirteen years ago. And I was hospitalized exactly seventeen days on the seventh floor of Holyoke Hospital. I would hardly call it an insane asylum like in 'One Flew Over the Cuckoo's Nest.'"

"That isn't what disturbs me the most, Wayne. I reviewed your personnel file this morning. It has your application for employment with the company. On the application it specifically asked if you had ever been hospitalized for any mental disorders. You checked 'No,' Wayne."

"Bill, do you know how many police departments and companies I applied to where I checked off 'Yes'? Probably about a hundred. And they all turned me down. You can't get a job as a dog catcher if you check off 'Yes' to that question."

"Wayne, you're putting me between a rock and a hard place. Let's say you built up evidence against an insurance fraud perpetrator. The lawyer for the bad guy goes to court and it comes out you were in a mental hospital. They'd sue Alco for every cent it had. This company couldn't afford lawsuits like that."

"Bill, they never sued before. I've been to court dozens of times."

"Because they didn't know before. Now with Dr. Baily on the loose who knows what might happen? I can't take a chance, Wayne. The Man Upstairs wants to see you."

When Sedlock returned to his office on the 9th floor his email informed him of a meeting on the 22nd floor with Jeremy Fondsworth. Sedlock had only met Fondsworth, the CEO of Alco Insurance Company, twice before in the years he had worked for Alco. He assumed, correctly, that the meeting was about the Miter case. Fondsworth's secretary escorted Sedlock into the CEO's office where the CEO's assistant, Clyde Persico, was already seated. Neither man said anything to each other. Sedlock sat down at an ornate mahogany conference table and looked around the room. Paintings, carvings and statues with a Wild West theme were spread out tastefully throughout the office. Sedlock heard a toilet flush. He had heard the chief executive officer had his own personal bathroom. Wouldn't dare want to mix with the employees, Sedlock thought.

Jeremy Fondsworth IV appeared from somewhere in the back recesses of his office.

"Wayne, how are you? Long time no see. When was the last time we got together? It was the Wilson case, wasn't it?"

Actually, it was the Rodriguez case, Sedlock thought. "Yes, the Wilson case," Sedlock said. "We wrapped that one up at no expense to Alco."

"This one's big, Wayne. Web Miter was well known throughout the business community. Throughout the world for that matter. I used to keep a copy of his management how-to book right here in the office. We modeled our computer programming outsourcing initiative after Miter's outsourcing model. Publicity wise, this case is big. Where do we stand on this one, Wayne?"

"Sir, we suspect somebody working in our company's computer department stole the social security number, drivers license number, telephone number, date of birth, name and address, etcetera, of one of our policy holders. Then we suspect that person or some person he gave the stolen identity to applied for a credit card and rented a car. This car was used the day before Miter was killed to transport two individuals who tested out explosives similar to that which killed Web Miter."

"Do you have any idea what the impact of what you just said would have on the company? Do you have any idea who in our computer department stole this identity?"

"It looks like it was done by somebody in the group which is developing the new Identity Theft software. It's an Indian group, Sir. A group of computer programmers over here from India."

Fondsworth leaned back in his chair, touched the fingers of both hands together in a steeple pose, and cleared his throat. "The problem," he said, "is one of image. We spent $13 million dollars last year in the television and print media defining Alco Insurance Company's image to the public. Thirty-six years ago, when I started at Alco right out of Yale, I came in to work one day wearing a rather loud plaid shirt. One of the older gentlemen in our department, who has long since passed away, advised me to wear conservative white shirts. 'Image is everything in this business,' he said. 'People won't buy insurance from a company where its employees wear loud clothes,' he said, 'any more than they would deposit their money in a bank where the tellers wore tie-dyed shirts or entrust the funerals of their loved ones with a funeral director who wore a black-leather motorcycle jacket.'"

The CEO stared up at the ceiling. "We are in a business where image, Wayne, is everything. That brings us to a couple complications in the investigation. The identity theft linked to the Miter case may have been stolen from our own I.D. theft software?" Fondsworth gave Sedlock a quizzical look when he spoke.

"Yes, Sir. The programmers who tested the software used a dozen real life identities to test with. One of the people used in the test case has definitely had his identity stolen. Somebody obtained at least one false credit card under his name, and rented a car that was used to transport two individuals to a site on the Ensign-Bickford property to test fire explosives the day before Miter was killed."

Fondsworth sat motionless for several seconds. "Three things, Sedlock. First, we've made a tremendous investment bringing computer programmers over from India. It's meant a substantial cost savings to the company. It would be a great embarrassment, and again I remind you of the word 'image,' if it was revealed that one of these Indian programmers stole an identity from among those he was using as a computer test case. Secondly, we are about to roll out our new Identity Theft coverage, and offer it as another option to our homeowners policy. Think how embarrassing it would be to the company, and I remind you again of the word 'image,' to have one our own employees involved in identity theft of one of our own policy holders, whose social security number, drivers license number, telephone number, date of birth, etcetera, are being used to test our own identity theft software. The third thing, Sedlock. You referred to those who killed Web Miter as individuals. I would prefer you start referring to them as terrorists. As you are probably aware, after 911 a law was passed relieving insurance companies from full liability for terrorist acts. The federal government pays most of the liability costs in cases of terrorism. Miter was killed by terrorists, Sedlock. Do you understand?"

Fondsworth stared hard at Sedlock. "Image, Mr. Sedlock. And good business. To the public at large this was a terrorist act. A random act of terror. Use the governor's description if you wish – golf terrorists. Mr. Miter was at the wrong place at the wrong time. Remember who you work for, Mr. Sedlock. We will have a story in the Hartford *Courant* tomorrow. Anonymous sources, of course. The story will be that as far as our investigation can tell, the murder of Web Miter was a terrorist act. That's all, Sedlock."

Sedlock's years of corporate conditioning told him to let it pass and go along with what the CEO said. But he had talked so much to Justin recently about honesty and telling the truth that he felt he just couldn't let it pass.

"Sir, there are just too many other possibilities to label Miter's murder a terrorist act. There is an anti-outsourcing group who tracked Miter for the better part of two years. Its leader was a consultant in the identity theft software project who was let go when the Indians took over the project. Furthermore, he may be connected to the type of explosive that killed Miter. Also, Miter was vehemently opposed to a new casino in western Connecticut and we've identified a member of the tribe that is agitating for that casino as having a connection to the type of explosive that was used in the murder. This type of explosive was commonly used in Vietnam and Web Miter was a company commander in Vietnam in the late sixties. Miter was awarded the second highest combat medal, the Navy Cross, for calling in artillery on his own position. There may be at least one of his former troops who harbored a grudge all these many years later because of what Miter did. There are a lot more possibilities in this crime than a random terrorist act, Sir." Sedlock was perspiring.

"All right, Wayne. You've made your point. You may go."

As Sedlock got up to leave he turned toward Fondsworth and asked, "Are you a golfer, Sir?"

"I carry a nine handicap. Why do you ask, Wayne?"

"Just wondered, Sir." Then Sedlock exited the office.

"Have you checked him out, Clyde?"

"Yes. Bill Walthrup confirmed he didn't tell the whole truth on his job application. Sedlock spent two years with the Lordship Police Department before he came to work for Alco. One of our investigators got friendly with an off-duty Lordship Police sergeant. The sergeant said Sedlock was let go by the police department because he lied on their job application because he spent some time in a mental hospital before he applied for the police job. We guessed based on his job history it was about 15 years ago, and we made inquiries at all the mental institutions in the area. Of course we made it appear that we were investigating an insurance claim. Turns out he spent 17 days on the seventh floor of Holyoke Hospital in Massachusetts in 1989. Our background checks in 1991 when he applied here didn't include out-of-state hospitals. We're much more thorough now. We checked out his medical pharmaceutical coverage. He's been taking a mood stabilizer drug, and as far as we can tell, has been since 1989."

"Did he put down on his job application that he had spent time in a mental institution?" Fondsworth asked.

"No, he did not," Persico said.

"Fire him. Use his lying on his job application as the reason."

"Yes, Sir. Should we give him a severance?"

"Give him a week's pay for every year he's been here. And when you fire him, make sure you get all the documentation on the Miter case before he goes. I don't want to see any of it showing up in the Hartford *Courant*."

When Sedlock returned to his desk he had a voice mail waiting for him from Carrie Edwards. He had talked to Carrie several times in the years he had worked for Alco. Carrie was the Hartford *Courant* reporter who covered the insurance industry. It was a major job for a Hartford newspaper, since Hartford was the Insurance Capitol of the World.

"Hello, Carrie, this is Wayne Sedlock returning your call."

"Hi, Wayne. I understand you're the investigator covering the Web Miter case. I'm looking to have a story in tomorrow's paper and I'd like to know how it's going on your end so far."

"Carrie, this has to be off the record. Do you agree?"

"If it has to be, it will be. Do you have any leads so far? The governor's statement that the murder was done by golf terrorists just doesn't seem to cut it."

"Carrie, we're looking at it as a terrorist act right now. That's all I can tell you."

"You can't give me anything more than that?"

"I'm afraid not."

"I got a strange call on my voice machine this morning, Wayne. He didn't leave a name or number. He said some of the Indian programmers at Alco, that is, programmers over here from India, were involved in an identity theft of an Alco client's identity, and there is a direct link with the Miter murder. Also, he said the Alco insurance investigators were aware of all this. Then he hung up. He called while I was in my daily meeting with my editor. Can you comment on this, Wayne?"

"I can't comment about any of that, Carrie. Even if I knew what you were talking about I couldn't comment about it."

"All right. I guess we go with terrorists in tomorrow's story. I was hoping to get more. Thanks, Wayne. Good-bye."

As Sedlock hung up he wondered who could have leaked the identity theft aspect of the investigation.

"I think it's enough to at least talk with Merriwether," Sedlock said to Bill Walthrup.

"He could be the tall, light complexioned one the E-B guard saw driving away the day before the Miter murder. He grew up near those woods. He would have known that area like the back of his hand. If he had anything to do with that explosion in 1972, he could have been the one that supplied the C-4."

"Well, he's not going anywhere, Wayne."

"Then let's concentrate on going after the other one, the shorter, dark-haired guy who was test firing explosives on July 23rd. And I would say Butch Tyler is a good candidate for that accomplice. I think we should look for some connection between Merriwether and Tyler. Let's find out if Tyler was in Connecticut that day. Tyler would be familiar with the C-4 explosive from his time in the Marine Corps in Vietnam."

"Wayne, I've got something to tell you. You better sit down."

"Uh oh. What now?"

"I have to let you go, Wayne. I'm sorry. I argued for you. I presented your record, which is one of the finest records I've ever known. But it's like I told you before. We can't afford to be sued every time you take the witness stand. And we just aren't a big enough department to have an office investigator who can't go out in the field. That's why we have college interns like Janie to do the paper shuffling. Besides, I know you wouldn't want a job like that. I'm sorry, Wayne. There was nothing more I could do for you. I'm suspending you as of right now. I want you to turn over everything you've got on the Miter case, including notebooks and emails on your computer. Give Janie your password and she'll print them all out."

"Will I get back on the job?" Sedlock asked.

Bill Walthrup started shuffling papers on his desk. "You're dismissed, Wayne."

"Thanks for trying, Bill," Sedlock said. There was nothing else he could say. He hurried out of Bill Walthrup's office because tears were welling up in his eyes and he didn't want Bill to notice them.

Sedlock thought about what Justin had said. "Shouldn't we always tell the truth?" What kind of a father am I, Sedlock asked himself, if I'm not going to live up to what I am trying to instill in my son?

He dialed Carrie Edwards, the Hartford *Courant* reporter who covered the insurance business. "This is Wayne Sedlock. We have to meet," he said when Carrie answered. "It's about the Miter case."

"Fine. We can meet here at the *Courant*," Carrie said.

"No. Let's meet halfway between the Alco building and the *Courant*. Do you know where the Indian fountain is in the middle of Bushnell Park?"

"I know it. Can you be there in half an hour?"

When Sedlock approached Carrie she was sitting on a bench next to Stu Merriwether.

"I believe you know Mr. Merriwether," Carrie said to Sedlock.

"What's he doing here?" Merriwether said. "I thought we were meeting to discuss 'Save Our Jobs.'"

"I brought you both together to clear up some things," Carrie said. "Over the past three weeks I've been getting unidentified voice mail messages on my phone concerning the Miter murder. I thought the two of you could just go down the list of what each of you knows about the case. You are no longer an insurance investigator for Alco Insurance, isn't that right, Wayne?"

"You have your sources in the insurance business, don't you, Carrie? My list starts and ends with Stu Merriwether. Mr. Merriwether worked for American Systems Corporation on the Alco Identity Theft project. ASC was responsible for establishing the test cases for the project, that is, copying the identities of real Alco clients down to be used on the test system. One of those copied down was Charlie Howell, a Mashicoke Indian whose Native American name was Little Coyote. Charlie sat on this very bench a few days ago and said he knew Stu Merriwether when both of them worked for an armored truck company when Stu was going to college. Charlie had been court-martialed and discharged from the Marine Corps for attempting to send C-4 explosives home through the mail while he was in Vietnam. By the way, Charlie's company commander in Vietnam was Web Miter. All these circumstances made Charlie one of our earliest suspects in the Miter murder."

"You believe that Stu knew about Charlie's court-martial for sending home the explosives?" Carrie asked.

"Yes, I do believe he knew about it. That's why he picked Charlie's name to be one of the test cases. He knew that stealing Charlie's identity would cast suspicion on Charlie when the police checked him out. Two men used Charlie's credit card to rent a car which was used to enter the Ensign-Bickford test site the day before the Miter murder. They set off two explosions of approximately the same size as that set off on the 17th green of the Lordship Country Club. I believe Merriwether was one of the men who set off the test explosives, and that he had an accomplice."

"This is all ridiculous," Stu Merriwether said. "You're jumping from one conclusion to another, when you don't even have any evidence for the first conclusion. Yes, I worked at Alco for ASC. But I had nothing to do with making test cases. As far as Charlie Howell goes, I don't even remember him from more than thirty years ago. And to conclude I was an accomplice in an identity theft is ludicrous. How can you possibly place me at the scene of a test explosion at E-B?"

"You were an E-B brat, weren't you, Stu? Your father worked for E-B for more than 40 years. You grew up living in E-B company housing. Most of the kids you grew up with had parents who worked at E-B. And you played in the Powder Woods as a boy. You knew those woods inside out. You knew test explosions were done at eleven and three every day."

"You've built a hypothetical case out of thin air. Where's the proof? Where's the evidence? Because I grew up next to the E-B woods, I'm a suspect in all this? Hundreds of kids grew up next to those Powder Woods. So what?"

"You could have grabbed a couple sticks of C-4 from a bunker when you worked as a college intern at E-B. That would explain why the ATF concluded the test explosions and the explosion that killed Miter were from a batch of C-4 that was more than 30 years old."

Merriwether shook his head. "Talk about far-fetched. Carrie, I hope you're not going to print any of this in the *Courant*. If you do you are opening yourself to a lawsuit. To say that an accident at E-B more than 30 years ago ties in with a murder today is ridiculous."

"Wayne, Stu's right. I can't print any of this. It's all circumstantial."

"Well, at least we aired it out," Sedlock said. "I still say he had access to 30-year-old C-4, and that he was an accomplice in the identity theft of Charlie Howell and at the test site of the explosives. The puzzle all fits."

"You're nuts!" Merriwether said, and he got up and trudged back up the hill toward the capitol building.

"Sorry, Wayne. I can't use any of it," Carrie said, and she headed back to the Hartford *Courant* building.

Sedlock stood up and stared at the statue of the Indian with the tomahawk raised, ready to scalp somebody.

Chapter 16 -
The Reluctant Hero

▼

Trooper Hank Wargo had been out of the Police Academy just seven weeks. For the third consecutive Saturday morning he sat in his Connecticut State Police issue Ford with his radar gun pointing up the long grade in front of him. The traffic was sparse at 7:30 in the morning, and the few cars that did pass kept well below the 65 MPH speed limit. Patrolling Route 8 north of Waterbury, a limited access highway that twisted through the Litchfield Hills, was a far cry from patrolling the heavily congested I-95 in the southern part of the state. But his supervisor warned him that the North-South artery connecting Massachusetts to Waterbury and Bridgeport was a conduit for drugs, and to be careful no matter who he pulled over.

Hank joined the Connecticut State Police for the adventure. He spent four years in the Air Force military police and longed to be in law enforcement. But his initial applications to police departments across the state got nowhere. He soon tired of the first shift job as a grinder at a plastics manufacturer downstate, and was finally accepted by the state police. He had kept himself in excellent shape, and passed all the entrance exams. When he graduated from the Academy in Meriden and was assigned to the Litchfield Barracks he was the happiest man in Connecticut. But here he was, seven weeks into the job, and he had to admit that there were times when being a state trooper was as boring as working in the shop.

A U-Haul rental truck approached. Trooper Wargo leveled the radar gun on it. It registered 58 MPH, well below the 65 MPH speed limit. He noted one occupant, middle- aged, dark beard, wearing a cowboy hat. A minute later he leveled his radar gun on a late model, light colored station wagon. It also was well within the limit. Single occupant, middle-aged, clean-shaven.

Five minutes later the U-Haul veered into the left hand median, which was about fifty yards wide at that point. The truck narrowly missed a twenty-foot tall rock outcropping on its left and the guardrails on its right. The driver hit his brakes in a wide meadow then crashed into a large pine tree. Smoke poured out of the cab. A minute later the light colored station wagon pulled over to the left hand side of the highway and stopped. Its driver ran from his car toward the smoking rental truck. He opened the cab door and unbuckled the seat belt of the truck's driver who was slouched out cold over the steering wheel. He dragged the man from the cab, then continued to drag him up the gradual slope toward the road. When he let him down on the grass the truck driver never moved.

Trooper Wargo got the call on his radio: "Accident left median Route 8 southbound between Exit 42 and Exit 41. Possible car fire. Harwinton fire apparatus on the way. Advise if you require an ambulance or wrecker."

Trooper Wargo turned on his flashers and sped south. He arrived at the scene in less than five minutes. A man was lying just off the road in the left median. A U-Haul rental truck was further down the slope wedged against a large pine tree. Trooper Wargo parked on the left hand side of the highway, ran up to the man lying on the ground and shook him.

"Are you OK?"

The man stirred. "Thanks for getting me out, man," he said to Wargo.

"Are you hurt?"

"No, I just bumped my head."

"Was anybody else in the truck?"

"No, but could you get my cowboy hat? Thanks again for getting me out."

Trooper Wargo ran to open the trunk of his cruiser, grabbed a fire extinguisher, and raced down to the smoking truck. He extinguished the smoke, pulled the cowboy hat from the front seat, and brought it back to the truck driver.

The driver was sitting up now. "Man, I could have roasted alive in there. Thanks again, man."

"What happened?"

"I guess I fell asleep. I was taking the truck down to my sister's place in New Jersey. I was going to help her move."

"What's in the truck?"

"Nothing. It's empty."

"Do you mind if I look?"

"Sure. Go ahead."

Trooper Wargo lifted up the latch, let the rear door up about a foot, assured himself there was nothing inside, and closed the latch shut again.

"I'm going to have to give you a ticket," Wargo said as he took some forms out of his cruiser. "And I have to fill out an accident report."

Seven miles north in Torrington a news team from Channel 8 News was getting on the southbound entrance to Route 8. They had just finished covering the dawn awards ceremony at Boy Scout Camp Strang in Goshen when they heard the accident call on their scanner. Accidents with fires played well on television, so they sped to the scene. When they arrived two state police cars were parked on the left median with their flashers going. A Harwinton fire truck was there, although the fire seemed to be out. A wrecker was just arriving. A U-Haul rental truck had run off the road and crashed into a large pine tree. Janice Walters exited the news truck and approached the state trooper nearest the road. "What happened?" she asked him.

"Guy fell asleep. Went off the road."

"Was there a fire?"

"Yeah, but the other trooper put it out before the fire truck got here."

A man with a cowboy hat on was arguing with the emergency medical team crew. He didn't want to go to the hospital. Janice approached him.

"Sir, were you the driver of the rental truck?" The cameraman was getting shots of the crashed vehicle before the wrecker towed it away.

"Sir, I'd like to do an interview with you on camera. What is your name?"

Janice Walters interviewed both the truck driver, who she called the Cowboy because he insisted in wearing his cowboy hat during the interview, and Trooper Wargo.

That night Channel 8 News dedicated a minute and a half to the "State Trooper Hero" story. The anchorman introduced the story: "In Harwinton a Connecticut State Trooper just seven weeks out of the State Police Academy saves a man's life. With the story is Janice Walters." With the videotape of the rental truck wedged against the pine tree in the background Janice Walters described the accident.

"Butch Tyler, of Coffeyville, Kansas, was the driver of the rental truck which caught on fire when it crashed into a tree off Route 8 in Harwinton at approximately eight o'clock this morning. Mr. Tyler, what happened?"

"I guess I fell asleep. Went off the road. Hit the tree and was knocked out. Next thing I know that state trooper over there is waking me up. He dragged me out of the cab. It was burning. Don't know what would have happened if he didn't get here when he did."

The tape shows Janice Walters interviewing Trooper Wargo.

"Trooper Wargo, how does it feel to be a hero just seven weeks out of the Academy?"

"Well, I don't know about being a hero, Ma'am. Helping people is what most of us joined the Connecticut State Police for."

Janice faces the camera. "He's too modest. Trooper Wargo dragged Mr. Tyler out of a burning truck. That's a hero, in my book."

Monday morning the Channel 8 news director held the daily status meeting.

"A viewer called me this morning. She said that state trooper we interviewed Saturday morning was no hero. She said she has videotape of the real hero, a Good Samaritan who stopped right after the accident, dragged the driver out of the burning cab and then drove away before the state police got there."

Janice Walters was skeptical. "She videotaped it?"

"She was up on a hill videotaping the scenery. Said she heard the brakes squeal then filmed the truck right after it hit the tree. She said she's the one who called 911 after the accident."

"Why was she up in the hills videotaping the scenery at eight o'clock Saturday morning?"

"She said she's an artist. Just here in Connecticut for a couple months. I guess she wanted to videotape the Litchfield Hills. A leaf peeper with a camera. She offered us the tape. Said she was upset the state cop was claiming to be a hero when all he did was extinguish the smoke in the truck."

"Did she ask for money for the tape?" Janice asked.

"No. Pick up the tape and take a camera crew to get her story. And let's see if we can locate the real hero. Maybe we can get his license plate number from the tape."

The Channel 8 News video department was able to enlarge the number on the license plate from the leaf peeper's tape. After a call to the Motor Vehicles Department in Wethersfield Janice Walters knew the owner of the vehicle was a James Joseph Wallace,who lived in Middletown. She got his phone number from information and dialed.

"Mr. Wallace? This is Janice Walters from Channel 8 News."

"Yes?"

"Do you own a cream colored VW station wagon?"

"Yes."

"Did you happen to see the Channel 8 News piece on the rental truck accident that happened last Saturday morning on Route 8 in Harwinton?"

"No, I didn't see it."

"We have videotape that shows you to be the first one at the scene of the accident. It shows you dragging the unconscious driver out of the burning vehicle…"

The phone was silent.

"Mr. Wallace? That was you, wasn't it? Mr. Wallace, we'd like to do an on-camera interview with you. Would that be a problem? Why did you leave the accident scene, Mr. Wallace?"

"Well, I didn't really leave. You see, my cell phone battery went dead, so I couldn't call 911. So I drove off the next exit to get to a gas station. The gas station I knew about in that area was one exit north of there. So I drove south and got off the first exit, then turned around and got back on driving north. I could see through the trees on the median where the rental truck was and I saw a state cop pulling up to the accident. So I knew everything was OK. So I got off the next exit and turned around to go south again. By the time I passed the accident this time there were two state cops there. I was going to pull over and tell them about being the first on the scene, but then

I thought, you know, it probably just meant more paperwork. I saw the situation was well in hand, so I just kept driving."

"Do you know, Mr. Wallace, a woman with a videotape camera filmed your heroics?"

"I don't think it was particularly heroic. It was what anybody would do in that situation."

"Could I ask you what you were doing on Route 8 that Saturday morning?"

"Well, I do volunteer work for the United Way. We were making a presentation of a check to Camp Strang, a Boy Scout Camp in Goshen. We were one of the contributors to their new outdoor theater at the camp. It was a dawn ceremony. I'd just finished up and was heading home."

"What a coincidence. I was there reporting on that ceremony. Do you remember the Channel 8 News crew there?"

"I got up so early that morning I don't remember much of anything," Wallace laughed.

"Tell me about it," Janice Walters laughed also. "When my news director told me our crew had to be at Goshen for a 6 A.M. ceremony, I told him he had to be kidding. I'm not used to getting up at 4 A.M. on a Saturday morning. Tell me, Mr. Wallace, will you do that on-camera interview? It's a great story. We can arrange to do it any time of the day or night, to accommodate your work schedule. By the way, where do you work?"

"I'm working for Aetna Insurance in Middletown. I'm a computer programmer."

"Is there a Mrs. Wallace? Do you have any kids?"

"No, my wife passed away several years ago. We didn't have any children."

"Why don't we meet at 6 P.M. tomorrow? Is your place all right? We could meet somewhere else, if you'd like."

"No, my place is ok."

When she arrived at James Wallace's condominium Janice gave Jim instructions while her cameraman set up.

"Just hold your head up and speak into the microphone. Just look at me when you give your responses. That way you won't be squinting from the glare of the light on the camera."

Janice took out a compact from her pocketbook and checked her face in the mirror.

"Now just stand facing this way. Feel free to answer the questions any way you like, we can always edit your answers. OK, Fred, we're ready to roll."

The interview lasted twenty minutes. As Janice was about to leave she said to Jim,

"This segment should be on tomorrow night's news. Thank you very much, Mr.

Wallace."

"I'll watch it," Jim said.

"Goodbye, Mr. Wallace."

"Just call me Bill," Wallace said softly to the door as it closed behind Janice Walters.

Janice Walters's interview of James Wallace first aired on the Wednesday evening 6 O'Clock Channel 8 News, four days after the accident. The segment also included an interview with the woman who shot the videotape of Wallace arriving at the accident scene, as well as the original interview with the rental truck driver and the state trooper who claimed to have rescued the driver. An interested viewer that evening was Wayne Sedlock.

He listened to the news expose. According to the reporter a Connecticut state trooper claimed to have pulled an unconscious man out of a burning vehicle. It happened early Saturday morning on Route 8 in Harwinton. Sedlock was familiar with that section of road up in the Litchfield Hills. There were no houses for miles. But a woman who was videotaping up in the hills filmed the real rescue. Channel

8 got the Good Samaritan's name from his license plate. He explained why he left the scene, and why he never bothered to come back. The Reluctant Hero.

But upon careful examination of the accident interviews it was clear to Sedlock that it was the truck driver who kept insisting the state trooper had pulled him out of the truck. The trooper never actually said he did so, he just never said he didn't. Sedlock came to believe there were stories and there were made up stories and this was the latter. He recorded the Channel 8 News stories of the Reluctant Hero on his VCR.

Chapter 17 – The Real James Wallace

Monday morning Wayne Sedlock drove through the Ensign-Bickford gate, waved to Mel, the guard, walked up to the south building and knocked on the door of Bob Corsino's little ATF office. Corsino waved him in and within fifteen minutes Sedlock had explained to Corsino that he had been taken off the Miter case, and why. Bob Corsino offered him a mug of coffee from the microwave.

"Freshest coffee free coffee can be, Wayne," Corsino said. "It happens. People have breakdowns. It happened to a buddy of mine from Vietnam. He was the Rock of Gibraltar in combat. Then he comes home and five years later he had a mental breakdown. He's been doing all right for the last several years, though."

"Did you see our boys James Wallace and Butch Tyler on the Six O'Clock News Saturday evening?"

"I did. Do you want to continue working on the Miter case? You can work right out of this office if you want. This little ATF office is a sideshow of a sideshow. Besides, what are they going to do to me if they catch you here? I've been thinking about retirement for a long time. Look at this."

Corsino focused Sedlock's attention on a topographic map he had spread out on the table.

"Look at this, Wayne." He bent over the topographic map of the Litchfield Hills in northwest Connecticut. Corsino pointed to Route 8 which wound its way among the hills and cut through the map in a generally north to south direction. "That rental truck went off the road here."

"Tyler fell asleep at the wheel. He got up about two in the morning according to the television interview. That was his story on Channel 8 News anyway."

"Yes. I'll come back to that. But from what I can read on the map, assuming you are not on the road itself, there is only one spot in the surrounding hills where the bird watcher could observe the accident."

"This position?"

"Exactly. Across the road she would have been too high up on top of the bluff. The accident would have happened underneath her. Anywhere south of the accident she would have been blocked by this curve. She had to be north of the accident on the opposite side of the road, close enough to the road and the accident to get it on tape." Corsino tapped his finger on the map. "This hill right here."

"What was she doing up there? Bird watching?"

"She's an artist. Recently came East from California. Wanted to get some shots of the changing colors of the hills to paint from."

"Could be just coincidence."

"Could be," Corsino said. "Yesterday I drove up Route 8 to the area where the accident took place. At the accident scene a wide meadow opened up in the median to the left, with a lone pine tree about fifty yards off the road. For the next two miles it's rocky cliff walls on one side and sheer drops on the other."

"I'd say our rental truck driver was about the luckiest son of a gun in the valley that day."

"What's the odds that you're driving and you fall asleep at the only spot in three miles where you could go off the road without even a guard rail to stop you, and not kill yourself?"

"And have it all filmed by a bird watcher."

Corsino put Sedlock's tape in the VCR and pressed Play. "Look at the time. 7:12 A.M. Almost an hour before the accident. She's panning the hills. Look here." Corsino stopped the tape.

"The accident scene. A rehearsal?"

"You saw that road. It winds through the Litchfield Hills. If all she wants is to paint those hills there's a hundred places to pull your car over and film the vista. Why hike all the way up that hill to see virtually the same thing?"

"And look here." Corsino pressed Fast Forward. When he pressed Play again a man was dragging the unconscious driver out of the burning rental truck. "Did you see it?"

"I didn't see anything."

Corsino pressed Rewind then played it again. "Watch as he drags him over that rocky ledge." The rescuer is having trouble dragging the other man over a rock ledge. The knee of the unconscious man bends and pushes off to propel himself over the obstacle.

"It's a setup. They setup the whole thing. James Wallace slash William W. Robinson and Butch Tyler and the Birdwatcher."

"What's the motive?"

"Maybe our hero wanted to be on the Channel 8 News."

"Then why did he drive away? Why didn't he just stay at the scene of the accident? One thing bothers me, Wayne. What that state trooper did was wrong, but it was natural. Hell, every state trooper wants to be a hero. That's why they join up in the first place. But why did Robinson and company stage this? He's stayed undercover for more than thirty years."

"You don't buy his explanation that he saw the situation was well in hand so he left?"

"It doesn't add up," Corsino said.

"What are we going to do about it?"

"Wayne, we've got to get Wallace's fingerprints. We have to confirm he is Corporal William Robinson."

It was a mystery to Sedlock. How can a man 50-years-old living as a citizen of the United States have no record of his fingerprints on file? That meant he had never been in the military, he had never applied for any defense contracting job, and had never even worked a security guard job to help put himself through college. For that matter, he had probably never worked as a sales clerk in retail. Even a computer programmer in a bank would probably have had his fingerprints taken in a background check.

So he was a programmer in an insurance company, Sedlock thought. Bob Corsino sat next to him in his car. They waited high up on the hilltop in Middletown that was the corporate headquarters of the Aetna Insurance Company. It was 11:30 A.M. Employees were starting to leave for lunch. They spotted Wallace as he drove out of the parking lot east toward the Peking Restaurant where Wallace ate every Friday. After a three-minute drive they parked on the other side of the restaurant parking lot and Corsino followed Wallace inside. The restaurant's owner sat them down at adjacent tables. Just like the previous Friday, Wallace looked over the entire menu, then ordered beef with broccoli and wonton soup. He didn't order anything to drink, just a glass of ice water. A man of steady habits, Corsino thought.

Wallace ate quickly, read the fortune in his fortune cookie then took his check up to the cash register to pay. After Wallace left, Corsino slipped a surgical glove over his right hand, walked over to Wallace's table, and picked up the clear acetate covered menu by one corner. Then he read Wallace's fortune: "Sometimes a stranger can bring great meaning to your life." He carried the menu out of the restaurant. The owner, tipped off by Corsino beforehand, had wiped the menu clean so only

James Wallace's fingerprints would be on it. The owner nodded as Corsino exited.

The Connecticut State Police Forensic Lab was only a short drive away. While Sedlock waited in the car reading a newspaper Corsino walked into the building, showed his ATF badge, filled out the proper paperwork, and deposited the menu in the fingerprint lab. Then he sat down to wait. Sedlock noticed that on page two of the newspaper there was a story of a high-ranking state police officer who accidentally left his gun and badge in a bag on the roof of his car, then drove off. A paper deliveryman found the gun and called the story in to the paper. Major story, Sedlock thought.

Within an hour the lab technician approached Corsino with a computer printout he had just torn off his printer.

"Well?" Corsino asked the lab man.

"William Wilson Robinson," the lab man said as he handed Corsino the printout.

"It's confirmed," Corsino said to Sedlock when he got back to the car. "He's William Wilson Robinson. Corporal William Wilson Robinson, USMC. He's been missing in action in Vietnam since August 1968. Other than that just your run of the mill identity theft case."

Sedlock and Corsino decided to interview John 'Butch' Tyler. Sedlock knew from his contacts with Aetna Security that Tyler was staying in Connecticut in a motel on the Berlin Turnpike about five miles southwest of Hartford. Tyler's emails to James Wallace said as much. On Tuesday morning Sedlock and Corsino knocked on Room 17 at the High Ridge Motel in Berlin.

When Butch opened the door Corsino showed him his ATF badge.

"Butch Tyler? We'd like to talk with you. We're investigating the murder of Web Miter. We understand he was your company commander in Vietnam in 1968."

"That's right. Come in. I don't have enough chairs for you, but one of us can sit on the bed."

They sat down, Butch and Sedlock on the bed, and Corsino on the only chair in the room.

"First of all, Butch, where were you on the afternoon of July 24th?"

"The afternoon Captain Miter was killed? I was at the casino, at Foxwoods. I'm sure there will be videos of me. I stayed at the same slot machine from about noon until five o'clock. Had my cowboy hat on." Butch picked up his cowboy hat off the bed stand and put it on his head. "You can check it out."

"We will, Butch. Second question. What is your relationship to James Wallace?"

"I've know Jim for about thirty years. We're friends, that's all."

"Butch, did you know a William Robinson when you were in the Marine Corps in Vietnam?"

Tyler seemed taken aback for a few seconds, then he smiled.

"You figured it out, huh? You finally figured it out."

"We've made a positive identification of James Joseph Wallace's fingerprints. They confirm that he is William Wilson Robinson, who has been missing in action in Vietnam since 1968."

"I guess there's no use hiding anything anymore," Tyler said. "I may as well start from the beginning." Thus Tyler told his story.

Corporal Bill Robinson, Butch's fire team leader in Bravo Company, never showed up living or dead after the Two August 1968 battle. Butch was depressed during the few days he was in the rear area for a minor wound he received in the battle, but soon he was back out humping on patrol and more or less forgot about his former comrade. Then Butch received a letter from a Jim Wallace in San Francisco. It was really from

Bill Robinson. The new Jim Wallace pleaded with Butch not to reveal his identity to anybody. It was all Butch could do to keep quiet, but most of Bravo Company were new guy replacements so hardly anybody remembered Bill Robinson anyway.

Butch Tyler claimed he arrived in San Francisco after being discharged from the Marine Corps in the fall of 1969. He had kept in touch with Jim via letters. When Butch was discharged Jim invited him to visit him in San Francisco on his way home. Jim greeted Butch at the airport. Butch had a short Marine haircut but he was in civilian clothes. Many soldiers were passing through the airport in uniform on their way home from Vietnam. After the two men shook hands Jim said, "Watch this. You're about to see a GI shower. Remember the Navy showers we had to take on board ship. This is the GI version."

A pretty hippie girl about twenty years old dressed in a floral pattern dress approached a soldier who had just exited a plane and was headed to the luggage area to pick up his duffel bag. The girl smiled as she held out a red rose and offered it to the GI. As the GI smiled in return and reached for the flower the girl spat in his face.

"Baby killer!" she shouted over and over again as she ran back into the crowd and disappeared. The soldier stood in shock wiping the spittle from his face. A janitor continued emptying ashtrays and a Red Cap hurried by with his cart full of luggage. None of the passengers nearby even gave a second look as they hurried through the terminal. It happened every day. Only Jim and Butch seemed to notice.

"Welcome home, brother," Jim said to Butch. Then, to the soldier he said, "Welcome home, war hero."

"Why did you leave me?" Jim asked his friend after each had had a couple beers in the airport lounge. "Why did you leave me on Two August?"

"I didn't have a choice, Robby. Right after you were knocked out Captain Miter called in artillery on top of us. A piece of shrapnel cut your arm. I tried to get you to come to, but I couldn't. I bandaged up your arm. Then a couple guys from the head of the column came running back past us. One of them had a radio. He said the captain wanted everybody to dee-dee to the rear of the column where they had a perimeter set up. I couldn't carry you by myself, you outweighed me by forty pounds. Your face was white as a sheet. So I threw clods of dirt on you as if an arty round landed in our crater. I figured if the NVA came by they would figure you were dead and they would move on. I couldn't even stay there to defend us. Both our rifles were jammed. What else could I do, Rob? What the hell else could I do?"

"Because of you I'm not Rob anymore, I'm Jim. Jim Wallace. Didn't you tell them when you got back to the perimeter? Didn't you tell them there was a Marine still alive up front in the column?"

"I told everybody. 'Robinson's still alive up there!' I screamed. They were saddling up and moving south. Everybody was carrying gear, carrying wounded. I told the captain, he said there were at least forty unaccounted for. He said we'd come back when we got reinforced. Then we all moved south to the Strip. Another battalion relieved us that night and went back out to pick up our dead the next day. They accounted for everybody but you. I figured you'd been captured and taken away. I tell you Rob, when I got that letter from you a couple months later I was the happiest grunt in Nam. It was all I could do not to tell everybody else."

"I couldn't believe they left me," Wallace said, shaking his head. "I was so pissed, the adrenalin was pumping so much I ran out of that jungle."

"How did you get home?"

For the next hour Jim Wallace told his combat buddy how me managed to get from the jungle near the DMZ to San Francisco.

"And what have you done to make a living since then?" Sedlock asked.

"I was a truck driver," Butch said. "A truck driver with a college major in history. But I built up my fleet to four trucks which I operated out of Kansas. I just sold the business a couple months ago. So I came out here to visit Robby. I wanted to get him to a battalion reunion in D.C."

"Butch, one thing doesn't add up," Sedlock said. "What are the odds that Web Miter would be playing in a PGA Pro-Am tournament thirty years after he was company commander for a unit in which one of his men became MIA, missing in action – what are the odds that man would be present as a PGA tournament volunteer at the very 17ᵗʰ hole at which Miter was killed?"

"I'd say the odds are about 50 to 1," Butch said.

"I would put those odds at more like 50,000 to 1. You and/or Robinson must have known something about this murder beforehand."

"I'm sorry, Gentlemen. It was as much a surprise to me and Robby as it was to everybody else. If there are no more questions, I'm going to drive over to Foxwoods."

"That's all for now, Butch."

Chapter 18 - The Miter Estate

Sedlock pondered whether to call Becky Miter. He didn't consider her a suspect in the case, although she was certainly on the list of people connected to it that Alco Insurance would frown on him contacting. Finally he called her.

"Looking for another golf match? I seem to shoot lower than my handicap when I play with you."

"I'll have to put that on hold, Becky. I need another copy of that manuscript your husband wrote. I can't explain now, but I don't have access to the copy you gave me. There are parts of it I just skimmed over. Would it be possible for me to stop by and read the master copy?"

"Why don't I just make you another copy, Wayne? I can email it to you, or copy it to a diskette and you can pick it up."

"I can't explain it all right now, but it would be better if you didn't give me anything. I've been suspended temporarily from the case, so any copy you give me might be evidence. I'll explain it all when I see you. Could I stop over today and read the original manuscript?"

"Sure, Wayne. I'm sorry to hear you've been suspended. You know where I live. Just use the intercom at the front gate and I'll buzz you in. I'm sure you're more computer literate than I am. You remember where Web's computer was. You can read the manuscript as long as you want."

"OK, I'll be there in about an hour and a half. See you then, Becky."

It was a beautiful, sunny late September morning and Sedlock made a mental note that he had his golf clubs in the trunk. Somehow during the Miter case he had been bitten by the golf bug, a sport for which he had lost interest since his breakdown thirteen years earlier. He had enjoyed his rounds of golf since the Miter case started, and even his frequent stops at the driving ranges where he belted golf balls and released whatever pent up frustrations he had from being let go by Alco. And although Sedlock knew another round with Becky today was probably out of the question, he knew of a couple driving ranges between Lordship and Greenwich and he intended to stop at one on the way home. After all, he reasoned, now that he was released from Alco he had nothing but time to work on his game.

Sedlock eased onto I-91 south. Bill Walthrup might be upset that Sedlock paid a visit to Web Miter's wife but if his ex-boss confronted him about it, Sedlock had a simple explanation. He'd simply say he visited the young widow to explain that he had been fired from the company, which was in fact partially why he was visiting her. He'd keep mum about his desire to read Web Miter's manuscript in full. If his ex-boss didn't like Sedlock's explanation, he thought, too bad.

Ninety minutes after he left his apartment Sedlock turned off the Greenwich exit on I-95. Ten minutes after that he drove on to the Miter estate gate, where he pressed the button to announce his arrival.

"Come on in, Wayne," Becky's voice came over the speaker box. Immediately the mammoth front gate opened. A minute later Wayne parked in the huge horseshoe driveway and Rebecca opened the front door.

"Would you like anything to drink?" Becky asked.

"No thanks, Becky. I'll just get on the computer if you don't mind. I want to read parts of Web's manuscript that I just skimmed over before."

"This way, Wayne." She pointed out her late husband's office where his computer sat in one corner. While Wayne was turning it on and getting familiar with it Becky said, "How can they suspend you from the case? You're further along in the investigation than anybody."

"I'm not only suspended from the case, I've been fired from Alco. Furthermore, I'm not supposed to see anybody connected with the case, either law enforcement or civilian."

"That's bizarre, Wayne."

"Bizarre it may be, but this is the situation. What's your password to get into Microsoft Windows?"

"Livingston. L-I-V-I-N-G-S-T-O-N."

"As in Dr. Livingston, I presume?"

"But there must be more to it than that. They wouldn't just kick you off the case just like that."

Sedlock searched the MS Word documents folder for Web Miter's manuscript.

"How's 'Memoir' for a document name? This must be it. There is more to it, Becky. Thirteen years ago I had a mental breakdown. I spent seventeen days in a mental hospital. I didn't put that down on my application for employment with Alco. It all came out after my psychiatrist retired. The doctor he referred me to contacted my boss about my background."

"But seventeen days in a hospital couldn't mean much after all these years."

"It's the wear-your-hat-rule."

"I don't understand, Wayne."

"I helped put myself through college by working summers as a security guard. We wore this military type uniform, with an awkward-looking barracks-type hat. Nobody wore the hat, at least none of the younger guys. And the higher ups never said anything about it. Until they wanted to fire somebody, and if they couldn't find any other reason, they'd say it was because the guy wasn't wearing his hat. Not filling out an application correctly is the same thing. It's the wear-your-hat rule, a convenient excuse to fire you if the company can't find any other reason."

"After all the good work you did for them? Just spend as long at the computer as you need to, Wayne. I have to go out. I'll be back in an hour or two."

Sedlock worked for three hours. He was hoping to find something in Web Miter's manuscript that somehow connected him with Stuart Merriwether, but no luck. He decided to copy the file onto a blank diskette and ask Becky permission to take it with him. Then he noticed the online version of the manuscript on the computer was dated July 25th, the day after Web was killed. He labeled the diskette "Miter Memoir" and put it in his pocket. He noticed another document called 'Memoir Backup' dated July 23ʳᵈ. It was slightly larger that the master copy memoir. He took another blank diskette, labeled it "Miter Memoir Backup," copied it and put it in his pocket. When Becky didn't return for another half hour he left a thank you note for her and left. He decided to go home via Route 7 toward Danbury and hit some practice balls at the driving range there. As he climbed into his car he took the two diskettes out of his pocket and put them, along with the notes he took, in his glove compartment.

Chapter 19 - Eleanor
North Again

▼

The story broke on the front page of the Hartford *Courant*, and was soon in every newspaper and on every television news channel in the country. Eleanor could hardly sleep after watching the 20/20 special about the Vietnam vet who turned up in Connecticut after being listed missing in action for thirty years. She drove to the Petaluma Public Library and looked up *Predictive Behavior* by Dr. Candice Wallace. As she had hoped, the library held a copy of the book, published in 1975. It was Candice Wallace Simpson's doctoral thesis, the same book Eleanor looked up at the Berkeley campus library when she discovered James Wallace's stolen identity. The only difference was the Petaluma copy had "Donated by the Author" penned on the title page, and "Petaluma native" written on the next page.

Eleanor turned to the back flap. The book cover showed a photo of the author, Dr. Candice Wallace Simpson. She would have been about 27 then, Eleanor thought. The hair was longer then, but the same eyes, mouth, and nose. It had to be her. She would be what, 55 now? It would be a little after noon on the East coast. She dialed Wayne Sedlock's number.

"Alco Insurance, Investigation Department," Janie answered.

"Could I speak to Mr. Sedlock?" Eleanor asked.

"I'm sorry, he's not available. Would you like to speak to another investigator?"

Eleanor didn't want to speak to anybody else.

"I really have to speak with Mr. Sedlock."

"M'am, if you leave a message, I'll try to get it to him."

Eleanor thought out her message carefully. She realized who the background check she did a month ago was for after watching the 20/20 special. She almost jumped out of her chair when she heard the identity of the returning M.I.A. He had been using the identity of James Joseph Wallace for thirty years.

According to the television report his real name was William Wilson Robinson, born in 1946 in Salem, Illinois. He walked away from the Marine Corps after a terrible battle in August 1968 and made it back to the States on a commercial jet by stealing another Marine's orders at the Marine airbase at Danang. He landed at Treasure Island just north of San Francisco and drifted into Haight-Ashbury. He used the identity of James Joseph Wallace, a young boy who was born in nearby Petaluma in 1946 who was killed by a hit-and-run driver in 1950. He was able to obtain the child's birth certificate at the Petaluma town hall, and with it a social security card and driver's license. In the early '70s Robinson-Wallace learned computer programming, and worked in San Francisco for several years. He married in 1972 and had no children. His wife died of cancer in the mid-1980s. Since then Robinson-Wallace had been a freelance independent contractor, working jobs all over the country. He was working in Connecticut when he happened on an accident and dragged an unconscious truck driver from a burning truck. The report then continued with the embarrassment of the Connecticut State Police when one of its troopers claimed to have dragged the driver out of the flames. A bird watcher had been videotaping from a nearby hill, and had captured the real rescue on tape. Her tape also captured the license plate number of the Good Samaritan, who had left the accident scene before the trooper arrived. There was a thirty-second on-camera interview with the bird watcher. That's when Eleanor sat up straight.

Eleanor said, "Tell Mr. Sedlock this: This is Eleanor North, the researcher in Petaluma, California, who did a background check on James Joseph Wallace. I watched the special on 20/20 last night showing the MIA who returned after 30 years. There was something about it that might be of the utmost importance to you. Please call me. Thank you."

Janie Caldwell took the message then called Sedlock at home on her cell phone.

"Wayne, I think this message could be important. It's from the researcher in California who discovered James Wallace was using a false identity. She wants you to call her."

It was almost five o'clock Eastern Daylight Time when Sedlock called. He knew that in all investigations, some breaks came through hard work, and some just fell onto your desk. Almost two o'clock in Petaluma, he thought. He dialed the number.

"Hello." Eleanor felt slightly groggy. She had been watching for more about Robinson-Wallace on the noon news and had fallen asleep in her chair in front of the television set.

"Hello, Miss North? This is Wayne Sedlock. I got your message. What is it you wanted to tell me?"

"Please call me Eleanor, Mr. Sedlock. I watched 20/20 last night. Did you see it?"

"Yes, I did, Eleanor."

"There was a very short piece about a woman. They called her the bird watcher."

"Yes. You could say, after your research work, she also started this whole thing."

"If you read the obituary of the real James Joseph Wallace, you will see that it mentions a sister named Candice Wallace. I don't know why, Mr. Sedlock, but I felt I had to contact this Candice and tell her about her brother's identity being stolen. I figured she was still alive. I traced her through the funeral home to UC Berkeley. She got her doctorate there. The thesis was published as a book. It was called *Predictive Behavior*, published in 1975. The book cover has her picture on the inside flap. Her hair was longer, but I swear to you, Mr. Sedlock…," Eleanor paused, "the bird watcher on television last night looked like her – Candice Wallace."

"Where could I get that book, Eleanor? What was it, *Predicting Behavior*?"

"You might get it in a public library. Every library wouldn't have it, but some nearby library might. And the title is *Predictive Behavior*."

That night Wayne Sedlock sat in his bed perusing the copy of *Predictive Behavior* that Janie checked out of a nearby library. He inserted the tape he had made on his VCR of the interview with Candice Simpson, pressed Play, and stopped it. He compared the picture on his television set with the photo on the back cover. It could be twins, he thought. The resemblance was amazing – same eyes, same mouth, same nose. He read the forward to the book: *Predictive behavior is the probability a human being will act a certain specific manner under certain circumstances not only as a result of that individual's background but also as a result of an individual's position in his peer group, and the expectations he has of that peer group. For example, within this theory we might be able to predict who might embezzle money from a bank, or who might desert from the military, or who might frequent prostitutes.*

Many tellers might be in need of money, but they all do not embezzle. But the embezzler might also feel wronged by the bank which is his employer. So two factors have to be present to conform to the predictive behavior model: there is the logical reason for the behavior (the embezzler needs money), and there is the reason he rationalizes his behavior through some radical shift in the relationship between himself and his peer group (perhaps a co-worker received a raise that the embezzler thought unfair).

As another example that illustrates predictive behavior there was the case of the Marine who deserted his platoon in Vietnam. He had been an exemplary Marine, then during a major battle he was knocked unconscious in the jungle. When he came to all his comrades had left him. The Marine Corps prided itself on never leaving Marines, dead or alive, behind. The deserted Marine worked his way back through the jungle to a base, and eventually managed to return to the U.S. He deserted not because of any particular belief about the legitimacy of the Vietnam War, which many soldiers felt doubt about, but because he felt his peer group, the U.S. Marine Corps, had wronged him.

Sedlock reread the paragraph again several times. If he was correct Candice Wallace must have known William Robinson sometime before 1975, the publication date of her dissertation. And it would have been too coincidental that Robinson just happened to choose her dead three-year-old brother's identity. She must have told him about her brother's death, and he established his new identity that way. And the bird watcher was certainly Candice Wallace Simpson. That, together with the tie between Wallace-Robinson and Butch Tyler, could prove the accident was a setup. But why? Wallace-Robinson was so careful to keep his real identity hidden for thirty years. It was almost as if the accident was a way of revealing his identity after all these years.

Chapter 20 – The Livingstons

▼

Sedlock and Corsino felt it was time to talk with William Robinson. When they rang the doorbell at his condo, the bird watcher answered the door.

"I'm Wayne Sedlock of Alco Insurance, and this is Agent Corsino of the Alcohol, Tobacco and Firearms Department." Corsino showed his badge. Sedlock was beyond worrying about the ramifications of him identifying himself as an investigator after he had been fired from the job. "We'd like to talk with William Robinson."

"You and every talk show in New York," the woman said. "Bill's in New York City for a few days. He's doing the Letterman show tonight and Oprah tomorrow. And I believe he's meeting with his publisher and his agent the day after that. I'm Candice Simpson. You're welcome to come in."

Both men followed Candice Wallace Simpson inside.

"You're the woman they call the bird watcher," Sedlock said. "And you're the author of the book *Predictive Behavior*."

"You're very thorough, Mr. Sedlock. But as you might guess, I predicted you would be here sooner or later. Sit down and I'll tell you how I met Bill, or Jim as I knew him, almost thirty-five years ago."

So Candice Simpson told the story of how she met Bill Robinson soon after he arrived on the UC Berkeley campus in the fall of 1968. She suggested he use her dead brother's name and switch identities with James Joseph Wallace. She told how she introduced Jim's Marine Corps friend Butch Tyler to Carla. And how Candice married another professor named Simpson, and Jim married and they all drifted apart, only keeping in touch with Christmas cards. And then after her husband died and Jim's wife died, Butch Tyler kept pressuring Jim to reveal his identity. Butch said it would help all Vietnam veterans by doing it. Jim might be elected to Congress, or who knows what? And part of Butch's plan was Jim Wallace being a tournament volunteer at the 17th hole of the Hartford Pro-Am and seeing his old company commander face to face. But then the terrible explosion happened and Butch talked Jim into revealing his true identity. Butch came up with the plan of the Reluctant Hero that he, Jim and Candice executed.

When Candice had finished her story, Sedlock asked, "What are the odds a man missing in action thirty years ago is a volunteer in a PGA Pro-Am at the same golf hole his former company commander is killed on, and he's not involved in the murder?"

"Whether you believe it or not, it's true," Candice said. "Butch thought if Jim, or Bill, saw his old company commander that day it might jolt him enough to sway him toward revealing his identity and becoming Bill Robinson again. As fate would have it, it was Jim witnessing his old commander dying that nudged him into agreeing with Butch to come back as Bill Robinson."

As Sedlock and Corsino drove away in Sedlock's car, Sedlock said, "If what Butch Tyler and Candice Simpson say are true, we are left with a coincidence of events on that 17th hole at the Lordship Country Club?"

"What they had in common," Bob Corsino said, "was a horrendous battle on Two August 1968. Miter. Robinson. Tyler. That's the one common thread. That never goes away.

Often I think of the Hue City battle where I was wounded, even all these years later."

"Could there be somebody else connected with that battle?" Sedlock asked. "Somebody we've completely overlooked? Do you think the answer could be on the Vietnam Wall?"

"It's possible," Bob Corsino said. "What else do we have to go on? Merriwether might have been one of the two test-firing explosive devices in the Ensign-Bickford woods the day before the Pro-Am. But Mel the E-B guard swears there were two of them that day. Who was the shorter, dark-haired man?"

"I've got to call Janie." Sedlock tapped in Janie Caldwell's work number on his cell phone.

"Janie, this is Wayne. Can you do something for me? Can you get me a list of all 84 Marines who were killed in the Two August battle in 1968? Their names would all be on Panel 94W of the Vietnam Memorial Wall."

"Let me Google it, Wayne." Sedlock could hear keys clicking over the phone. "This looks promising," Janie said. "There's an Internet website called VietnamWallOnline dot com. It lists all the 59,000 names alphabetically. It also gives their date of death and their unit. I could select all the names and load the information into an Excel spreadsheet. Then I could sort them on date of death and have a secondary sort on unit. The 84 names of the Greatest Groundpounders who were killed on August 2nd, 1968, would be together, and I could select them and print them out. Or if you want, I can put the names in an Access Database and…"

Sedlock felt he had to interrupt. "Janie, just print them out for me for now. Fax the list to me at Bob Corsino's office. You know the fax number."

Sedlock and Corsino arrived at Corsino's office a few minutes later. Twenty minutes later Corsino's fax machine came to life. Four pages printed out, with exactly twenty-one names on each page.

"The names are so neat, lined up so perfectly when printed out by a computer," Bob Corsino said. "It could be a list of men in a local golf league. All that's missing is the starting times. But they were all young men with parents and brothers and sisters. Some may have been married and had children. They all had a story. Chances are their lives ended abruptly on the battlefield. Those sheets of paper you're holding in your hands, Wayne, tell such a sad story. They'd all be about my age now, had they lived. Who knows what they might have done with their lives?"

Sedlock pored over the names.

"Smith, Parker, Ortiz, Kosecki. Where do we start? Here's one. Thaddeus A. Livingston."

"Livingston," Corsino repeated. He took his notebook out of his pocket and leafed through it. "When I was standing next to Robinson and Tyler at the Vietnam Wall one of their comrades they talked about was Livingston. He was a descendent of one of the signers of the Declaration of Independence. As Janie would say, 'Let's Google it.'"

They found this brief biography: *'Philip Livingston was born in Albany, New York, in 1716. He graduated from Yale College in 1737. He was a successful businessman in New York City. In 1776 he was selected as a delegate to the Continental Congress. He was a signer of the Declaration of Independence, and he died in 1778.'*

"The name Livingston rings a bell. When I used Rebecca Miter's computer to copy her husband's memoirs she was using 'Livingston' as a password."

"Her maiden name?"

"I had a society page from the Danbury newspaper. Here it is." He picked up a folded newspaper page from his case folder. The caption under Rebecca's photo read 'Rebecca Livingston Miter.'

Sedlock called Janie again.

"Janie, does that Vietnam Wall website give the hometowns of the men whose names are on it? Can you look up Thaddeus A. Livingston?"

After a minute Janie responded, "He was from Bridgeport, New York."

"Thanks, Janie. That's all for now." To Corsino he said, "Bridgeport, New York. Check it on the map and see if it's near Syracuse. Rebecca told me she was from the Syracuse area and she graduated from Syracuse University."

Corsino took out a New York State road map from a drawer in his desk. "Just outside Syracuse, like you said."

"Maybe Sanjay Gupta, the Miters' chauffeur, would know something about this. Thaddeus Livingston couldn't have been Rebecca's father, she's too young. Besides, I saw Rebecca with her parents at Web Miter's funeral."

Sedlock punched in Gupta's number on his cell phone.

"Sanjay, this is Wayne Sedlock. Have you ever been to Rebecca Miter's parents' house?"

"Yes, I drove her to her parents' house two or three times. It's a five-hour drive just north of Syracuse, New York. Once I drove both the Miters to a funeral near Syracuse. I believe it was when Rebecca's aunt passed away."

"What town was that funeral in, Sanjay? Was it Bridgeport, New York?"

"Yes, that was it. The funeral was about this time of year two years ago. The services and the cemetery were in Bridgeport."

"Did you ever meet Rebecca's parents?"

"Oh, yes. Very nice people."

"Sanjay, would you be willing to drive me to Rebecca's parents' house in New York State? And I would appreciate it if you didn't mention this to Rebecca."

"Certainly, Mr. Sedlock. I'm still the Miter family chauffeur for five more days. Then I go back to India. Is it all right if I meet you tomorrow morning?"

"Let's meet at the Lordship Country Club parking lot."

Two hours into their drive the next morning as they passed through Albany on I-90 west to Syracuse, Sedlock said, "Sanjay, you knew both Web Miter and his wife Rebecca. What kind of a marriage would you say they had?"

"Oh, you mean because of their age difference? Well, they weren't like young honeymooners, but I think they had an affection for each other. Rebecca struck me as being very ambitious when she worked at United Eastern. Perhaps marrying Web was the ultimate promotion. And Web was finally retired. He was able to enjoy life, and his young wife was one of his enjoyments. I hated to see Web divorce Donna. They'd worked as a team for so many years. But who knows what goes through the minds of powerful men like Web Miter? Who knows how they think? I don't think either of the two Mrs. Miters could have been involved in Web's death, if that's what you are driving at."

Sedlock decided to drop the subject. He was hoping to find out more when he visited Rebecca's parents.

When they drove into Rebecca's parents' driveway Sedlock said, "Sanjay, would you mind walking up to the door with me? They know you, but they don't know me."

"Certainly, Mr. Sedlock."

Philip Livingston opened the door when Sedlock rang the bell. "Sir, I'm Wayne Sedlock of the Alco Insurance Company and I'm investigating the Web Miter case."

"Yes, certainly, come in. Hello, Sanjay. Haven't seen you for a while."

"Hello, Mr. Livingston. Rebecca is fine. We figured it would be easier if I drove Mr. Sedlock, rather than give him directions."

"Yes, come in and sit down. If I had known you were coming we might have prepared lunch."

"We won't be here long, Sir. I just have a few questions. First, are you related to a Thaddeus A. Livingston?"

Philip Livingston hesitated a few seconds and looked slightly stunned.

"Yes, Tad was my older brother. He was killed in Vietnam in 1968. He was a Marine."

"You called him Tad, Sir."

"Yes, we all called him Tad. The name Thaddeus has been kicking around in our family since before the Revolutionary War. But everybody called him Tad. We are direct descendents of one of the signers of the Declaration of Independence, Philip Livingston of New York. We've had both Philips and Thaddeuses in our family for generations."

"Did your brother Tad have a son, Sir?"

"Yes, he did, but Tad never knew him. His son was born a month after Tad was killed. They named him Thaddeus, also."

"Did Tad's wife remarry after he was killed?"

"Yes, she did. Married a fellow named Reincke. The fellow adopted Tad junior. I begged him not to change his name. Let him be another Thaddeus Livingston, I said. But he wouldn't listen. He didn't give a damn any more about American history than he did about a bucket of spit. We didn't have much to do with the Reinckes after that. Just an occasional Christmas card. Last I saw young Tad was two years ago at his mother's funeral. He's a cameraman, works for one of the television networks."

CHAPTER 21 -
THE VIETNAM WALL

▼

Sedlock stood at the east entrance to the Vietnam Memorial Wall. There were about a dozen people walking by it on this warm Saturday late September night, and a few stood transfixed searching for particular names. He approached Panel 94W, which held the 84 names from the Two August battle. A compactly built man with dark hair stood staring at the black panel as if mesmerized by those names in front of him. Sedlock walked up behind him.

"Good evening, Tad," he said. The man turned around and faced Sedlock. "My name is Wayne Sedlock. I was an insurance investigator for Alco Insurance, investigating the Miter murder. I was working on the case with Detective Geany of the Lordship Police Department."

Tad Reincke acted as if he had suddenly been shaken awake from a sound sleep.

"Yes, I talked with Detective Geany."

"I didn't mean to startle you," Sedlock said. "This Wall is quite powerful, isn't it? Especially for Vietnam vets and relatives who lost loved ones over in Vietnam."

"I'm a cameraman working the Congressional tournament over in Potomac, Maryland. Believe it or not John Rollings is leading it by three strokes. Ever since the Hartford tournament he's been on fire. Looks like he finally got rid of the yips." Tad hesitated for a few seconds. "Whenever I'm in town I come down here. It's peaceful here, you know? What are you doing here, Mr. Sedlock?"

"I'm just wrapping up the case, Tad. Just trying to tie up some loose ends. It's quite a coincidence you were looking at the names that were a keystone to the case. All those killed in one Marine battle on Two August 1968. It was the bloodiest single day battle of the Vietnam War, you know? Too many names on this Wall to even comprehend what they mean to their loved ones. Luckily I had this fantastic college intern working with me this past summer. She's back in school now. But I called her and asked if she could get me a list from Panel 94W of all those Marines killed in the Two August 1968 battle. She got it right off the Internet, sorted by last name. These kids are really something with their computers." Sedlock waited for a response. When he got none, he said, "Tad's your nickname, isn't it? Short for Thaddeus? You don't hear names like Thaddeus much anymore. But there's a Thaddeus on the Wall you were just staring at. Thaddeus A. Livingston, killed August 2nd, 1968. He was with a battalion nicknamed the 'Greatest Groundpounders.' You were born in September, 1968, the month after the battle. Corporal Thaddeus A. Livingston was your father, wasn't he, Tad?"

Tad turned and faced the Wall. "Yes, he was my father. Whenever I'm in town I come down here after my golf tournament shift and just stare at his name and wonder what it would have been like to have a father. A real father, I mean."

"You had a stepfather named Reincke who adopted you when your mother re-married."

"He was a father to my stepbrother, but he wasn't much of a father to me. Forget it. It doesn't matter now."

"Now I know why it happened on a golf course. But why did you kill Web Miter, Tad?" Sedlock asked.

"Why? He killed my father, that's why. He ordered artillery on top of his own men." Then Tad spit out, "Then he was awarded the Navy Cross for doing it!"

"It was war, Tad. People die in wars. Miter used to say 'sometimes you have to sacrifice a few to save many.' He lived by that creed all through his business career. Your father made the ultimate sacrifice. Who knows how many lives he saved by doing that?"

"Don't give me that 'ultimate sacrifice' garbage. I didn't have a father because Captain Web Miter killed him. Right on this spot I talked with an ex-Marine who was in that battle. He told me what really happened on Two August, 1968."

"Tyler? You talked to Butch Tyler? Did Tyler tell you how he deserted his best friend on that battlefield? Did he tell you that part of the story?" Sedlock paused for several seconds. "One question, Tad. Where did you get the explosive? Where did you get the C-4? Did Tyler give it to you?"

"No. It was all my idea from the start. My father sent a stick of C-4 home in the mail from Vietnam. I don't think my mother, and later my stepfather, ever even knew what it was. My mother kept all my father's things from Vietnam in a cedar chest in her bedroom. It had his letters, pictures, ribbons, even a Marine uniform of his. When I was a kid I used to open up that cedar chest and smell his uniform. You know, hoping I could get a whiff of what he smelled like. And with all that stuff, there was that stick of C-4."

"When did you get the idea of killing Web Miter?" Sedlock asked.

"I worked the Hartford Open for five years. It was always at the Lordship Country Club. Year before last I was the cameraman on the 14th hole. We have all the schedules of who's playing in the Pro-Am. I never even noticed his name until his group got on the green. There he was, the great Web Miter. When I saw him I hated him like I've never hated anybody in my life. My mother passed away a couple months after that. My stepfather had already died earlier so my stepbrother and I put her house up for sale. I was cleaning out the cedar chest and found the C-4. Then the idea came to me. I cut up the C-4, got some blasting caps and figured out how to make a remote control detonator from an automatic garage door opener. Over the next several months I did some demolition tests in whatever woods were nearby, wherever I happened to be. By the time this year's Hartford Open rolled around, I was a certified demolitions expert. I was just hoping Web Miter would show up again."

"Was there any reason you picked the 17th hole? Was that just the hole you were assigned to cover?"

"No, that was kind of strange. I ran into Tyler here a couple weeks before the tournament. He asked me if I could cover the 17th hole. He said one of his buddies was going to be a volunteer on seventeen. He said the guy had political ambitions and could I take some shots of him that they could use later in political ads? I told him I would trade off with somebody and cover seventeen."

"But Tyler knew nothing of the plan to kill Web Miter?"

"Nothing. It was my show."

"What did you do with the remote after Miter was dead?"

"We're up in those towers from 6:30 in the morning till 6:30 in the evening. And it gets mighty hot and you have to drink fluids, so we have a giant thermos. I just tossed the remote into that and walked away with it when I finished my shift. Nobody notices anybody carrying a thermos at a golf tournament."

"I guess that's all I've got, Tad. I was just curious."

"Just curious? Aren't you going to arrest me?"

"I'm not an investigator anymore, Tad. In fact, I'm no longer with Alco. I plan to start up a private detective business. You're free to go as far as I'm concerned. I just had to know who did it and why. Good luck."

Sedlock handed Tad Reincke his business card, then turned to go. He had a long drive ahead of him.

Chapter 22 – Sedlock, Private Investigator

▼

"It's great to see you again, Wayne," Becky said as she drove a golf cart up to Wayne's car in The Greenwich Club parking lot. "We'll finally get to finish that match."

Sedlock lifted his golf bag out of his trunk and strapped it on to the back of the golf cart.

"Would you like to drive?" Becky laughed. "When I share a cart with a man I always have to ask."

"No, be my guest, Becky. I've been driving all night."

They drove straight to the first tee.

"Would you like to go over to the range and warm up?" Becky asked.

"No, let's get right out. There's nobody in front of us."

Sedlock took out his driver and swung it three times. Then he teed up his ball and poked it down the middle 240 yards.

"You've been practicing," Becky said.

She walked down to the ladies tee and promptly hit her drive down the middle.

"So have you," Sedlock said as he drove the cart to pick her up.

"A much better start than the last time we played together," Becky said. "I heard about Stuart Merriwether.

Carbon monoxide poisoning. He turned on the ignition of his car inside his garage. Because of his stand on outsourcing Merriwether was willing to kill Web. And in the end he killed himself."

"Maybe that was part of it," Sedlock said. "But mainly it was what Web was going to write in his memoirs. Stu Merriwether had political ambitions. He had been a mild-mannered, even what you might call timid, computer programmer for thirty years. Then two years ago he founded 'Save Our Jobs.' It was an organization for the right place and the right time. Suddenly the Wall Street *Journal* and the New York *Times* were calling Merriwether up for quotes about outsourcing. He was appearing on radio talk shows and television news shows. He became a lobbyist, rubbing shoulders with state legislators, congressmen and senators. He began to see himself in Congress. Many people in his movement encouraged him to run for office.

"I had this great college intern helping me at Alco. I picked up two computer diskettes when I visited you last month. One was the backup of the full text of Web Miter's memoirs, and one was a shorter version that you gave me made after he was dead. My intern friend Janie compared the text of both diskettes. A section describing Web meeting Stu Merriwether had been removed from the later disk.

"That's the most ironic part of this whole thing. Eighteen months ago whenever Web made a speech, 'Save Our Jobs' people would be outside the hall picketing with signs. Web met Stu Merriwether to try to hammer out a truce between them. Then Web paid Merriwether off. He wrote the checks out as donations to SOJ, but they were really bribes. Suddenly the picketing by 'Save Our Jobs' people stopped. About six months ago Merriwether realized he could never run for Congress with the payoff hanging over his head. He ran into Charlie Howell in the state capitol. Howell was there lobbying for his Indian tribe's casino. They had both worked together as drivers for the same armored truck company years earlier before Merriwether became a computer programmer. Then Merriwether developed a plan. He had stashed some C-4 explosives and blasting caps which he had stolen from the Ensign-Bickford Company just before an explosion in 1972. He remembered that when they worked together years earlier Howell had told him the story that Howell had gone to Leavenworth Prison for two years for trying to send explosives home from Vietnam. Merriwether thought he could get away with murder and shift the blame to Howell."

Sedlock paused while Becky hit her 5-iron just short of the first green. They drove up to Sedlock's ball. He stood over it with an 8-iron, swung with a perfect tempo, and lofted a soft shot onto the green. The ball skipped twice and ended up pin high ten feet to the left of the cup.

"Uphill putt," said Sedlock. "That's what I was trying to do."

"You have been practicing, haven't you?" Rebecca said.

"No, it's just that I'm very relaxed. I don't have the Web Miter murder case on my mind anymore."

"You mean now that you've solved it, you'll be working for some other insurance company?"

"No, actually it's doubtful I'll ever be able to get insurance work again. Now I know how those computer programmers who lost there jobs must feel when their jobs got outsourced."

"Because of what happened to you a dozen years ago? That's just not right. What are you going to do now, Wayne?"

"Private investigator, Becky."

They approached the first green in the golf cart. Both took out their putters. Becky decided to putt on. She stood still over her ball and stroked the putt firmly. It rolled smoothly over the fringe and ended up three feet from the cup. Sedlock lined up his putt then stroked it into the back of the cup.

"Great putt, Wayne! You're playing this hole two under in two rounds."

Becky then putted her ball into the cup for a par.

"Nice par, Becky," Sedlock said.

"I'll help you in any way I can, Wayne," Becky said as she got back into the cart. They motored over to the second tee.

"When Merriwether was alive you didn't want any connection between he and Web to appear in Web's manuscript. So you deleted his meetings with Web from the master copy. But you forgot to delete them from the backup copy. You were protecting somebody. There's an old saying in detective work, Becky. 'Don't believe in coincidences.' The password I used on your computer last month was 'Livingston.' That was your maiden name. Your uncle was Corporal Thaddeus A. Livingston, who was killed in the Two August 1968 battle, and whose name is on the Vietnam Memorial Wall. That makes Thaddeus 'Tad' Reincke your cousin. He was the cameraman on the 17th hole at Lordship Country Club when your husband was killed."

Tears started to creep down Becky's cheeks.

"When I heard what had happened on the golf course that day," she said, "I knew Tad did it. I didn't know he was going to do it. Even though Web was my husband, after it happened, I felt I had to protect Tad. He was my cousin. I'd last seen him at my aunt's funeral. But he didn't want anything to do with me after I married Web. When I married Web I didn't know Web was my uncle's commander in Vietnam."

"Did you ever see explosives in your aunt's cedar chest in her bedroom along with your uncle's ribbons and letters from Vietnam? It would have looked like a giant stick of butter in a sheath of clear plastic."

"No. I never saw anything like that."

"Merriwether must have supplied the C-4 and the blasting caps. What was the connection between Merriwether and Tad Reincke? The Ensign-Bickford guard spotted two men who were test-firing C-4 driving away the day before the Pro-Am. They had set off two explosives. One man was tall and fair.

The other man was short and darker. Sounds like Merriwether and Reincke."

Becky sobbed.

"Web was at my aunt's funeral. There was a 'Save Our Jobs' picketer outside the church. Tad asked me after the funeral what kind of organization SOJ was. I told him about their website. I guess he wanted to know more about any organization that picketed against Web Miter. So Tad got in touch with Stu Merriwether. They must have planned the murder together. Are you going to have Tad arrested?"

Becky stopped sobbing.

"No, Becky. I've talked with Tad. I wanted to solve this case for my own satisfaction. Just to prove to myself that Alco Insurance fired a damned good investigator. Stu Merriwether is dead. And dead men tell no tales. The only people who know Tad did it are you, me and Tad."

Sedlock stood over his golf ball on the tee of the 150-yard second hole. He made a pass at the ball that was slow and smooth, and the ball sailed high into the air toward the green. Sedlock watched the flight of the ball. He didn't have a care in the world.

When they finished their round Sedlock and Becky stopped in at the snack bar for coffees. As they sat down a political ad was playing on the television. Sedlock's first thought was that it was slick, produced by real professionals. And it must have cost a lot of money. With the background music of the 'Battle Hymn of the Republic' and displaying a battle scene from the Vietnam War the announcer read the following in a deep, resonant voice: *"When he was still a teenager he fought in the longest, most divisive war in our country's history. He's a survivor of the deadliest single day battle of that war. And like most of his countrymen he knew it was the wrong war, at the wrong time and the wrong place.* (Pause, 'When Johnny Comes Marching Home Again' plays in the background.) *So he came home.* (Pause, there is a picture of a smiling William Robinson.)

Connecticut has a history of giving us men who had the courage of their convictions – Nathan Hale, John Brown, Ralph Nadar (Pictures of all three move across the screen) *– men who stood up for what they believed in. Isn't it time we elected a senator who has the courage of HIS convictions?"*

Next is a scene of a computer tape spinning.

"They called William Wilson Robinson missing in action for three decades, but Bill Robinson was not missing. He was taking part in the computer revolution. He worked, he married, he paid taxes. He was just like you. Isn't it about time we had a senator who was not owned by the corporations, by the lobbyists, by the special interests? With Bill Robinson we have a chance for a fresh start in politics. Sign the petition that puts Bill Robinson on the Independent slate for senator. (A smiling Bill Robinson again). *Then vote for Bill Robinson. Vote for a fresh start."*

"We'll see what kind of a fresh start we get with Bill Robinson," Sedlock said.

Next on the television was the wrap-up of the PGA Congressional Tournament at Potomac, Maryland. The final group of the day, led by John Rollings, was walking up the 18ᵗʰ fairway. The crowd was cheering enthusiastically as he walked toward the green.

"This is Josh Parrow with Bill Wyner in the tower at the 18ᵗʰ green at the Congressional. It looks like that journeyman pro John Rollings is finally going to win his first tournament on the PGA Tour. Bill, how many PGA tournaments has this 42-year-old touring pro played?"

"We're trying to get that number right now, Josh. He's been on and off the Tour for nineteen years now. He's lost his player's card seven times that we know of. You called him a journeyman, and that's exactly what he is."

"Ever since that terrible explosion at the 17ᵗʰ hole of the Hartford Pro-Am two months ago that killed one of his amateur playing partners, John Rollings has been on fire."

"Since Hartford John's had a fifth-place finish, a fourth-place and two third-place finishes. You might say John was ready to break through. This is an unbelievable statistic I've just been handed. With his win today, John will have won more in the past five tournaments than he has won in official prize money on the PGA Tour in his entire nineteen-year career."

"We all know John had a terrible case of the yips, meaning he just couldn't putt. But in the past two months he's been sinking every putt he's looked at. It looks like he exorcised his demons at Lordship."

"I'm happy for him," Sedlock said to Becky. "Anybody who works that hard for that many years deserves some kind of reward. I even wish Bill Robinson luck in his campaign. He and Tyler have exorcised some demons too. So have I, for that matter.

"By the way, Tyler called me. He wanted me to try to help him find the members of Bravo Company who survived the Two August 1968 battle. He said he came into a sizable sum of money and he wants to divide it up among the survivors."

"This could be your first P.I. case. Are you going to do it?"

"Yes, I think I will. Alco gave me about three months severance pay. We could start by getting their military personnel records to find out where they lived when they enlisted in the Marine Corps. We have experience doing that with Bill Robinson and Butch Tyler."

"How many survivors of Bravo Company were there?"

"About twenty. And who knows how many have passed away in the past 35 years?"

"If you need any help at all, I'm behind you, Wayne."

"Well, Janie Caldwell said she could do the Internet research even though she's back in school. I didn't understand it all but she talked about setting up a web site that had search engines on 'Web Miter' and 'Two August' and 'Greatest Groundpounders.' And she'll set up a way for any of the survivors to send an email if they want to get in touch with Bill or Butch. And Bob Corsino said he could try to find some of the survivors by placing ads in veterans' magazines and through different veterans' organizations he belongs to. It might be a tough assignment. Butch says he thinks most of these guys have just disappeared. Only a few have ever shown up at the Greatest Groundpounders reunions. One thing that might be to our advantage, and I hate to say it, Becky, but it's Web's death. All the publicity might bring some of these men out in the open."

"You'll do a good job finding them, Wayne. I know you will."

Sedlock raised his coffee cup toward Becky. She raised her cup and touched it to his.

"And here's the best to you, Becky, and to my new venture as a private detective."

Becky handed Wayne a baseball card in a plastic case holder.

"A present for Justin. I just couldn't resist getting on Ebay and getting this for him," Becky said.

"The 1952 Eddie Mathews rookie card!" Sedlock exclaimed. "You're a princess, Becky."

CHAPTER 23 - AFTERWARD

▼

The day before Thanksgiving Carrie Edwards covered a news conference at the Alco Insurance building. The next day's Hartford *Courant* headline on page three read 'Golf Terrorists Still At Large.' The full text of the article follows:

Richard Geany, the insurance investigator at Alco Insurance Company in charge of that company's investigation of the murder of United Eastern's former CEO and managerial guru Web Miter at last July's Hartford Open at the Lordship Country Club, declared in a news conference today that Alco agrees with the governor that the crime was committed by a terrorist group.

Geany recently went to work for Alco as an insurance investigator after retiring from the Lordship Police Department as the detective in charge of that department's investigation of the Miter murder.

"Dick Geany has a more extensive background in this investigation than anybody," said Alco CEO Jeremy Fondsworth IV when he introduced Geany at the news conference.

"All indicators are that this crime was a terrorist act," Geany said. "Organizations like al-Qaida have made it known they will strike at the heart of America's economy. Golf is the most popular recreational sport in the United States - nearly twenty percent of all Americans play golf. We believe these terrorists thought by killing a world famous amateur golfer such as Web Miter, during

a televised professional golf tournament, that Americans would be afraid to play the game. The economy would have suffered significantly if the terrorists had succeeded."

"But the golf terrorists misjudged the backbone and the mettle of the American people," Fondsworth said.

When asked if authorities had any concrete proof that the crime was committed by terrorists, Geany said that the modus operandi pointed to terrorists. He cited the military-like execution of the operation's planning and the stolen identities used by two men who apparently test-fired an explosive the day before the murder. Also, he noted that the type of explosive used in the crime was most likely smuggled into the U.S. from a terrorist state, since that type of explosive hasn't been made in this country for more than 30 years.

When asked if he believed the golf terrorists were still in the U.S. Geany said it was "highly unlikely."

When a Courant reporter asked if investigators had found any link between an anti-outsourcing advocate who had committed suicide and Web Miter, who was a pioneer in outsourcing computer work overseas, Geany replied, "We considered a dozen suspects in the investigation, and could find no evidence linking any of them to the Miter murder."

When asked if Alco Insurance would still be one of the sponsors of the Hartford Open next summer Fondsworth said it was under consideration. Fondsworth then announced Alco was sponsoring a "one-day celebrity golf tournament at the Lordship Country Club next summer to show golf terrorists throughout the world that their tactics are futile against a determined golfing population."

Wayne Sedlock became a private investigator. He, Janie Caldwell, Bob Corsino and Butch Tyler managed to locate 13 survivors of the Two August battle from Bravo Company. Sedlock spent more and more time with Justin, whose grades improved markedly the more time he spent with his father. They fished and played golf together and Wayne rarely missed one of Justin's Babe Ruth baseball games. As a result of spending more time with his son, Wayne spent more time with his ex-wife, Nancy. Within a year Nancy admitted she had made a mistake to divorce Wayne because of his breakdown. After Nancy made Wayne promise to always take his "meds," they re-married, and for the first time in his life Wayne Sedlock became a full-time Dad.

In two years Janie Caldwell graduated with honors from Wesleyan.

Eleanor North continued to do genealogical research and background checks.

Bill Robinson received only seventeen percent of the vote the following November in his Independent bid for senator. But that took enough votes away from the popular Democratic attorney general to give the Republican Gray Standard the victory in heavily Democratic Connecticut. Bill Robinson and Candice Wallace Simpson then lived together in a two-bedroom cape in the Litchfield Hills area of northwestern Connecticut. He settled down to write his memoirs, for which a publisher had given him a six-figure advance. Candice had become an accomplished artist, specializing in landscapes, and she spent many summer weekends with Bill selling her paintings at craft fairs on the small town village greens in that area of the state.

Bill Walthrup retired after 35 years at Alco Insurance. Dick Geany took over Bill's job as head of the insurance investigative staff.

The next summer Becky Miter asked Jason Sombery to continue giving her golf lessons. One lesson led to another, and after a year Jason asked Becky to marry him. Their wedding was on all the Fairfield County society pages. Jason finally got to play the Greenwich Country Club.

Sanjay Gupta, the one-time orphan whose parents were killed in a United Eastern chemical accident, retired to India where his savings from working many years in the United States made him a relatively wealthy man.

'Save Our Jobs' disappeared as a functioning organization after Stu Merriwether died. Its web site remains on the Internet.

Carl Buffsky's machine shop could no longer compete with cheap foreign labor. He declared bankruptcy and laid off his ten employees.

Bob Corsino retired from the ATF, bought a Winnebego motor home and is following the sun.

Gray Standard was elected Connecticut's junior senator by a slim margin. While in the Senate he was a staunch supporter of veterans' causes.

Chief Herbert Livy stepped down after 40 years with the Lordship Police Department.

Steven Miter passed away at 92.

Jeremy Fondsworth IV was indicted by the Connecticut attorney general for manipulating the price of Alco stock. He was convicted on four counts and sentenced to serve 19 months at the minimum security prison in Devonwood, Massachusetts. His former assistant, Clyde Persico, testified against Fondsworth to get a lighter sentence for himself. While at Devonwood, known as "the country club" because it sits next to a golf course, Fondsworth brought his golf handicap down to a seven.

John Rollings continued rolling, winning two more PGA tournaments in the next 18 months. He was named to the American Ryder Cup team, brought Chump Williams over to Great Britain for the matches, and won one match and halved another.

Three more Bravo Company survivors surfaced, for a total of 18 including Dan Sullivan, Butch Tyler and Bill Robinson. Eleven of them lined up on the stage of Hartford's Bushnell Auditorium behind Bill Robinson on the last day of his senatorial campaign.

Carrie Edwards was awarded first place for in depth news from the Connecticut Journalism Society for the Sunday article she wrote after interviewing the Bravo survivors during their visit to Hartford. The headline of the article read "Two August – The Battle Nobody Knew."

Janice Walters became an anchorwoman at Channel 8 News. She became embroiled in a sexual harassment lawsuit against one of the anchormen at the station.

Ensign-Bickford came upon hard times, also because of foreign competition. It moved much of its operation to its Colorado facility where it had the wide-open spaces to test-fire its explosives. It determined it didn't need the Powder Woods anymore. When a reporter writing about the two terrorists who test-fired explosives in those woods wrote that the company had owned the Powder Woods for more than 200 years and that the woods had never been logged, three competing logging companies bid to log them. Within a month the several hundred-year-old trees were cut down and hauled away. E-B then sold the woods to developers, who are clearing them away to erect upscale housing and condominiums.

Charlie Howell continued lobbying for the Mashicoke tribe, which is still awaiting recognition from the Bureau of Indian Affairs.

Tad Reincke was found in his apartment dead from a self-inflicted gunshot wound two years after the Miter murder. Sedlock, Becky, Tad's stepbrother and Becky's parents attended his small, private burial. Philip Livingston read a simple eulogy at the graveside.

"Tad is descended from a great man, Philip Livingston, a signer of the Declaration of Independence. But he never knew another great man, his father, my brother, Thaddeus A. Livingston, who we also called Tad. His father died before Tad was even born, in a far-off land, on an unknown battlefield, fighting for a questionable cause. But whether by living on this earth we become known to the Ages, or whether we are hardly known at all, we are all part of the fabric of history. Tad was part of the Livingston history, part of the Livingston family, part of the Livingston story.

Some in our family risked their fortunes, some risked their lives, and others in our family bore the consequences of those risks. Tad certainly bore the consequences of never knowing his father. Now Tad will lie forever next to his father, and he will know him at last in Eternity. May he also finally know Peace."

THE END